Deemed 'the father of the scientific ⌐
Austin Freeman had a long and distin⌐
a writer of detective fiction. He was born in London, the son of a
tailor who went on to train as a pharmacist. After graduating as a
surgeon at the Middlesex Hospital Medical College, Freeman
taught for a while and joined the colonial service, offering his skills
as an assistant surgeon along the Gold Coast of Africa. He became
embroiled in a diplomatic mission when a British expeditionary
party was sent to investigate the activities of the French. Through
his tact and formidable intelligence, a massacre was narrowly
avoided. His future was assured in the colonial service. However,
after becoming ill with blackwater fever, Freeman was sent back to
England to recover and finding his finances precarious, embarked
on a career as acting physician in Holloway Prison. In desperation,
he turned to writing and went on to dominate the world of
British detective fiction, taking pride in testing different criminal
techniques. So keen were his powers as a writer that part of one of
his best novels was written in a bomb shelter.

BY THE SAME AUTHOR
ALL PUBLISHED BY HOUSE OF STRATUS

A Certain Dr Thorndyke

Dr Thorndyke Intervenes

Dr Thorndyke's Casebook

The Eye of Osiris

Felo De Se

Flighty Phyllis

The Golden Pool: A Story of a Forgotten Mine

The Great Portrait Mystery

Helen Vardon's Confession

John Thorndyke's Cases

Mr Polton Explains

Mr Pottermack's Oversight

The Mystery of 31 New Inn

The Mystery of Angelina Frood

The Penrose Mystery

The Puzzle Lock

The Red Thumb Mark

The Shadow of the Wolf

The Singing Bone

A Silent Witness

The D'Arblay Mystery

R Austin Freeman

HOUSE OF
STRATUS

This edition published in 2001 by House of Stratus, an imprint of Stratus Holdings plc, 24c Old Burlington Street, London, W1X 1RL, UK.

www.houseofstratus.com

Typeset, printed and bound by House of Stratus.

A catalogue record for this book is available from the British Library.

ISBN 0-7551-0350-5

CONTENTS

CHAPTER ONE

The Pool in the Wood

There are certain days in our lives which, as we recall them, seem to detach themselves from the general sequence as forming the starting-point of a new epoch. Doubtless, if we examined them critically, we should find them to be but links in a connected chain. But in a retrospective glance their continuity with the past is unperceived, and we see them in relation to the events which followed them rather than to those which went before.

Such a day is that on which I look back through a vista of some twenty years; for on that day I was, suddenly and without warning, plunged into the very heart of a drama so strange and incredible that in the recital of its events I am conscious of a certain diffidence and hesitation.

The picture that rises before me as I write is very clear and vivid. I see myself, a youngster of twenty-five, the owner of a brand-new medical diploma, wending my way gaily down Wood Lane, Highgate, at about eight o'clock on a sunny morning in early autumn. I was taking a day's holiday, the last I was likely to enjoy for some time; for on the morrow I was to enter on the duties of my first professional appointment. I had nothing in view today but sheer, delightful idleness. It is true that a sketch-book in one pocket and a box of collecting-tubes in another suggested a bare hint of purpose in the expedition; but primarily it was a holiday, a

1

pleasure jaunt, to which art and science were no more than possible sources of contributory satisfaction.

At the lower end of the Lane was the entrance to Churchyard Bottom Wood, then open and unguarded save by a few hurdles (it has since been enclosed and re-named "Queen's Wood"). I entered and took my way along the broad, rough path, pleasantly conscious of the deep silence and seeming remoteness of this surviving remnant of the primeval forest of Britain, and letting my thoughts stray to the great plague-pit in the haunted bottom that gave the wood its name. The foliage of the oaks was still unchanged, despite the waning of the year. The low-slanting sunlight spangled it with gold and made rosy patterns on the path, where lay a few prematurely-fallen leaves; but in the hollows among the undergrowth traces of the night-mists lingered, shrouding tree-bole, bush and fern in a mystery of gauzy blue.

A turn of the path brought me suddenly within a few paces of a girl who was stooping at the entrance to a side-track and seemed to be peering into the undergrowth as if looking for something. As I appeared, she stood up and looked round at me with a startled, apprehensive manner that caused me to look away and pass as if I had not seen her. But the single glance had shown me that she was a strikingly handsome girl – indeed, I should have used the word "beautiful" – that she seemed to be about my own age, and that she was evidently a lady.

The apparition, pleasant as it was, set me speculating as I strode forward. It was early for a girl like this to be afoot in the woods, and alone, too. Not so very safe, either, as she had seemed to realize, judging by the start that my approach seemed to have given her. And what could it be that she was looking for? Had she lost something at some previous time and come to search for it before anyone was about? It might be so. Certainly she was not a poacher, for there was nothing to poach, and she hardly had the manner or appearance of a naturalist.

A little farther on I struck into a side-path which led, as I knew, in the direction of a small pond. That pond I had had in my mind when I put the box of collecting-tubes in my pocket, and I now made my way to it as directly as the winding track would let me; but still, it was not the pond or its inmates that occupied my thoughts, but the mysterious maiden whom I had left peering into the undergrowth. Perhaps if she had been less attractive I might have given her less consideration. But I was twenty-five; and if a man at twenty-five has not a keen and appreciative eye for a pretty girl, there must be something radically wrong with his mental make-up.

In the midst of my reflections I came out into a largish opening in the wood, at the centre of which, in a slight hollow, was the pond – a small oval piece of water, fed by the trickle of a tiny stream, the continuation of which carried away the overflow towards the invisible valley. Approaching the margin, I brought out my box of tubes, and uncorking one, stooped and took a trial dip. When I held the glass tube against the light and examined its contents through my pocket-lens, I found that I was in luck. The "catch" included a green hydra, clinging to a rootlet of duckweed, several active water-fleas, a scarlet water-mite and a beautiful sessile rotifer. Evidently this pond was a rich hunting-ground.

Delighted with my success, I corked the tube, put it away and brought out another, with which I took a fresh dip. This was less successful; but the naturalist's ardour and the collector's cupidity being thoroughly aroused, I persevered, gradually enriching my collection and working my way slowly round the margin of the pond, forgetful of everything – even of the mysterious maiden – but the objects of my search: indeed, so engrossed was I with my pursuit of the minute denizens of this watery world that I failed to observe a much larger object which must have been in view most of the time. Actually, I did not see it until I was right over it. Then, as I was stooping to clear away the duckweed for a fresh dip, I found myself confronted by a human face; just below the surface and half-concealed by the pondweed.

It was a truly appalling experience. Utterly unprepared for this awful apparition, I was so overcome by astonishment and horror that I remained stooping, with motion arrested, as if petrified, staring at the thing in silence and hardly breathing. The face was that of a man of about fifty or a little more; a handsome, refined, rather intellectual face with a moustache and Vandyke beard, and surmounted by a thickish growth of iron-grey hair. Of the rest of the body little was to be seen, for the duckweed and water-crowfoot had drifted over it, and I had no inclination to disturb them.

Recovering somewhat from the shock of this sudden and fearful encounter, I stood up and rapidly considered what I had better do. It was clearly not for me to make any examination or meddle with the corpse in any way; indeed, when I considered the early hour and the remoteness of this solitary place, it seemed prudent to avoid the possibility of being seen there by any chance stranger. Thus reflecting, with my eyes still riveted on the pallid, impassive face, so strangely sleeping below the glassy surface and conveying to me somehow a dim sense of familiarity, I pocketed my tubes and, turning back, stole away along the woodland track, treading lightly, almost stealthily, as one escaping from the scene of a crime.

Very different was my mood, as I retraced my steps, from that in which I had come. Gone was all my gaiety and holiday spirit. The dread meeting had brought me into an atmosphere of tragedy, perchance even of something more than tragedy. With death I was familiar enough – death as it comes to men, prefaced by sickness or even by injury. But the dead man who lay in that still and silent pool in the heart of the wood had come there by none of the ordinary chances of normal life. It seemed barely possible that he could have fallen in by mere misadventure, for the pond was too shallow and its bottom shelved too gently for accidental drowning to be conceivable. Nor was the strange, sequestered spot without significance. It was just such a spot as might well be chosen by one who sought to end his life – or another's.

I had nearly reached the main path when an abrupt turn of the narrow track brought me once more face to face with the girl whose existence I had till now forgotten. She was still peering into the dense undergrowth as if searching for something; and again, on my sudden appearance, she turned a startled face towards me. But this time I did not look away. Something in her face struck me with a nameless fear. It was not only that she was pale and haggard, that her expression betokened anxiety and even terror. As I looked at her I understood in a flash the dim sense of familiarity of which I had been conscious in the pallid face beneath the water. It was her face that it had recalled.

With my heart in my mouth, I halted, and, taking off my cap, addressed her.

"Pray pardon me; you seem to be searching for something. Can I help you in any way or give you any information?"

She looked at me a little shyly and, as I thought, with slight distrust, but she answered civilly enough though rather stiffly:

"Thank you, but I am afraid you can't help me. I am not in need of any assistance."

This, under ordinary circumstances, would have brought the interview to an abrupt end. But the circumstances were not ordinary, and, as she made as if to pass me, I ventured to persist.

"Please," I urged, "don't think me impertinent, but would you mind telling me what you are looking for? I have a reason for asking, and it isn't curiosity."

She reflected for a few moments before replying and I feared that she was about to administer another snub. Then, without looking at me, she replied:

"I am looking for my father," (and at these words my heart sank). "He did not come home last night. He left Hornsey to come home and he would ordinarily have come by the path through the wood. He always came that way from Hornsey. So I am looking through the wood in case he missed his way, or was taken ill, or – "

Here the poor girl suddenly broke off, and, letting her dignity go, burst into tears. I huskily murmured a few indistinct words of condolence, but, in truth, I was little less affected than she was. It was a terrible position, but there was no escape from it. The corpse that I had just seen was almost certainly her father's corpse. At any rate, the question whether it was or was not had to be settled now, and settled by me – and her. That was quite clear; but yet I could not screw my courage up to the point of telling her. While I was hesitating, however, she forced the position by a direct question.

"You said just now that you had a reason for asking what I was searching for. Would it be – ?" She paused and looked at me inquiringly as she wiped her eyes.

I made a last, frantic search for some means of breaking the horrid news to her. Of course there was none. Eventually I stammered:

"The reason I asked was – er – the fact is that I have just seen the body of a man lying – "

"Where?" she demanded. Show me the place!"

Without replying, I turned and began quickly to retrace my steps along the narrow track. A few minutes brought me to the opening in which the pond was situated, and I was just beginning to skirt the margin, closely followed by my companion, when I heard her utter a low, gasping cry. The next moment she had passed me and was running along the bank towards a spot where I could now see the toe of a boot just showing through the duckweed. I stopped short and watched her with my heart in my throat. Straight to the fatal spot she ran, and for a moment stood on the brink, stooping over the weedy surface. Then, with a terrible, wailing cry she stepped into the water.

Instantly, I ran forward and waded into the pond to her side. Already she had her arms round the dead man's neck and was raising the face above the surface. I saw that she meant to bring the body ashore, and, useless as it was, it seemed a natural thing to do. Silently I passed my arms under the corpse and lifted it; and as she supported the head, we bore it through the shallows and up the bank, where I laid it down gently in the high grass.

Not a word had been spoken, nor was there any question that need be asked. The pitiful tale told itself only too plainly. As I stood looking with swimming eyes at the tragic group, a whole history seemed to unfold itself – a history of love and companionship, of a happy, peaceful past made sunny by mutual affection, shattered in an instant by the hideous present, with its portent of a sad and lonely future. She had sat down on the grass and taken the dead head on her lap, tenderly wiping the face with her handkerchief, smoothing the grizzled hair and crooning or moaning words of endearment into the insensible ears. She had forgotten my presence; indeed, she was oblivious of everything but the still form that bore the outward semblance of her father.

Some minutes passed thus. I stood a little apart, cap in hand, more moved than I had ever been in my life, and, naturally enough, unwilling to break in upon a grief so overwhelming and, as it seemed to me, so sacred. But presently it began to be borne in on me that something had to be done. The body would have to be removed from this place, and the proper authorities ought to be notified. Still, it was some time before I could gather courage to intrude on her sorrow, to profane her grief with the sordid realities of everyday life. At last I braced myself up for the effort and addressed her.

"Your father," I said gently – I could not refer to him as "the body" – "will have to be taken away from here; and the proper persons will have to be informed of what has happened. Shall I go alone, or will you come with me? I don't like to leave you here."

She looked up at me and, to my relief, answered me with quiet composure:

"I can't leave him here all alone. I must stay with him until he is taken away. Do you mind telling whoever ought to be told" – like me, she instinctively avoided the word "police" – "and making what arrangements are necessary?"

There was nothing more to he said; and loath as I was to leave her alone with the dead, my heart assented to her decision. In her place, I should have had the same feeling. Accordingly, with a promise to return as quickly as I could, I stole away along the woodland track. When I turned to take a last glance at her before plunging into the wood, she was once more leaning over the head that lay in her lap, looking with fond grief into the impassive face and stroking the dank hair.

My intention had been to go straight to the police station, when I had ascertained its whereabouts, and make my report to the officer in charge. But a fortunate chance rendered this proceeding unnecessary, for, at the moment when I emerged from the top of Wood Lane, I saw a police officer, mounted on a bicycle – a road patrol, as I assumed him to be – approaching along the Archway Road. I hailed him to stop, and as he dismounted and stepped on to the footway, I gave him a brief account of the finding of the body and my meeting with the daughter of the dead man. He listened with calm, businesslike interest, and, when I had finished, said:

"We had better get the body removed as quickly as possible. I will run along to the station and get the wheeled stretcher. There is no need for you to come. If you will go back and wait for us at the entrance to the wood, that will save time. We shall be there within a quarter of an hour."

I agreed gladly to this arrangement, and when I had seen him mount his machine and shoot away along the road, I turned back down the Lane and re-entered the wood. Before taking up my post, I walked quickly down the path and along the track to the opening by the pond. My new friend was sitting just as I had left her, but she looked up as I told her briefly what had happened, and was about to retire when she asked: "Will they take him to our house?"

"I am afraid not," I replied. "There will have to be an inquiry by the coroner, and until that is finished, his body will have to remain in the mortuary."

"I was afraid it might be so," she said with quiet resignation; and as she spoke she looked down with infinite sadness at the waxen face in her lap. A good deal relieved by her reasonable acceptance of the painful necessities, I turned back and made my way to the rendezvous at the entrance to the wood.

As I paced to and fro on the shady path, keeping a look-out up the Lane, my mind was busy with the tragedy to which I had become a party. It was a grievous affair. The passionate grief which I had witnessed spoke of no common affection. On one life at least this disaster had inflicted irreparable loss, and there were probably others on whom the blow had yet to fall. But it was not only a grievous affair; it was highly mysterious. The dead man had apparently been returning home at night in a customary manner and by a familiar way. That he could have strayed by chance from the open, well-worn path into the recesses of the wood was inconceivable, while the hour and the circumstances made it almost as incredible that he should have been wandering in the wood by choice. And again, the water in which he had been lying was quite shallow; so shallow as to rule out accidental drowning as an impossibility.

What could the explanation be? There seemed to be but three possibilities, and two of them could hardly be entertained. The idea of intoxication I rejected at once. The girl was evidently a lady, and her father was presumably a gentleman who would not be likely to be wandering abroad drunk; nor could a man who was sober enough to have reached the pond have been so helpless as to be drowned in its shallow waters. To suppose that he might have fallen into the water in a fit was to leave unexplained the circumstance of his being in that remote place at such an hour. The only possibility that remained was that of suicide; and I could not but admit that some of the appearances seemed to support that view. The solitary place – more solitary still at night – was precisely such as an intending suicide might he expected to seek; the shallow water presented no inconsistency; and when I recalled how I had found his daughter searching the wood with evident foreboding of evil, I could not escape the feeling that the dreadful possibility had not been entirely unforeseen.

My meditations had reached this point when, as I turned once more towards the entrance and looked up the Lane, I saw two constables approaching, trundling a wheeled stretcher, while a third man, apparently an inspector, walked by its side. As the little procession reached the entrance and I turned back to show the way, the latter joined me and began at once to interrogate me. I gave him my name, address and occupation, and followed this with a rapid sketch of the facts as known to me, which he jotted down in a large note-book, and he then said:

"As you are a doctor, you can probably tell me how long the man had been dead when you first saw him."

"By the appearance and the rigidity," I replied, "I should say about nine or ten hours; which agrees pretty well with the account his daughter gave of his movements."

The inspector nodded. "The man and the young lady," said he, "are strangers to you, I understand. I suppose you haven't picked up anything that would throw any light on the affair?"

"No," I answered; "I know nothing but what I have told you."

"Well," he remarked, "it's a queer business. It is a queer place for a man to be in at night, and he must have gone there of his own accord. But there, it is no use guessing. It will all be thrashed out at the inquest."

As he reached this discreet conclusion, we came out into the opening and I heard him murmur very feelingly, "Dear, dear! Poor thing!" The girl seemed hardly to have changed her position since I had last seen her, but she now tenderly laid the dead head on the grass and rose as we approached; and I saw with great concern that her skirts were soaked almost from the waist downwards.

The officer took off his cap and as he drew near looked down gravely but with an inquisitive eye at the dead man. Then he turned to the girl and said in a singularly gentle and deferential manner:

"This is a very terrible thing, miss. A dreadful thing. I assure you that I am more sorry for you than I can tell; and I hope you will forgive me for having to intrude on your sorrow by asking questions. I won't trouble you more than I can help."

"Thank you," she replied quietly. "Of course I realize your position. What do you want me to tell you?"

"I understand," replied the inspector, "that this poor gentleman was your father. Would you mind telling me who he was and where he lived and giving me your own name and address?"

"My father's name," she answered, "was Julius D'Arblay. His private address was Ivy Cottage, North Grove, Highgate. His studio and workshop, where he carried on the profession of a modeller, is in Abbey Road, Hornsey. My name is Marion D'Arblay and I lived with my father. He was a widower and I was his only child."

As she concluded, with a slight break in her voice, the inspector shook his head and again murmured, "Dear, dear!" as he rapidly entered her answers in his note-book. Then, in a deeply apologetic tone, he asked: "Would you mind telling us what you know as to how this happened?"

"I know very little," she replied. "As he did not come home last night, I went to the studio quite early this morning to see if he was there. He sometimes stayed there all night when he was working very late. The woman who lives in the adjoining house and looks after the studio, told me that he had been working late last night, but that he left to come home soon after ten. He always used to come through the wood, because it was the shortest way and the most pleasant. So when I learned that he had started to come home, I came to the wood to see if I could find any traces of him. Then I met this gentleman and he told me that he had seen a dead man in the wood and – " Here she suddenly broke down and, sobbing passionately, flung out her hand towards the corpse.

The inspector shut his note-book, and murmuring some indistinct words of sympathy, nodded to the constables, who had drawn up the stretcher a few paces away and lifted off the cover. On this silent instruction, they approached the body and, with the inspector's assistance and mine, lifted it on to the stretcher without removing the latter from its carriage. As they picked up the cover, the inspector turned to Miss D'Arblay and said gently but finally: "You had better not come with us. We must take him to the mortuary, but you will see him again after the inquest, when he will be brought to your house if you wish it."

She made no objection; but as the constables approached with the cover, she stooped over the stretcher and kissed the dead man on the forehead.

Then she turned away; the cover was placed in position, the inspector and the constables saluted reverently, and the stretcher was wheeled away along the narrow track.

For some time after it had gone, we stood in silence at the margin of the pond with our eyes fixed on the place where it had disappeared. I considered in no little embarrassment what was to be done next. It was most desirable that Miss D'Arblay should be got home as soon as possible, and I did not at all like the idea of her going alone, for her appearance, with her drenched skirts and her dazed and rather wild expression, was such as to attract unpleasant attention. But I was a total stranger to her and I felt a little shy of pressing my company on her. However, it seemed a plain duty, and, as I saw her shiver slightly, I said:

"You had better go home now and change your clothes. They are very wet. And you have some distance to go."

She looked down at her soaked dress and then she looked at me.

"You are rather wet, too," she said. "I am afraid I have given you a great deal of trouble."

"It is little enough that I have been able to do," I replied. "But you must really go home now; and if you will let me walk with you and see you safely to your house, I shall be much more easy in my mind."

"Thank you," she replied. "It is kind of you to offer to see me home, and I am glad not to have to go alone."

With this, we walked together to the edge of the opening and proceeded in single file along the track to the main path, and so out into Wood Lane, at the top of which we crossed the Archway Road into Southwood Lane. We walked mostly in silence, for I was unwilling to disturb her meditations with attempts at conversation, which could only have seemed banal or impertinent. For her part, she appeared to be absorbed in reflections the nature of which I could easily guess, and her grief was too fresh for any thought of distraction. But I found myself speculating with profound discomfort on what might be awaiting her at home. It is true that her own desolate state as an orphan without brothers or sisters had its compensation in that there was no wife to whom the dreadful tidings had to be imparted, nor any fellow-orphans to have their bereavement broken to them. But there must be someone who cared; or if there were not, what a terrible loneliness would reign in that house!

"I hope," I said as we approached our destination, "that there is someone at home to share your grief and comfort you a little."

"There is," she replied. "I was thinking of her and how grievous it will be to have to tell her – an old servant and a dear friend. She was my mother's nurse when the one was a child and the other but a young girl. She came to our house when my mother married and has managed our home ever since. This will be a terrible shock to her, for she loved my father dearly – everyone loved him who knew him. And she has been like a mother to me since my own mother died. I don't know how I shall break it to her."

Her voice trembled as she concluded and I was deeply troubled to think of the painful homecoming that loomed before her; but still it was a comfort to know that her sorrow would be softened by sympathy and loving companionship, not heightened by the empty desolation that I had feared.

A few minutes more brought us to the little square – which, by the way, was triangular – and to a pleasant little old-fashioned house, on the gate of which was painted the name "Ivy Cottage". In the bay window on the ground floor I observed a formidable-looking elderly woman, who was watching our approach with evident curiosity; which, as we drew nearer and the state of our clothing became visible, gave place to anxiety and alarm. Then she disappeared suddenly, to reappear a few moments later at the open door, where she stood viewing us both with consternation and me in particular with profound disfavour.

At the gate Miss D'Arblay halted and held out her hand. "Goodbye," she said. "I must thank you some other time for all your kindness," and with this she turned abruptly and, opening the gate, walked up the little paved path to the door where the old woman was waiting.

CHAPTER TWO

A Conference with Dr Thorndyke

The sound of the closing door seemed, as it were, to punctuate my experiences and to mark the end of a particular phase. So long as Miss D'Arblay was present, my attention was entirely taken up by her grief and distress; but now that I was alone I found myself considering at large the events of this memorable morning. What was the meaning of this tragedy? How came this man to be lying dead in that pool? No common misadventure seemed to fit the case. A man may easily fall into deep water and be drowned; may step over a quay-side in the dark or trip on a mooring-rope or ring-bolt. But here there was nothing to suggest any possible accident. The water was hardly two feet deep where the body was lying and much less close to the edge. If he had walked in the dark, he would simply have walked out again. Besides, how came he there at all? The only explanation that was intelligible was that he went there with the deliberate purpose of making away with himself.

I pondered this explanation and found myself unwilling to accept it, notwithstanding that his daughter's presence in the wood, her obvious apprehension and her terrified searching among the underwood, seemed to hint at a definite expectation on her part. But yet that possibility was discounted by what his daughter had told me of him. Little as she had said, it was clear that he was a man universally beloved. Such men, in making the world a pleasant place for others, make it pleasant for themselves. They are usually happy men; and happy men do not commit suicide. Yet, if the idea of suicide were rejected, what was left? Nothing but an insoluble mystery.

I turned the problem over again and again as I sat on the top of the tram (where I could keep my wet trousers out of sight), not as a matter of mere curiosity but as one in which I was personally concerned. Friendships spring up into sudden maturity under great emotional stress. I had known Marion D'Arblay but an hour or two, but they were hours which neither of us would ever forget; and in that brief space she had become to me a friend who was entitled, as of right, to sympathy and service. So, as I revolved in my mind the mystery of this man's death, I found myself thinking of him not as a chance stranger but as the father of a friend; and thus it seemed to devolve upon me to elucidate the mystery, if possible.

It is true that I had no special qualifications for investigating an obscure case of this kind, but yet I was better equipped than most young medical men. For my hospital, St Margaret's, though its medical school was but a small one, had one great distinction; the chair of Medical Jurisprudence was occupied by one of the greatest living authorities on the subject, Dr John Thorndyke. To him and his fascinating lectures my mind naturally turned as I ruminated on the problem; and presently, when I found myself unable to evolve any reasonable suggestion, the idea occurred to me to go and lay the facts before the great man himself.

Once started, the idea took full possession of me, and I decided to waste no time but to seek him at once. This was not his day for lecturing at the hospital, but I could find his address in our school calendar; and as my means, though modest, allowed of my retaining him in a regular way, I need have no scruples as to occupying his time. I looked at my watch. It was even now but a little past noon. I had time to change and get an early lunch and still make my visit while the day was young.

A couple of hours later found me walking slowly down the pleasant, tree-shaded footway of King's Bench Walk in the Inner Temple, looking up at the numbers above the entries. Dr Thorndyke's number was 5A, which I presently discovered inscribed on the keystone of a fine, dignified brick portico of the seventeenth century, on the jamb whereof was painted his name as the occupant of the "1st pair". I accordingly ascended the first pair and was relieved to find that my teacher was apparently at home; for a massive outer door, above which his name was painted, stood wide open, revealing an inner door, furnished with a small, brilliantly-burnished brass knocker, on which I ventured to execute a modest rat-tat. Almost immediately the door was opened by a small, clerical-looking gentleman who wore a black linen apron – and ought, from his appearance, to have had black gaiters to match – and who regarded me with a look of polite inquiry.

"I wanted to see Dr Thorndyke," said I, adding discreetly, "on a matter of professional business."

The little gentleman beamed on me benevolently. "The doctor," said he, "has gone to lunch at his club, but he will be coming in quite shortly. Would you like to wait for him?"

"Thank you," I replied, "I should, if you think I shall not be disturbing him."

The little gentleman smiled – that is to say, the multitudinous wrinkles that covered his face arranged themselves into a sort of diagram of geniality. It was the crinkliest smile that I have ever seen, but a singularly pleasant one.

"The doctor," said he, "is never disturbed by professional business. No man is ever disturbed by having to do what he enjoys doing."

As he spoke, his eyes turned unconsciously to the table, on which stood a microscope, a tray of slides and mounting material and a small heap of what looked like dressmaker's cuttings.

"Well," I said, "don't let me disturb you, if you are busy."

He thanked me very graciously, and, having installed me in an easy-chair, sat down at the table and resumed his occupation, which apparently consisted in isolating fibres from the various samples of cloth and mounting them as microscopic specimens. I watched him as he worked, admiring his neat, precise, unhurried methods and speculating on the purpose of his proceedings: whether he was preparing what one might call museum specimens, to be kept for reference, or whether these preparations were related to some particular case. I was considering whether it would be admissible for me to ask a question on the subject when he paused in his work, assuming a listening attitude, with one hand – holding a mounting-needle – raised and motionless.

"Here comes the doctor," said he.

I listened intently and became aware of footsteps, very faint and far away, and only barely perceptible. But my clerical friend – who must have had the auditory powers of a watch-dog – had no doubts as to their identity, for he began quietly to pack all his material on the tray. Meanwhile the footsteps drew nearer, they turned in at the entry and ascended the "first pair", by which time my crinkly-faced acquaintance had the door open. The next moment Dr Thorndyke entered and was duly informed that "a gentleman was waiting to see" him.

"You under-estimate my powers of observation, Polton," he informed his subordinate, with a smile. "I can see the gentleman distinctly with my naked eye. How do you do, Gray?" and he shook my hand cordially.

"I hope I haven't come at the wrong time, sir," said I. "If I have, you must adjourn me. But I want to consult you about a rather queer case."

"Good," said Thorndyke. "There is no wrong time for a queer case. Let me hang up my hat and fill my pipe and then you can proceed to make my flesh creep."

He disposed of his hat, and when Mr Polton had departed with his tray of material, he filled his pipe, laid a note-block on the table and invited me to begin; whereupon I gave him a detailed account of what had befallen me in the course of the morning, to which he listened with close attention, jotting down an occasional note, but not interrupting my narrative. When I had finished, he read through his notes and then said:

"It is, of course, evident to you that all the appearances point to suicide. Have you any reasons, other than those you have mentioned, for rejecting that view?"

"I am afraid not," I replied gloomily. "But you have always taught us to beware of too ready acceptance of the theory of suicide in doubtful cases."

He nodded approvingly. "Yes," he said, "that is a cardinal principle in medico-legal practice. All other possibilities should be explored before suicide is accepted. But our difficulty in this case is that we have hardly any of the relevant facts. The evidence at the inquest may make everything clear. On the other hand, it may leave things obscure. But what is your concern with the case? You are merely a witness to the finding of the body. The parties are all strangers to you, are they not?"

"They were," I replied. "But I feel that someone ought to keep an eye on things for Miss D'Arblay's sake, and circumstances seem to have put the duty on me. So, as I can afford to pay any costs that are likely to be incurred, I proposed to ask you to undertake the case – on a strict business footing, you know, sir."

"When you speak of my undertaking the case," said he, "what is it that is in your mind? What do you want me to do in the matter?"

"I want you to take any measures that you may think necessary," I replied, "to ascertain definitely, if possible, how this man came by his death."

He reflected a while before answering. At length he said:

"The examination of the body will be conducted by the person whom the coroner appoints, probably the police surgeon. I will write to the coroner for permission to be present at the post-mortem examination. He will certainly make no difficulties. I will also write to the police surgeon, who is sure to be quite helpful. If the post-mortem throws no light on the case – in fact, in any event – I will instruct a first-class shorthand writer to attend at the inquest and make a verbatim report of the evidence, and you, of course, will be present as a witness. That, I think, is about all that we can do at present. When we have heard all the evidence, including that furnished by the body itself, we shall be able to judge whether the case calls for further investigation. How will that do?"

"It is all that I could wish," I answered, "and I am most grateful to you, sir, for giving your time to the case. I hope you don't think I have been unduly meddlesome."

"Not in the least," he replied warmly. "I think you have shown a very proper spirit in the way you have interpreted your neighbourly duties to this poor, bereaved girl, who, apparently, has no one else to watch over her interests. And I take it as a compliment from an old pupil that you should seek my help."

I thanked him again, very sincerely, and had risen to take my leave, when he held up his hand.

"Sit down, Gray, if you are not in a hurry," said he. "I hear the pleasant clink of crockery. Let us follow the example of the eminent Mr Pepys – though it isn't always a safe thing to do – and taste of the 'China drinke called Tee', while you tell me what you have been doing since you went forth from the fold."

It struck me that the sense of hearing was uncommonly well developed in this establishment, for I had heard nothing; but a few moments later the door opened very quietly and Mr Polton entered with a tray on which was a very trim, and even dainty, tea-service, which he set out, noiselessly and with a curious neatness of hand, on a small table placed conveniently between our chairs.

"Thank you, Polton," said Thorndyke. "I see you diagnosed my visitor as a professional brother."

Polton crinkled benevolently and admitted that he "thought the gentleman looked like one of us"; and with this he melted away, closing the door behind him without a sound.

"Well," said Thorndyke, as he handed me my tea-cup, "what have you been doing with yourself since you left the hospital?"

"Principally looking for a job," I replied; "and now I've found one — a temporary job, though I don't know how temporary. Tomorrow I take over the practice of a man named Cornish in Mecklenburgh Square. Cornish is a good deal run down and wants to take a quiet holiday on the East Coast. He doesn't know how long he will be away. It depends on his health; but I have told him that I am prepared to stay as long as he wants me to. I hope I shan't make a mess of the job, but I know nothing of general practice."

"You will soon pick it up," said Thorndyke; "but you had better get your principal to show you the ropes before he goes, particularly the dispensing and book-keeping. The essentials of practice you know, but the little practical details have to be learnt, and you are doing well to make your first plunge into professional life in a practice that is a going concern. The experience will be valuable when you make a start on your own account."

On this plane of advice and comment our talk proceeded until I thought that I had stayed long enough, when I once more rose to depart. Then, as we were shaking hands, Thorndyke reverted to the object of my visit.

"I shall not appear in this case unless the coroner wishes me to," said he. "I shall consult with the official medical witness and he will probably give our joint conclusions in his evidence — unless we should fail to agree, which is very unlikely. But you will be present, and you had better attend closely to the evidence of all the witnesses and let me have your account of the inquest as well as the shorthand writer's report. Goodbye, Gray. You won't be far away if you should want my help or advice."

I left the precincts of the Temple in a much more satisfied frame of mind. The mystery which seemed to me to surround the death of Julius D'Arblay would be investigated by a supremely competent observer, and I need not further concern myself with it. Perhaps there was no mystery at all. Possibly the evidence at the inquest would supply a simple explanation. At any rate, it was out of my hands and into those of one immeasurably more capable, and I could now give my undivided attention to the new chapter of my life that was to open on the morrow.

CHAPTER THREE

The Doctor's Revelations

It was in the evening of the very day on which I took up my duties at number 61 Mecklenburgh Square that the little blue paper was delivered summoning me to attend at the inquest on the following day. Fortunately, Dr Cornish's practice was not of a highly strenuous type, and the time of year tended to a small visiting-list, so that I had no difficulty in making the necessary arrangements. In fact, I made them so well that I was the first to arrive at the little building in which the inquiry was to be held and was admitted by the caretaker to the empty room. A few minutes later, however, the inspector made his appearance, and while I was exchanging a few words with him, the jury began to straggle in, followed by the reporters, a few spectators and witnesses, and finally the coroner, who immediately took his place at the head of the table and prepared to open the proceedings.

At this moment I observed Miss D'Arblay standing hesitatingly in the doorway and looking into the room as if reluctant to enter. I at once rose and went to her, and as I approached, she greeted me with a friendly smile and held out her hand; and then I perceived, lurking just outside, a tall, black-apparelled woman, whose face I recognized as that which I had seen at the window.

"This," said Miss D'Arblay, presenting me, "is my friend Miss Boler, of whom I spoke to you. This, Arabella, dear, is the gentleman who was so kind to me on that dreadful day."

I bowed deferentially and Miss Boler recognized my existence by a majestic inclination, remarking that she remembered me. As the coroner now began his preliminary address to the jury, I hastened to find three chairs near the table, and having inducted the ladies into two of them, took the third myself, next to Miss D'Arblay. The coroner and the jury now rose and went out to the adjacent mortuary to view the body, and during their absence I stole an occasional critical glance at my fair friend.

Marion D'Arblay was, as I have said, a strikingly handsome girl. The fact seemed now to dawn on me afresh, as a new discovery; for the harrowing circumstances of our former meeting had so preoccupied me that I had given little attention to her personality. But now, as I looked her over anxiously to see how the grievous days had dealt with her, it was with a sort of surprised admiration that I noted the beautiful, thoughtful face, the fine features and the wealth of dark, gracefully disposed hair. I was relieved, too, to see the change that a couple of days had wrought. The wild, dazed look was gone. Though she was pale and heavy-eyed and looked tired and infinitely sad, her manner was calm, quiet and perfectly self-possessed.

"I am afraid," said I, "that this is going to be rather a painful ordeal for you."

"Yes," she agreed, "it is all very dreadful. But it is a dreadful thing in any case to be bereft in a moment of the one whom one loves best in all the world. The circumstances of the loss cannot make very much difference. It is the loss itself that matters. The worst moment was when the blow fell – when we found him. This inquiry and the funeral are just the drab accompaniments that bring home the reality of what has happened."

"Has the inspector called on you?" I asked.

"Yes," she replied. "He had to, to get the particulars; and he was so kind and delicate that I am not in the least afraid of the examination by the coroner. Everyone has been kind to me, but none so kind as you were on that terrible morning."

I could not see that I had done anything to call for so much gratitude, and I was about to enter a modest disclaimer when the coroner and the jury returned and the inspector approached somewhat hurriedly.

"It will be necessary," said he, "for Miss D'Arblay to see the body – just to identify deceased; a glance will be enough. And, as you are a witness, Doctor, you had better go with her to the mortuary. I will show you the way."

Miss D'Arblay rose without any comment or apparent reluctance and we followed the inspector to the adjoining mortuary, where, having admitted us, he stood outside awaiting us. The body lay on the slate-topped table, covered with a sheet excepting the face, which was exposed and was undisfigured by any traces of the examination. I watched my friend a little nervously as we entered the grim chamber, fearful that this additional trial might be too much for her self-control. But she kept command of herself, though she wept quietly as she stood beside the table looking down on the still, waxen-faced figure. After standing thus for a few moments, she turned away with a smothered sob, wiped her eyes and walked out of the mortuary.

When we re-entered the court-room, we found our chairs moved up to the table and the coroner waiting to call the witnesses. As I had expected, my name was the first on the list, and on being called, I took my place by the table near to the coroner and was duly sworn.

"Will you give us your name, occupation and address?" the coroner asked.

"My name is Stephen Gray," I replied. "I am a medical practitioner and my temporary address is 61 Mecklenburgh Square, London."

"When you say your 'temporary address', you mean – ?"

"I am taking charge of a medical practice at that address. I shall be there six weeks or more."

"Then that will be your address for our purposes. Have you viewed the body that is now lying in the mortuary, and, if so, do you recognize it?"

"Yes. It is the body which I saw lying in a pond in Churchyard Bottom Wood on the morning of the 16th instant – last Tuesday."

"Can you tell us how long deceased had been dead when you first saw the body?"

"I should say he had been dead nine or ten hours."

"Will you relate the circumstances under which you discovered the body?"

I gave a circumstantial account of the manner in which I made the tragic discovery, to which not only the jury but also the spectators listened with eager interest. When I had finished my narrative, the coroner asked:

"Did you observe anything which led you, as a medical man, to form any opinion as to the cause of death?"

"No," I replied. "I saw no injuries or marks of violence or anything which was not consistent with death by drowning."

This concluded my evidence, and when I had resumed my seat, the name of Marion D'Arblay was called by the coroner, who directed that a chair should be placed for the witness. When she had taken her seat, he conveyed to her, briefly but feelingly, his own and the jury's sympathy.

"It has been a terrible experience for you," he said, "and we are most sorry to have to trouble you in your great affliction, but you will understand that it is unavoidable."

"I quite understand that," she replied, "and I wish to thank you and the jury for your kind sympathy."

She was then sworn, and having given her name and address, proceeded to answer the questions addressed to her, which elicited a narrative of the events substantially identical with that which she had given to the inspector and which I have already recorded.

"You have told us," said the coroner, "that when Dr Gray spoke to you, you were searching among the bushes. Will you tell us what was in your mind – what you were searching for and what induced you to make that search?"

"I was very uneasy about my father," she replied. "He had not been home that night and he had not told me that he intended to stay at the studio – as he sometimes did when he was working very late. So, in the morning I went to the studio in Abbey Road to see if he was there; but the caretaker told me that he had started for home about ten o'clock. Then I began to fear that something had happened to him, and as he always came home by the path through the wood, I went there to see if – if anything had happened to him."

"Had you in your mind any definite idea as to what might have happened to him?"

"I thought he might have been taken ill or have fallen down dead. He once told me that he would probably die quite suddenly. I believe that he suffered from some affection of the heart, but he did not like speaking about his health."

"Are you sure that there was nothing more than this in your mind?"

"There was nothing more. I thought that his heart might have failed and that he might have wandered, in a half-conscious state, away from the main path and fallen dead in one of the thickets."

The coroner pondered this reply for some time. I could not see why, for it was plain and straightforward enough. At length he said, very gravely and with what seemed to me unnecessary emphasis:

"I want you to be quite frank and open with us, Miss D'Arblay. Can you swear that there was no other possibility in your mind than that of sudden illness?"

She looked at him in surprise, apparently not understanding the drift of the question. As to me, I assumed that he was endeavouring delicately to ascertain whether deceased was addicted to drink.

"I have told you exactly what was in my mind," she replied.

"Have you ever had any reason to suppose, or to entertain the possibility, that your father might take his own life?"

"Never," she answered emphatically. "He was a happy, even-tempered man, always interested in his work and always in good spirits. I am sure he would never have taken his own life."

The coroner nodded with a rather curious air of satisfaction, as if he were concurring with the witness' statement. Then he asked in the same grave, emphatic manner:

"So far as you know, had your father any enemies?"

"No," she replied confidently. "He was a kindly, amiable man who disliked nobody, and everyone who knew him loved him."

As she uttered this panegyric (and what prouder testimony could a daughter have given?), her eyes filled, and the coroner looked at her with deep sympathy but yet with a somewhat puzzled expression.

"You are sure," he said gently, "that there was no one whom he might have injured – even inadvertently – or who bore him any grudge or ill-will?"

"I am sure," she answered, "that he never injured or gave offence to anyone, and I do not believe that there was any person in the whole world who bore him anything but good-will."

The coroner noted this reply, and as he entered it in the depositions, his face bore the same curious puzzled or doubtful expression. When he had written the answer down, he asked:

"By the way, what was the deceased's occupation?"

"He was a sculptor by profession, but in late years he worked principally as a modeller for various trades – pottery manufacturers, picture-frame makers, carvers and the makers of high-class wax figures for shop windows."

"Had he any assistants or subordinates?"

"No. He worked alone. Occasionally I helped him with his moulds when he was very busy or had a very large work on hand; but usually he did everything himself. Of course, he occasionally employed models."

"Do you know who those models were?"

"They were professional models. The men, I think, were all Italians and some of the women were, too. I believe my father kept a list of them in his address book."

"Was he working from a model on the night of his death?"

"No. He was making the moulds for a porcelain statuette."

"Did you ever hear that he had any kind of trouble with his models?"

"Never. He seemed always on the best of terms with them and he used to speak of them most appreciatively."

"What sort of persons are professional models? Should you say they are a decent, well-conducted class?"

"Yes. They are usually most respectable, hardworking people; and, of course, they are sober and decent in their habits or they would be of no use for their professional duties."

The coroner meditated on these replies with a speculative eye on the witness. After a short pause, he began along another line.

"Did deceased ever carry about with him property of any considerable value?"

"Never, to my knowledge."

"No jewellery, plate or valuable material?"

"No. His work was practically all in plaster or wax. He did no goldsmith's work and he used no precious material."

"Did he ever have any considerable sums of money about him?"

"No. He received all his payments by cheque and he made his payments in the same way. His habit was to carry very little money on his person – usually not more than one or two pounds."

Once more the coroner reflected profoundly. It seemed to me that he was trying to elicit some fact – I could not imagine what – and was failing utterly. At length, after another puzzled look at the witness, he turned to the jury and inquired if any of them wished to put any questions; and when they had severally shaken their heads, he thanked Miss D'Arblay for the clear and straightforward way in which she had given her evidence and released her.

While the examination had been proceeding, I had allowed my eyes to wander round the room with some curiosity, for this was the first time that I had ever been present at an inquest. From the jury, the witnesses in waiting and the reporters – among whom I tried to identify Dr Thorndyke's stenographer – my attention was presently transferred to the spectators. There were only a few of them, but I found myself wondering why there should be any. What kind of person attends as a spectator at an ordinary inquest such as this appeared to be? The newspaper reports of the finding of the body were quite unsensational and promised no startling developments. Finally, I decided that they were probably local residents who had some knowledge of the deceased and were just indulging their neighbourly curiosity.

Among them my attention was particularly attracted by a middle-aged woman who sat near me – at least I judged her to be middle-aged, though the rather dense black veil that she wore obscured her face to a great extent. Apparently she was a widow, and advertised the fact by the orthodox, old-fashioned "weeds". But I could see that she had white hair and wore spectacles. She held a folded newspaper on her knee, apparently dividing her attention between the printed matter and the proceedings of the court. She gave me the impression of having come in to spend an idle hour, combining a somewhat perfunctory reading of the paper with a still more perfunctory attention to the rather gruesome entertainment that the inquest afforded.

The next witness called was the doctor who had made the official examination of the body; on whom the – presumed – widow bestowed a listless, incurious glance and then returned to her newspaper. He was a youngish man, though his hair was turning grey, with a quiet but firm and confident manner and a very clear, pleasant voice. The preliminaries having been disposed of, he coroner led off with the question:

"You have made an examination of the body of the deceased?

"Yes. It is that of a well-proportioned, fairly muscular man of about sixty, quite healthy with the exception of the heart, one of the valves of which – the mitral valve – was incompetent and allowed some leakage of blood to take place."

"Was the heart affection sufficient to account for the death of deceased?"

"No. It was quite a serviceable heart. There was good compensation – that is to say, there was extra growth of muscle to make up for the leaky valve. So far as his heart was concerned, deceased might have lived for another twenty years."

"Were you able to ascertain what actually was the cause of death?"

"Yes. The cause of death was aconitine poisoning."

At this reply a murmur of astonishment arose from the jury, and I heard Miss D'Arblay suddenly draw in her breath. The spectators sat up on their benches, and even the veiled lady was so far interested as to look up from her paper.

"How had the poison been administered?" the coroner asked.

"It had been injected under the skin by means of a hypodermic syringe."

"Can you give an opinion as to whether the poison was administered to deceased by himself or by some other person?"

"It could not have been injected by deceased himself," the witness replied. "The needle-puncture was in the back, just below the left shoulder-blade. It is, in my opinion, physically impossible for anyone to inject with a hypodermic syringe into his own body in that spot. And, of course, a person who was administering an injection to himself would select the most convenient spot – such as the front of the thigh. But apart from the question of convenience, the place in which the needle-puncture was found was actually out of reach." Here the witness produced a hypodermic syringe, the action of which he demonstrated with the aid of a glass of water; and having shown the impossibility of applying it to the spot that he had described, passed the syringe round for the jury's inspection.

"Have you formed any opinion as to the purpose for which this drug was administered in this manner?"

"I have no doubt that it was administered for the purpose of causing the death of deceased."

"Might it not have been administered for medicinal purposes?"

"That is quite inconceivable. Leaving out of consideration the circumstances − the time and place where the administration occurred − the dose excludes the possibility of medicinal purposes. It was a lethal dose. From the tissues round the needle puncture we recovered the twelfth of a grain of aconitine. That alone was more than enough to cause death. But a quantity of the poison had been absorbed, as was shown by the fact that we recovered a recognizable trace from the liver."

"What is the medicinal dose of aconitine?"

"The maximum medicinal dose is about the four-hundredth of a grain, and even that is not very safe. As a matter of fact, aconitine is very seldom used in medical practice. It is a dangerous drug and of no particular value."

"How much aconitine do you suppose was injected?"

"Not less than the tenth of a grain − that is, about forty times the maximum medicinal dose. Probably more."

"There can, I suppose, be no doubt as to the accuracy of the facts that you have stated − as to the nature and quantity of the poison?"

"There can be no doubt whatever. The analysis was made in my presence by Professor Woodford of St Margaret's Hospital after I had removed the tissues from the body in his presence. He has not been called because, in accordance with the procedure under Coroner's Law, I am responsible for the analysis and the conclusions drawn from it."

"Taking the medical facts as known to you, are you able to form an opinion as to what took place when the poison was administered?"

"That," the witness replied, "is a matter of inference or conjecture. I infer that the person who administered the poison thrust the needle violently into the back of the deceased, intending to inject the poison into the chest. Actually, the needle struck a rib and bent up sharply, so that the contents of the syringe were delivered just under the skin. Then I take it that the assailant ran away – probably towards the pond – and deceased pursued him. Very soon the poison would take effect, and then deceased would have fallen. He may have fallen into the pond, or more probably was thrown in. He was alive when he fell into the pond, as is proved by the presence of water in the lungs; but he must then have been insensible and in a dying condition, for there was no water in the stomach, which proves that the swallowing reflex had already ceased."

"Your considered opinion, then, based on the medical facts ascertained by you, is, I understand, that deceased died from the effects of a poison injected into his body by some other person with homicidal intent?"

"Yes; that is my considered opinion, and I affirm that the facts do not admit of any other interpretation."

The coroner looked towards the jury. "Do any of you gentlemen wish to ask the witness any questions?" he inquired; and when the foreman had replied that the jury were entirely satisfied with the doctor's explanations, he thanked the witness, who thereupon retired. The medical witness was succeeded by the inspector, who made a short statement respecting the effects found on the person of deceased. They comprised a small sum of money – under two pounds – a watch, keys and other articles, none of them of any appreciable value, but such as they were, furnishing evidence that at least petty robbery had not been the object of the attack.

When the last witness had been heard, the coroner glanced at his notes and then proceeded to address the jury.

"There is little, gentlemen," he began, "that I need say to you. The facts are before you and they seem to admit of only one interpretation. I remind you that, by the terms of your oath, your finding must be 'according to the evidence'. Now, the medical evidence is quite clear and definite. It is to the effect that deceased met his death by poison administered violently by some other person; that is, by homicide. Homicide is the killing of a human being, and it may or may not be criminal. But if the homicidal act is done with the intent to kill, if that intention has been deliberately formed – that is to say, if the homicidal act has been premeditated – then that homicide is wilful murder.

"Now, the person who killed the deceased came to the place where the act was done provided with a solution of a very powerful and uncommon vegetable poison. He was also provided with a very special appliance – to wit, a hypodermic syringe – for injecting it into the body. The fact that he was furnished with the poison and the appliance creates a strong presumption that he came to this place with the deliberate intention of killing the deceased. That is to say, this fact constitutes strong evidence of premeditation.

"As to the motive for this act, we are completely in the dark; nor have we any evidence pointing to the identity of the person who committed that act. But a coroner's inquest is not necessarily concerned with motives, nor is it our business to fix the act on any particular person. We have to find how and by what means the deceased met his death; and for that purpose we have clear and sufficient evidence. I need say no more, but will leave you to agree upon your finding."

There was a brief interval of silence when the coroner had finished speaking. The jury whispered together for a few seconds; then the foreman announced that they had agreed upon their verdict.

"And what is your decision, gentlemen?" the coroner asked.

"We find," was the reply, "that deceased met his death by wilful murder, committed by some person unknown."

The coroner bowed. "I am in entire agreement with you, gentlemen," said he. "No other verdict was possible; and I am sure you will join with me in the hope that the wretch who committed this dastardly crime may he identified and in due course brought to justice."

This brought the proceedings to an end. As the court rose, the spectators filed out of the building and the coroner approached Miss D'Arblay to express once more his deep sympathy with her in her tragic bereavement. I stood apart with Miss Boler, whose rugged face was wet with tears, but set in a grim and wrathful scowl.

"Things have taken a terrible turn," I ventured to observe.

She shook her head and uttered a sort of low growl. "It won't bear thinking of," she said gruffly.

"There is no possible retribution that would meet the case. One has thought that some of the old punishments were cruel and barbarous; but if I could lay my hands on the villain that did this – " She broke off, leaving the conclusion to my imagination, and in an extraordinarily different voice, said: "Come, Miss Marion; let us get out of this awful place."

As we walked away slowly and in silence, I looked at Miss D'Arblay, not without anxiety. She was very pale, and the dazed expression that her face had borne on the fatal day of the discovery had, to some extent, reappeared. But now, the signs of bewilderment and grief were mingled with something new. The rigid face, the compressed lips and lowered brows spoke of a deep and abiding wrath.

Suddenly she turned to me and said, abruptly, almost harshly:

"I was wrong in what I said to you before the inquiry. You remember that I said the circumstances of the loss could make no difference; but they make a whole world of difference. I had supposed that my dear father had died as he had thought he would die; that it was the course of Nature, which we cannot rebel against. Now I know, from what the doctor said, that he might have lived on happily for the full span of human life but for the malice of this unknown wretch. His life was not lost; it was stolen – from him and from me."

"Yes," I said somewhat lamely. "It is a horrible affair."

"It is beyond bearing!" she exclaimed. "If his death had been natural, I would have tried to resign myself to it. I would have tried to put my grief away. But to think that his happy, useful life has been snatched from him, that he has been torn from us who loved him, by the deliberate act of this murderer – it is unendurable. It will be with me every hour of my life until I die. And every hour I shall call on God for justice against this wretch."

I looked at her with a sort of admiring surprise. A quiet, gentle girl as I believed her to be at ordinary times, now, with her flushed cheeks, her flashing eyes and ominous brows, she reminded me of one of the heroines of the French Revolution. Her grief seemed to be merged in a longing for vengeance.

While she had been speaking, Miss Boler had kept up a running accompaniment in a deep, humming bass. I could not catch the words – if there were any – but was aware only of a low, continuous bourdon. She now said with grim decision:

"God will not let him escape. He shall pay the debt to the uttermost farthing." Then, with sudden fierceness, she added: "If I should ever meet with him, I could kill him with my own hand."

After this, both women relapsed into silence, which I was loath to interrupt. The circumstances were too tragic for conversation. When we reached their gate, Miss D'Arblay held out her hand and once again thanked me for my help and sympathy.

"I have done nothing," said I, "that any stranger would not have done, and I deserve no thanks. But I should like to think that you will look on me as a friend, and if you should need any help will let me have the privilege of being of use to you."

"I look on you as a friend already," she replied; "and I hope you will come and see us sometimes – when we have settled down to our new conditions of life."

As Miss Boler seemed to confirm this invitation, I thanked them both and took my leave, glad to think that I had now a recognized status as a friend and might pursue a project which had formed in my mind even before we had left the court-house.

The evidence of the murder, which had fallen like a thunderbolt on us all, had a special significance for me; for I knew that Dr Thorndyke was behind this discovery, though to what extent I could not judge. The medical witness was an obviously capable man, and it might be that he would have made the discovery without assistance. But a needle-puncture in the back is a very inconspicuous thing. Ninety-nine doctors in a hundred would almost certainly have overlooked it, especially in the case of a body apparently "found drowned" and seeming to call for no special examination beyond the search for gross injuries. The revelation was very characteristic of Thorndyke's methods and principles. It illustrated in a most striking manner the truth which he was never tired of insisting on: that it is never safe to accept obvious appearances, and that every case, no matter how apparently simple and commonplace, should be approached with suspicion and scepticism and subjected to the most rigorous scrutiny. That was precisely what had been done in this case; and thereby an obvious suicide had been resolved into a cunningly planned and skilfully executed murder. It was quite possible that, but for my visit to Thorndyke, those cunning plans would have succeeded and the murderer have secured the cover of a verdict of "death by misadventure" or "suicide while temporarily insane". At any rate, the results had justified me in invoking Dr Thorndyke's aid; and the question now arose whether it would be possible to retain him for the further investigation of the case.

This was the project that had occurred to me as I listened to the evidence and realized how completely the unknown murderer had covered up his tracks. But there were difficulties. Thorndyke might consider such an investigation outside his province. Again, the costs involved might be on a scale entirely beyond my means. The only thing to be done was to call on Thorndyke and hear what he had to say on the subject, and this I determined to do on the first opportunity. And having formed this resolution, I made my way back by the shortest route to Mecklenburgh Square, where the evening consultations were now nearly due.

CHAPTER FOUR

Mr Bendelow

There are certain districts in London the appearance of which conveys to the observer the impression that the houses, and indeed the entire streets, have been picked up second-hand. There is in their aspect a grey, colourless, mouldy quality, reminiscent, not of the antique shop, but rather of the marine-store dealers; a quality which even communicates itself to the inhabitants, so that one gathers the impression that the whole neighbourhood was taken as a going concern.

It was on such a district that I found myself looking down from the top of an omnibus a few days after the inquest (Dr Cornish's brougham being at the moment under repairs and his horse "out to grass" during the slack season), being bound for a street in the neighbourhood of Hoxton – Market Street by name – which abutted, as I had noticed when making out my route, on the Regent's Canal. The said route I had written out, and now, in the intervals of my surveys of the unlovely prospect, I divided my attention between it and the note which had summoned me to these remote regions.

Concerning the latter I was somewhat curious, for the envelope was addressed, not to Dr Cornish but to "Dr Stephen Gray". This was really quite an odd circumstance. Either the writer knew me personally or was aware that I was acting as locum tenens for Cornish. But the name – James Morris – was unknown to me, and a careful inspection of the index of the ledger had failed to bring to light anyone answering to the description. So Mr Morris was presumably a stranger to my principal also. The note, which had been left by hand in the morning, requested me to call "as early in the forenoon as possible", which seemed to hint at some degree as of urgency. Naturally, as a young practitioner, I speculated with interest, not entirely unmingled with anxiety, on the possible nature of the case, and also on the patient's reasons for selecting a medical attendant whose residence was so inconveniently far away.

In accordance with my written route, I got off the omnibus at the corner of Shepherdess Walk, and pursuing that pastoral thoroughfare for some distance, presently plunged into a labyrinth of streets adjoining it and succeeded most effectually in losing myself. However, inquiries addressed to an intelligent fish-vendor elicited a most lucid direction and I soon found myself in a little, drab street which justified its name by giving accommodation to a row of stationary barrows loaded with what looked like the "throw-outs" from a colossal spring-clean. Passing along this kerb-side market and reflecting (like Diogenes, in similar circumstances) how many things there were in the world that I did not want, I walked slowly up the street looking for number 23 – my patient's number – and the canal which I had seen on the map. I located them both at the same instant, for number 23 turned out to be the last house on the opposite side, and a few yards beyond it the street was barred by a low wall, over which, as I looked, the mast of a sailing-barge came into view and slowly crept past. I stepped up to the wall and looked over. Immediately beneath me was the towing-path, alongside which the barge was now bringing up and beginning to lower her mast, apparently to pass under a bridge that spanned the canal a couple of hundred yards farther along.

From these nautical manœuvres I transferred my attention to my patient's house – or at least, so much of it as I could see; for number 23 appeared to consist of a shop with nothing over it. There was, however, in a wall which extended to the canal wall, a side door with a bell and knocker, so I inferred that the house was behind the shop and that the latter had been built on a formerly existing front garden. The shop itself was somewhat reminiscent of the stalls down the street, for though the fascia was newly painted (with the inscription "J. Morris, Dealer in Antiques"), the stock-in-trade exhibited in the window was in the last stage of senile decay. It included, I remember, a cracked Toby jug, a mariner's sextant of an obsolete type, a Dutch clock without hands, a snuff-box, one or two plaster statuettes, an invalid punch-bowl, a shiny, dark and inscrutable oil-painting and a plaster mask, presumably the death-mask of some celebrity whose face was unknown to me.

My examination of this collection was brought to a sudden end by the apparition of a face above the half-blind of the grazed shop door; the face of a middle-aged woman who seemed to be inspecting me with malevolent interest. Assuming – rather too late – a brisk, professional manner, I opened the shop door, thereby setting a bell jangling within, and confronted the owner of the face.

"I am Dr Gray," I began to explain.

"Side-door," she interrupted brusquely. "Ring the bell and knock."

I backed out hastily and proceeded to follow the directions, giving a tug at the bell and delivering a flourish on the knocker. The hollow reverberations of the latter almost suggested an empty house, but my vigorous pull at the bell-handle produced no audible result, from which I inferred – wrongly, as afterwards appeared – that it was out of repair. After waiting quite a considerable time, I was about to repeat the performance when I heard sounds within; and then the door was opened, to my surprise, by the identical sour-faced woman whom I had seen in the shop. As her appearance and manner did not invite conversation, and as she uttered no word, I followed her in silence through a long passage, or covered way, which ran parallel to the side of the shop and presumably crossed the site of the garden. It ended at a door which opened into the hall proper; a largish square space into which the doors of the ground-floor rooms opened. It contained the main staircase and was closed in at the farther end by a heavy curtain which extended from wall to wall.

We proceeded in this funereal manner up the stairs to the first floor on the landing of which my conductress halted and for the first time broke the silence.

"You will probably find Mr Bendelow asleep or dozing," she said in a rather gruff voice. "If he is, there is no need for you to disturb him."

"Mr Bendelow!" I exclaimed. "I understood that his name was Morris."

"Well, it isn't," she retorted. "It is Bendelow. My name is Morris and so is my husband's. It was he who wrote to you."

"By the way," said I, "how did he know my name? I am acting for Dr Cornish, you know."

"I *didn't* know," said she, "and I don't suppose he did. Probably the servant told him. But it doesn't matter. Here you are, and you will do as well as another. I was telling you about Mr Bendelow. He is in a pretty bad way. The specialist whom Mr Morris took him to – Dr Artemus Cropper – said he had cancer of the bilorus, whatever that is – "

"Pylorus," I corrected.

"Well, pylorus, then, if you prefer it," she corrected impatiently. "At any rate, whatever it is, he's got cancer of it; and as I said before, he is in a pretty bad way. Dr Cropper told us what to do, and we are doing it. He wrote out full directions as to diet – I will show them to you presently – and he said that Mr Bendelow was to have a dose of morphia if he complained of pain – which he does, of course; and that, as there was no chance of his getting better, it didn't matter how much morphia he had. The great thing was to keep him out of pain. So we give it to him twice a day – at least, my husband does – and that keeps him fairly comfortable. In fact he sleeps most of the time and is probably dozing now; so you are not likely to get much out of him, especially as he is rather hard of hearing even when he is awake. And now you had better come in and have a look at him."

She advanced to the door of a room and opened it softly, and I followed in a somewhat uncomfortable frame of mind. It seemed to me that I had no function but that of a mere figure-head. Dr Cropper, whom I knew by name as a physician of some reputation, had made the diagnosis and, prescribed the treatment, neither of which I, as a mere beginner, would think of contesting. It was an unsatisfactory, even an ignominious position, from which my professional pride revolted. But apparently it had to be accepted.

Mr Bendelow was a most remarkable-looking man. Probably he had always been; but now the frightful emaciation (which strongly confirmed Cropper's diagnosis) had so accentuated his original peculiarities that he had the appearance of some dreadful, mirthless caricature. Under the influence of the remorseless disease, every shrinkable structure had shrunk to the vanishing-point, leaving the unshrinkable skeleton jutting out with a most horrible and grotesque effect. His great hooked nose, which must always have been strikingly prominent, stuck out now, thin and sharp, like the beak of some bird of prey. His heavy beetling brows, which must always have given to his face a frowning sullenness, now overhung sockets which had shrunk away into mere caverns. His naturally-high cheek-bones were now not only prominent but exhibited the details of their structure as one sees them in a dry skull. Altogether, his aspect was at once pitiable and forbidding. Of his age I could form no estimate. He might have been a hundred. The wonder was that he was still alive; that there was yet left in that shrivelled body enough material to enable its mechanism to continue its functions.

He was not asleep, but was in that somnolent, lethargic state that is characteristic of the effects of morphia. He took no notice of me when I approached the bed, nor even when I spoke his name somewhat loudly.

"I told you wouldn't get much out of him," said Mrs Morris, looking at me with a sort of grim satisfaction. "He doesn't have a great deal to say to any of us nowadays."

"Well," said I, "there is no need to rouse him, but I had better just examine him, if only as a matter of form. I can't take the case entirely on hearsay."

"I suppose not," she agreed. "You know best. Do what you think necessary, but don't disturb him more than you can help."

It was not a prolonged examination. The first touch of my fingers on the shrunken abdomen made me aware of the unmistakable hard mass and rendered further exploration needless. There could be no doubt as to the nature of the case or of what the future held in store. It was only a question of time, and a short time at that.

The patient submitted to the examination quite passively, but he seemed to be fully aware of what was going on, for he looked at me in a sort of drunken, dreamy fashion but without any sign of interest in my proceedings. When I had finished, I looked him over again, trying to reconstitute him as he might have been before this deadly disease fastened on him. I observed that he "seemed" to have a fair crop of hair of a darkish iron-grey. I say seemed, because the greater part of his head was covered by a skull-cap of black silk; but a fringe of hair straying from under it on to the forehead suggested that he was not bald. His teeth, too, which were rather conspicuous, were natural teeth and in good preservation. In order to confirm this fact, I stooped and raised his lip the better to examine them. But at this point Mrs Morris intervened.

"There, that will do," she said impatiently. "You are not a dentist, and his teeth will last as long as he will want them. If you have finished, you had better come with me and I will show you Dr Cropper's prescriptions. Then you can tell me if you have any further directions to give."

She led the way out of the room, and when I had made a farewell gesture to the patient (of which he took no notice) I followed her down the stairs to the ground-floor, where she ushered me into a small, rather elegantly furnished room. Here she opened the flap of a bureau and from one of the little drawers took an open envelope, which she handed to me. It contained one or two prescriptions for occasional medicines and a sheet of directions relative to the diet and general management of the patient, including the administration of morphia. The latter read, under the general heading, "Simon Bendelow, Esq.,"

"As the case progresses, it will probably be necessary to administer morphine regularly, but the amount given should, if possible, be restricted to $1/4$ gr. Morph. Sulph. not more than twice a day; but, of course, the hopeless prognosis and probable early termination of the case make some latitude admissible."

Although I was in complete agreement with the writer, I was a little puzzled by these documents. They were signed "Artemus Cropper, MD," but they were not addressed to any person by name. They appeared to have been given to Mr Morris, in whose possession they now were; but the use of the word "morphine" instead of the more familiar "morphia" and the general technical phraseology seemed inappropriate to directions addressed to lay persons. As I returned them I remarked:

"These directions read as if they had been intended for the information of a medical man."

"They were," she replied. "They were meant for the doctor who was attending Mr Bendelow at the time. When we moved to this place, I got them from him to show to the new doctor. You are the new doctor."

"Then you haven't been here very long?"

"No," she replied. "We have only just moved in. And that reminds me that our stock of morphia is running out. Could you bring a fresh tube of the tabloids next time you call? My husband left an empty tube for me to give you to remind you what size the tabloids are. He gives Mr Bendelow the injections."

"Thank you," said I, "but I don't want the empty tube. I read the prescription and shan't forget the dose. I will bring a new tube tomorrow – that is, if you want me to call every day. It seems hardly necessary."

"No, it doesn't," she agreed. "I should think twice a week would be quite enough. Monday and Thursday would suit me best; if you could manage to come about this time I should be sure to be in. My time is rather taken up, as I haven't a servant at present."

It was a bad arrangement. Fixed appointments are things to avoid in medical practice. Nevertheless I agreed to it – subject to unforeseen obstacles – and was forthwith conducted back along the covered way and launched into the outer world with a farewell which it would be inadequate to describe as unemotional.

As I turned away from the door I cast a passing glance at the shop-window; and once again I perceived a face above the half-blind. It was a man's face this time; presumably the face of Mr Morris. And like his wife, he seemed to be "taking stock of me". I returned the attention and carried away with me the instantaneous mental photograph of a man in that unprepossessing transitional state between being clean-shaved and wearing a beard which is characterized by a sort of grubby prickliness that disfigures the features without obscuring them. His stubble was barely a week old, but as his complexion and hair were dark the effect was very untidy and disreputable. And yet, as I have said, it did not obscure the features. I was even able, in that momentary glance, to note a detail which would probably have escaped a non-medical eye: the scar of a hare-lip which had been very neatly and skilfully mended and which a moustache would probably have concealed altogether.

I did not, however, give much thought to Mr Morris. It was his dour-faced wife with her gruff, overbearing manner who principally occupied my reflections. She seemed to have divined in some way that I was but a beginner – perhaps my youthful appearance gave her the hint – and to have treated me with almost open contempt. In truth, my position was not a very dignified one. The diagnosis of the case had been made for me, the treatment had been prescribed for me and was being carried out by other hands than mine. My function was to support a kind of legal fiction that I was conducting the case, but principally to supply the morphia (which a chemist might have refused to do) and, when the time came, to sign the death-certificate. It was an ignominious rôle for a young and ambitious practitioner and my pride was disposed to boggle at it. But yet there was nothing to which I could object. The diagnosis was undoubtedly correct and the treatment and management of the case exactly such as I should have prescribed. Finally, I decided that my dissatisfaction was principally due to the unattractive personality of Mrs Morris; and with this conclusion I dismissed the case from my mind and let my thoughts wander into more agreeable channels.

CHAPTER FIVE

Inspector Follett's Discovery

To a man whose mind is working actively, walking is a more acceptable mode of progression than riding in a vehicle. There is a sort of reciprocity between the muscles and the brain – possibly due to the close association of the motor and psychical centres – whereby the activity of the one appears to act as a stimulus to the other. A sharp walk sets the mind working; and, conversely, a state of lively reflection begets an impulse to bodily movement.

Hence, when I had emerged from Market Street and set my face homewards, I let the omnibuses rumble past unheeded. I knew my way now. I had but to retrace the route by which I had come and, preserving my isolation amidst the changing crowd, let my thoughts keep pace with my feet. And I had, in fact, a good deal to think about – a general subject for reflection which arranged itself around two personalities, Miss D'Arblay and Dr Thorndyke.

To the former I had written suggesting a call on her, "subject to the exigencies of the service," on Sunday afternoon, and had received a short but cordial note definitely inviting me to tea. So that matter was settled and really required no further consideration, though it did actually occupy my thoughts for an appreciable part of my walk. But that was mere self-indulgence; the preliminary savouring of an anticipated pleasure. My cogitations respecting Dr Thorndyke were, on the other hand, somewhat troubled. I was eager to invoke his aid in solving the hideous mystery which his acuteness had (I felt convinced) brought into view. But it would probably be a costly business and my pecuniary resources were not great. To apply to him for services of which I could not meet the cost was not to be thought of. The too-common meanness of sponging on a professional man was totally abhorrent to me.

But what was the alternative? The murder of Julius D'Arblay was one of those crimes which offer the police no opportunity; at least, so it seemed to me. Out of the darkness this fiend had stolen to commit this unspeakable atrocity, and into the darkness he had straightway vanished, leaving no trace of his identity nor any hint of his diabolical motive. It might well be that he had vanished for ever; that the mystery of the crime was beyond solution. But if any solution was possible, the one man who seemed capable of discovering it was John Thorndyke.

This conclusion, to which my reflections led again and again, committed me to the dilemma that either this villain must be allowed to go his way unmolested, if the police could find no clue to his identity – a position that I utterly refused to accept – or that the one supremely skilful investigator should be induced, if possible, to take up the inquiry. In the end I decided to call on Thorndyke and frankly lay the facts before him; but to postpone the interview until I had seen Miss D'Arblay and ascertained what view the police took of the case and whether any new facts had transpired.

The train of reflection which brought me to this conclusion had brought me also, by way of Pentonville, to the more familiar neighbourhood of Clerkenwell; and I had just turned into a somewhat squalid by-street which seemed to bear in the right direction, when my attention was arrested by a brass plate affixed to the door of one of those hybrid establishments, intermediate between a shop and a private house, known by the generic name of "open surgery". The name upon the plate – "Dr Solomon Usher" – awakened certain reminiscences. In my freshman days there had been a student of that name at our hospital; a middle-aged man (elderly, we considered him, seeing that he was near upon forty) who, after years of servitude as an unqualified assistant, had scraped together the means of completing his curriculum. I remembered him very well: a facetious, seedy, slightly bibulous but entirely good-natured man, invincibly amiable (as he had need to be), and always in the best of spirits. I recalled the quaint figure that furnished such rich material for our school-boy wit: the solemn spectacles, the ridiculous side-whiskers, the chimney-pot hat, the formal frock-coat (too often decorated with a label secretly pinned to the coat-tail and bearing some such inscription as "This style 10*s*. 6*d*." or other scintillations of freshman humour), and, looking over the establishment, decided that it seemed to present a complete congruity with that well-remembered personality. But the identification was not left to mere surmise, for even as my eye roamed along a range of stoppered bottles that peeped over the wire blind, the door opened and there he was, spectacles, side-whiskers, top-hat and frock-coat, all complete, plus an oedematous-looking umbrella.

He did not recognize me at first – naturally, for I had changed a good deal more than he had in the five or six years that had slipped away – but inquired gravely if I wished to see him. I replied that it had been the dearest wish of my heart, now at length gratified. Then, as I grinned in his face, my identity suddenly dawned on him.

"Why, it's Gray!" he exclaimed, seizing my hand.

"God bless me, what a surprise! I didn't know you. Getting quite a man. Well, I am delighted to see you. Come in and have a drink."

He held the door open invitingly, but I shook my head.

"No, thanks," I replied. "Not at this time in the day."

"Nonsense," he urged. "Do you good. I've just had one myself. Can't say more than that, excepting that I am ready to have another. Won't you really? Pity. Should never waste an opportunity. Which way are you going?"

It seemed that we were going the same way for some distance and we accordingly set off together.

"So you've flopped out of the nest," he remarked, looking me over — "at least, so I judge by the adult clothes that you are wearing. Are you in practice in these parts?"

"No," I replied; "I am doing a locum. Only just qualified, you know."

"Good," said he. "A locum's the way to begin. Try your prentice hand on somebody else's patients and pick up the art of general practice, which they don't teach you at the hospital."

"You mean book-keeping and dispensing and the general routine of the day's work?" I suggested.

"No, I don't," he replied. "I mean practice; the art of pleasing your patients and keeping your end up. You've got a lot to learn, my boy. Experientia does it. Scientific stuff is all very well at the hospital, but in practice it is experience, gumption, tact, knowledge of human nature, that counts."

"I suppose a little knowledge of diagnosis and treatment is useful?" I suggested.

"For your own satisfaction, yes," he admitted; "but for practical purposes, a little knowledge of men and women is a good deal better. It isn't your scientific learning that brings you kudos, nor is it out-of-the-way cases. It is just common sense brought to bear on common ailments. Take the case of an aurist. You think that he lives by dealing with obscure and difficult middle and internal care cases. Nothing of the kind. He lives on wax. Wax is the foundation of his practice. Patient comes to him as deaf as a post. He does all the proper jugglery – tuning-fork, otoscope, speculum and so on, for the moral effect. Then he hikes out a good old plug of cerumen and the patient hears perfectly. Of course, he is delighted. Thinks a miracle has been performed. Goes away convinced that the aurist is a genius; and so he is if he has managed the case properly. I made my reputation here on a fishbone."

"Well, a fish-bone isn't always so very easy to extract," said I.

"It isn't," he agreed. "Especially if it isn't there."

"What do you mean?" I asked.

"I'll tell you about it," he replied. "A chappie here got a fish-bone stuck in his throat. Of course it didn't stay there. They never do. But the prick in his soft palate did, and he was convinced that the bone was still there. So he sent for a doctor. Doctor came, looked in his throat. Couldn't see any fish-bone and, like a fool, said so. Tried to persuade the patient that there was no bone there. But the chappie said it was his throat and he knew better. He could feel it there. So he sent for another doctor and the same thing happened. No go. He had four different doctors and they hadn't the sense of an infant among them. Then he sent for me.

"Now, as soon as I heard how the land lay, I nipped into the surgery and got a fish-bone that I keep there in a pill-box for emergencies, stuck it into the jaws of a pair of throat-forceps, and off I went. 'Show me whereabouts it is,' says I, handing him a probe to point with. He showed me the spot and nearly swallowed the probe. 'All right,' said I. 'I can see it. Just shut your eyes and open your mouth wide and I will have it out in a jiffy.' I popped the forceps into his mouth, gave a gentle prod with the point on the soft palate, patient hollered out, 'Hoo!' I whisked out the forceps and held them up before his eyes with the fish-bone grasped in their jaws.

" 'Ha!' says he. 'Thank Gawd! What a relief! I can swallow quite well now.' And so he could. It was a case of suggestion and counter-suggestion. Imaginary fish-bone cured by imaginary extraction. And it made my local reputation. Well, goodbye, old chap. I've got a visit to make here. Come in one evening and smoke a pipe with me. You know where to find me. And take my advice to heart. Never go to extract a fish-bone without one in your pocket; and it isn't a bad thing to keep a dried earwig by you. I do. People will persist in thinking they've got one in their ears. So long. Look me up soon," and with a farewell flourish of the umbrella, he turned to a shabby street-door and began to work the top bell-pull as if it were the handle of an air-pump.

I went on my way, not a little amused by my friend's genial cynicism, nor entirely uninstructed. For "there is a soul of truth in things erroneous", as the philosopher reminds us; and if the precepts of Solomon Usher did not sound the highest note of professional ethics, they were based on a very solid foundation of worldly wisdom.

When, having finished my short round of visits, I arrived at my temporary home, I was informed by the housemaid in a mysterious whisper that a police officer was waiting to see me. "Name of Follett," she added. "He's waiting in the consulting-room."

Proceeding thither, I found my friend, the Highgate inspector, standing with one eye closed before a card of test-types that hung on the wall. We greeted one another cordially and then, as I looked at him inquiringly, he produced from his pocket without remark an official envelope, from which he extracted a coin, a silver pencil-case and a button. These objects he laid on the writing-table and silently directed my attention to them. A little puzzled by his manner, I picked up the coin and examined it attentively. It was a Charles the Second guinea, dated 1663, very clean and bright and in remarkably perfect preservation. But I could not see that it was any concern of mine.

"It is a beautiful coin," I remarked; "but what about it?"

"It doesn't belong to you, then?" he asked.

"No. I wish it did."

"Have you ever seen it before?"

"Never, to my knowledge."

"What about the pencil-case?"

I picked it up and turned it over in my fingers. "No," I said, "it is not mine and I have no recollection of ever having seen it before."

"And the button?"

"It is apparently a waistcoat button," I said after having inspected it, "which seems to belong to a tweed waistcoat; and judging by the appearance of the thread and the wisp of cloth that it still holds, it must have been pulled off with some violence. But it isn't off my waistcoat, if that is what you want to know."

"I didn't much think it was," he replied, "but I thought it best to make sure. And it didn't come from poor Mr D'Arblay's waistcoat, because I have examined that and there is no button missing. I showed these things to Miss D'Arblay and she is sure that none of them belonged to her father. He never used a pencil-case – artists don't, as a rule – and as to the guinea, she knew nothing about it. If it was her father's, he must have come by it immediately before his death; otherwise she felt sure he would have shown it to her, seeing that they were both interested in anything in the nature of sculpture."

"Where did you get these things?" I asked.

"From the pond in the wood," he replied. "I will tell you how I came to find them – that is, if I am not taking up too much of your time."

"Not at all," I assured him; and even as I spoke. I thought of Solomon Usher. He wouldn't have said that. He would have anxiously consulted his engagement-book to see how many minutes he could spare. However, Inspector Follett was not a patient, and I wanted to hear his story. So having established him in the easy-chair, I sat down to listen.

"The morning after the inquest," he began, "an officer of the CID came up to get particulars of the case and see what was to be done. Well, as soon as I had told him all I knew and shown him our copy of the depositions, it was pretty clear to me that he didn't think there was anything to be done but wait for some fresh evidence. Mind you, Doctor, this is in strict confidence."

"I understand that. But if the Criminal Investigation Department doesn't investigate crime, what the deuce is the good of it?"

"That is hardly a fair way of putting it," he protested. "The people at Scotland Yard have got their hands pretty full and they can't spend their time in speculating about cases in which there is no evidence. They can't create evidence; and you can see for yourself that there isn't the ghost of a clue to the identity of the man who committed this murder. But they are keeping the case in mind, and meanwhile we have got to report any new facts that may turn up. Those were our instructions, and when I heard them I decided to do a bit of investigating on my own, with the superintendent's permission, of course.

"Well, I began by searching the wood thoroughly, but I got nothing out of that excepting Mr D'Arblay's hat, which I found in the undergrowth not far from the main path.

"Then I thought of dragging the pond; but I decided that, as it was only a small pond and shallow, it would be best to empty it and expose the bottom completely. So I dammed up the little stream that feeds it and deepened the outflow, and very soon I had it quite empty excepting a few small puddles. And I think it was well worth the trouble. These things don't tell us much, but they may be useful one day for identification. And they do tell us something. They suggest that this man was a collector of coins; and they make it fairly clear that there was a struggle in the pond before Mr D'Arblay fell down."

"That is, assuming that the things belonged to the murderer," I interposed. "There is no evidence that they did."

"No, there isn't," he admitted; "but if you consider the three things together, they suggest a very strong probability. Here is a waistcoat button violently pulled off, and here are two things such as would be carried in a waistcoat pocket and might fall out if the waistcoat were dragged at violently when the wearer was stooping over a fallen man and struggling to avoid being pulled down with him. And then there is this coin. Its face-value is a guinea, but it must be worth a good deal more than that. Do you suppose anybody would leave a thing of that kind in a shallow pond from which it could be easily recovered with a common landing-net? Why, it would have paid to have had the pond dragged or even emptied. But, as I say, that wouldn't have been necessary."

"I am inclined to think you are right, Inspector," said I, rather impressed by the way in which he had reasoned the matter out;

"but even so, it doesn't seem to me that we are much more forward. The things don't point to any particular person."

"Not at present," he rejoined. "But a fact is a fact and you can never tell in advance what you may get out of it. If we should get a hint of any other kind pointing to some particular person, these things might furnish invaluable evidence connecting that person with the crime. They may even give a clue now to the people at the CID, though that isn't very likely."

"Then you are going to hand them over to the Scotland Yard people?"

"Certainly. The CID are the lions, you know. I'm only a jackal."

"I was rather sorry to hear this, for the idea had floated into my mind that I should have liked Thorndyke to see these waifs, which, could they have spoken, would have had much to tell. To me they conveyed nothing that threw any light on the ghastly events of that night of horror. But to my teacher, with his vast experience and his wonderful power of analysing evidence, they might convey some quite important significance.

I reflected rapidly on the matter. It would not be wise to say anything to the inspector about Thorndyke, and it was quite certain that a loan of the articles would not be entertained. Probably a description of them would be enough for the purpose; but still I had a feeling that an inspection of them would be better. Suddenly I had a bright idea and proceeded cautiously to broach it.

"I should rather like to have a record of these things," said I, "particularly of the coin. Would you object to my taking an impression of it in sealing-wax?"

Inspector Follett looked doubtful. "It would be a bit irregular," he said. "It is a bit irregular for me to have shown it to you, but you are interested in the case, and you are a responsible person. What did you want the impression for?"

"Well," I said, "we don't know much about that coin. I thought I might be able to pick up some further information. Of course, I understand that what you have told me is strictly confidential. I shouldn't go showing the thing about, or talking. But I should like to have the impression to refer to, if necessary."

"Very well," said he. "On that understanding, I have no objection. But see that you don't leave any wax on the coin, or the CID people will be asking questions."

With this permission, I set about the business gleefully, determined to get as good an impression as possible. From the surgery I fetched an ointment slab, a spirit-lamp, a stick of sealing-wax, a teaspoon, some powder-papers, a bowl of water and a jar of vaseline. Laying a paper on the slab, I put the coin on it and traced its outline with a pencil. Then I broke off a piece of sealing-wax, melted it in the teaspoon and poured it out carefully into the marked circle so that it formed a round, convex button of the right size. While the wax was cooling to the proper consistency, I smeared the coin with vaseline and wiped the excess off with my handkerchief. Then I carefully laid it on the stiffening wax and made steady pressure. After a few moments, I cautiously lifted the paper and dropped it into the water, leaving it to cool completely. When, finally, I turned it over under water, the coin dropped away by its own weight.

"It is a beautiful impression," the inspector remarked, as he examined it with the aid of my pocket-lens, while I prepared to operate on the reverse of the coin. "As good as the original. You seem rather a dab at this sort of thing, Doctor. I wonder if you would mind doing another pair for me?"

Of course, I complied gladly; and when the inspector departed a few minutes later he took with him a couple of excellent wax impressions to console him for the necessity of parting with the original.

As soon as he was gone, I proceeded to execute a plan that had already formed in my mind. First, I packed the two wax impressions very carefully in lint and bestowed them in a tin tobacco-box, which I made up into a neat parcel and addressed it to Dr Thorndyke. Then I wrote him a short letter giving him the substance of my talk with Inspector Follett and asking for an appointment early in the following week to discuss the situation with him. I did not suppose that the wax impressions would convey, even to him, anything that would throw fresh light on this extraordinarily obscure crime. But one never knew. And the mere finding of the coin might suggest to him some significance that I had overlooked. In any case, the new incident gave me an excuse for reopening the matter with him.

I did not trust the precious missive to the maid, but as soon as the letter was written I took it and the parcel in my own hands to the post, dropping the letter into the box but giving the parcel the added security of registration. This business being thus dispatched, my mind was free to occupy itself with pleasurable anticipations of the projected visit to Highgate on the morrow and to deal with whatever exigencies might arise in the course of the Saturday evening consultations.

CHAPTER SIX
Marion D'Arblay at Home

Most of us have, I imagine, been conscious at times of certain misgivings as to whether the Progress of which we hear so much has done for us all that it is assumed to have done; whether the undoubted gain of advancing knowledge has not a somewhat heavy counterpoise of loss. We moderns are accustomed to look upon a world filled with objects that, would have made our forefathers gasp with admiring astonishment; and we are accordingly a little puffed up by our superiority. But the museums and galleries and ancient buildings sometimes tell a different tale. By them we are made aware that these same "rude forefathers" were endowed with certain powers and aptitudes that seem to be denied to the present generation.

Some such reflections as these passed through my mind as I sauntered about the ancient village of Highgate, having arrived in the neighbourhood nearly an hour too early. Very delightful the old village was to look upon, and so it had been even when the mellow red brick was new and the plaster on the timber houses was but freshly laid; when the great elms were saplings and the stage-wagon with its procession of horses rumbled along the road which now resounds to the thunder of the electric tram. It was not Time that had made beautiful its charming old houses and pleasant streets and closes, but fine workmanship guided by unerring taste.

At four o'clock precisely, by the chime of the church clock, I pushed open the gate of Ivy Cottage, and as I walked up the flagged path, read the date, 1709, on a stone tablet let into the brickwork. I had no occasion to knock, for my approach had been observed, and as I mounted the threshold the door opened and Miss D'Arblay stood in the opening.

"Miss Boler saw you coming up the Grove," she explained, as we shook hands. "It is surprising how much of the outer world you can see from a bay window. It is as good as a watch-tower." She disposed of my hat and stick and then preceded me into the room to which the window appertained, where, beside a bright fire, Miss Boler was at the moment occupied with a brilliantly-burnished copper kettle and a silver teapot. She greeted me with an affable smile and as much of a bow as was possible under the circumstances, and then proceeded to make the tea with an expression of deep concentration.

"I do like punctual people," she remarked, placing the teapot on a carved wooden stand. "You know where you are with them. At the very moment when you turned the corner, sir, Miss Marion finished buttering the last muffin and the kettle boiled over. So you won't have to wait a moment."

Miss D'Arblay laughed softly. "You speak as if Dr Gray had staggered into the house in a famished condition, roaring for food," said she.

"Well," retorted Miss Boler, "you said 'tea at four o'clock', and at four o'clock the tea was ready and Dr Gray was here. If he hadn't been, he would have had to eat leathery muffins, that's all."

"Horrible!" exclaimed Miss D'Arblay. "One doesn't like to think of it; and there is no need to as it hasn't happened. Remember that this is a gate-legged table, Dr Gray, when you sit down. They are delightfully picturesque, but exceedingly bad for the knees of the unwary."

I thanked her for the warning and took my seat with due caution. Then Miss Boler poured out the tea and uncovered the muffins with the grave and attentive air of one performing some ceremonial rite.

As the homely, simple meal proceeded, to an accompaniment of desultory conversation on everyday topics, I found myself looking at the two women with a certain ill-defined surprise. Both were garbed in unobtrusive black, and both, in moments of repose, looked somewhat tired and worn. But in their manner and the subjects of their conversation they were astonishingly ordinary and normal. No stranger, looking at them and listening to their talk, would have dreamed of the tragedy that over-shadowed their lives. But so it constantly happens. We go into a house of mourning and are almost scandalized by its cheerfulness, forgetting that whereas to us the bereavement is the one salient fact, to the bereaved there is the necessity of taking up afresh the threads of their lives. Food must be prepared even while the corpse lies under the roof, and the common daily round of duty stands still for no human affliction.

But, as I have said, in the pauses of the conversation when their faces were in repose, both women looked strained and tired. Especially was this so in the case of Miss D'Arblay. She was not only pale, but she had a nervous, shaken manner which I did not like. And as I looked anxiously at the delicate, pallid face, I noticed, not for the first time, several linear scratches on the cheek and a small cut on the temple.

"What have you been doing to yourself?" I asked. "You look as if you have had a fall."

"She has," said Miss Boler in an indignant tone. "It is a marvel that she is here to tell the tale. The wretches!"

I looked at Miss D'Arblay in consternation.

"What wretches?" I asked.

"Ah! indeed!" growled Miss Boler. "I wish I knew. Tell him about it, Miss Marion."

"It was really rather a terrifying experience," said Miss D'Arblay, "and most mysterious. You know Southwood Lane and the long, steep hill at the bottom of it?" I nodded, and she continued: "I have been going down to the studio every day on my bicycle, just to tidy up, and of course I went by Southwood Lane. It is really the only way. But I always put on the brake at the top of the hill and go down quite slowly because of the crossroads at the bottom. Well, three days ago I started as usual and ran down the Lane pretty fast until I got on the hill. Then I put on the brake; and I could feel at once that it wasn't working."

"Has your bicycle only one brake?" I asked.

"It had. I am having a second one fixed now. Well, when I found that the brake wasn't acting, I was terrified. I was already going too fast to jump off, and the speed increased every moment. I simply flew down the hill, faster and faster, with the wind whistling about my ears and the trees and houses whirling past like express trains. Of course, I could do nothing but steer straight down the hill; but at the bottom there was the Archway Road with the trams and buses and wagons. I knew that if a tram crossed the bottom of the Lane as I reached the road, it was practically certain death. I was horribly frightened.

"However, mercifully the Archway Road was clear when I flew across it, and I steered to run on down Muswell Hill Road, which is nearly in a line with the Lane. But suddenly I saw a steam roller and a heavy cart, side by side and taking up the whole of the road. There was no room to pass. The only possible thing was to swerve round, if I could, into Wood Lane. And I just managed it. But Wood Lane is pretty steep, and I flew down it faster than ever. That nearly broke down my nerve; for at the bottom of the Lane is the wood – the horrible wood that I can never even think of without a shudder. And there I seemed to be rushing towards it to my death."

She paused and drew a deep breath, and her hand shook so that the cup which it held rattled on the saucer.

"Well," she continued, "down the Lane I flew with my heart in my mouth and the entrance to the wood rushing to meet me. I could see that the opening in the hurdles was just wide enough for me to pass through, and I steered for it. I whizzed through into the wood and the bicycle went bounding down the steep, rough path at a fearful pace until it came to a sharp turn; and then I don't quite know what happened. There was a crash of snapping branches and a violent shock, but I must have been partly stunned, for the next thing that I remember is opening my eyes and looking stupidly at a lady who was stooping over me. She had seen me fly down the Lane and had followed me into the Wood to see what happened to me. She lived in the Lane and she very kindly took me to her house and cared for me until I was quite recovered; and then she saw me home and wheeled the bicycle."

"It is a wonder you were not killed outright!" I exclaimed.

"Yes," she agreed, "it was a narrow escape. But the odd thing is that, with the exception of these scratches and a few slight bruises, I was not hurt at all; only very much shaken. And the bicycle was not damaged a bit."

"By the way," said I, "what had happened to the brake?"

"Ah!" exclaimed Miss Boler. "There you are. The villains!"

Miss D'Arblay laughed softly. "Ferocious Arabella!" said she. "But it is really a most mysterious affair. Naturally, I thought that the wire of the brake had snapped. But it hadn't. It had been cut."

"Are you quite sure of that?" I asked.

"Oh, there is no doubt at all," she replied. "The man at the repair shop showed it to me. It wasn't merely cut in one place. A length of it had been cut right out. And I can tell within a few minutes when it was done; for I had been riding the machine in the morning and I know the brake was all right then. But I left it for a few minutes outside the gate while I went into the house to change my shoes, and when I came out, I started on my adventurous journey. In those few minutes someone must have come along and just snipped the wire through in two places and taken away the piece."

"Scoundrel!" muttered Miss Boler; and I agreed with her most cordially.

"It was an infamous thing to do," I exclaimed, "and the act of an abject fool. I suppose you have no idea or suspicion as to who the idiot might be?"

"Not the slightest," Miss D'Arblay replied. "I can't even guess at the kind of person who would do such a thing. Boys are sometimes very mischievous, but this is hardly like a boy's mischief."

"No," I agreed; "it is more like the mischief of a mentally defective adult; the sort of half-baked larrikin who sets fire to a rick if he gets the chance."

Miss Boler sniffed. "Looks to me more like deliberate malice," said she.

"Mischievous acts usually do," I rejoined; "but yet they are mostly the outcome of stupidity that is indifferent to consequences."

"And it is of no use arguing about it," said Miss D'Arblay, "because we don't know who did it or why he did it, and we have no means of finding out. But I shall have two brakes in future and I shall test them both every time I take the machine out."

"I hope you will," said Miss Boler; and this closed the topic so far as conversation went, though I suspect that, in the interval of silence that followed, we all continued to pursue it in our thoughts. And to all of us, doubtless, the mention of Churchyard Bottom Wood had awakened memories of that fatal morning when the pool gave up its dead. No reference to the tragedy had yet been made, but it was inevitable that the thoughts which were at the back of all our minds should sooner or later come to the surface. They were in fact brought there by me, though unintentionally; for, as I sat at the table, my eyes had strayed more than once to a bust – or rather a head, for there were no shoulders – which occupied the centre of the mantelpiece. It was apparently of lead and was a portrait, and a very good one, of Miss D'Arblay's father. At the first glance I had recognized the face which I had first seen through the water of the pool. Miss D'Arblay, who was sitting facing it, caught my glance and said: "You are looking at that head of my dear father. I suppose you recognized it?"

"Yes, instantly. I should take it to be an excellent likeness."

"It is," she replied; "and that is something of an achievement in a self-portrait in the round."

"Then he modelled it himself?"

"Yes, with the aid of one or two photographs and a couple of mirrors. I helped him by taking the dimensions with callipers and drawing out a scale. Then he made a wax cast and a fireproof mould and we cast it together in type-metal, as we had no means of melting bronze. Poor Daddy! How proud he was when we broke away the mould and found the casting quite perfect!"

She sighed as she gazed fondly on the beloved features, and her eyes filled. Then, after a brief silence, she turned to me and asked:

"Did Inspector Follett call on you? He said he was going to."

"Yes; he called yesterday to show me the things that he had found in the pond. Of course they were not mine, and he seemed to have no doubt – and I think he is right – that they belonged to the – to the – "

"Murderer," said Miss Boler.

"Yes. He seemed to think that they might furnish some kind of clue, but I am afraid he had nothing very clear in his mind. I suppose that coin suggested nothing to you?"

Miss D'Arblay shook her head. "Nothing," she replied. "As it is an ancient coin, the man may he a collector or a dealer – "

"Or a forger," interposed Miss Boler.

"Or a forger. But no such person is known to us. And even that is mere guess-work."

"Your father was not interested in coins, then?"

"As a sculptor, yes, and more especially in medals and plaquettes. But not as a collector. He had no desire to possess; only to create. And so far as I know, he was not acquainted with any collectors. So this discovery of the inspector's, so far from solving the mystery, only adds a fresh problem."

She reflected for a few moments with knitted brows; then, turning to me quickly, she asked:

"Did the inspector take you into his confidence at all? He was very reticent with me, though most kind and sympathetic. But do you think that he, or the others, are taking any active measures?"

"My impression," I answered reluctantly, "is that the police are not in a position to do anything. The truth is that this villain seems to have got away without leaving a trace."

"That is what I feared," she sighed. Then with sudden passion, though in a quiet, suppressed voice, she exclaimed: "But he must not escape! It would be too hideous an injustice. Nothing can bring back my dear father from the grave; but if there is a God of Justice, this murderous wretch must be called to account and made to pay the penalty of his crime."

"He must," Miss Boler assented in deep, ominous tones, "and he shall; though God knows how it is to be done."

"For the present," said I, "there is nothing to he done but to wait and see if the police are able to obtain any fresh information; and meanwhile to turn over every circumstance that you can think of; to recall the way your father spent his time, the people he knew and the possibility in each case that some cause of enmity may have arisen."

"That is what I have done," said Miss D'Arblay. "Every night I lie awake, thinking, thinking; but nothing comes of it. The thing is incomprehensible. This man must have been a deadly enemy of my father's. He must have hated him with the most intense hatred; or he must have had some strong reason, other than mere hatred, for making away with him. But I cannot imagine any person hating my father and I certainly have no knowledge of any such person; nor can I conceive of any reason that any human creature could have had for wishing for my father's death. I cannot begin to understand the meaning of what has happened."

"But yet," said I, "there must be a meaning. This man – unless he was a lunatic, which he apparently was not – must have had a motive for committing the murder. That motive must have had some background, some connexion with circumstances of which somebody has knowledge. Sooner or later those circumstances will almost certainly come to light and then the motive for the murder will come into view. But, once the motive is known, it should not be difficult to discover who could be influenced by such a motive. Let us, for the present, be patient and see how events shape; but let us also keep a constant watch for any glimmer of light, for any fact that may bear on either the motive or the person."

The two women looked at me earnestly and with an expression of respectful confidence of which I knew myself to be wholly undeserving.

"It gives me new courage," said Miss D'Arblay, "to hear you speak in that reasonable, confident tone. I was in despair, but I feel that you are right. There must be some explanation of this awful thing; and if there is, it must be possible to discover it. But we ought not to put the burden of our troubles on you, though you have been so kind."

"You have done me the honour," said I, "to allow me to consider myself your friend. Surely friends should help to bear one another's burdens."

"Yes," she replied, "in reason; and you have given most generous help already. But we must not put too much on you. When my father was alive, he was my great interest and chief concern. Now that he is gone, the great purpose of my life is to find the wretch who murdered him and to see that justice is done. That is all that seems to matter to me. But it is my own affair. I ought not to involve my friends in it."

"I can't admit that," said I. "The foundation of friendship is sympathy and service. If I am your friend, then what matters to you matters to me; and I may say that in the very moment when I first knew that your father had been murdered, I made the resolve to devote myself to the discovery and punishment of his murderer by any means that lay in my power. So you must count me as your ally as well as your friend."

As I made this declaration – to an accompaniment of approving growls from Miss Boler – Marion D'Arblay gave me one quick glance and then looked down; and once more her eyes filled. For a few moments she made no reply; and when, at length, she spoke, her voice trembled.

"You leave me nothing to say," she murmured, "but to thank you from my heart. But you little know what it means to us, who felt so helpless, to know that we have a friend so much wiser and stronger than ourselves."

I was a little abashed, knowing my own weakness and helplessness, to find her putting so much reliance on me. However, there was Thorndyke in the background; and now I was resolved that, if the thing was in any way to be compassed, his help must be secured without delay.

A longish pause followed; and as it seemed to me that there was nothing more to say on this subject until I had seen Thorndyke, I ventured to open a fresh topic.

"What will happen to your father's practice?" I asked. "Will you be able to get anyone to carry it on for you?"

"I am glad you asked that," said Miss D'Arblay, "because, now that you are our counsellor, we can take your opinion. I have already talked the matter over with Arabella — with Miss Boler."

"There's no need to stand on ceremony," the latter lady interposed. "Arabella is good enough for me."

"Arabella is good enough for anyone," said Miss D'Arblay. "Well, the position is this. The part of my father's practice that was concerned with original work — pottery figures and reliefs and models for goldsmith's work — will have to go. No one but a sculptor of his own class could carry that on. But the wax figures for the shop-windows are different. When he first started, he used to model the heads and limbs in clay and make plaster casts from which to make the gelatine moulds for the wax-work. But as time went on, these casts accumulated and he very seldom had need to model fresh heads or limbs. The old casts could be used over and over again. Now there is a large collection of plaster models in the studio — heads, arms, legs and faces, especially faces — and as I have a fair knowledge of the wax-work, from watching my father and sometimes helping him, it seemed that I might be able to carry on that part of the practice."

"You think you could make the wax figures yourself?" I asked.

"Of course she could," exclaimed Miss Boler. "She's her father's daughter. Julius D'Arblay was a man who could do anything he turned his hand to and do it well. And Miss Marion is just like him. She is quite a good modeller – so her father said; and she wouldn't have to make the figures. Only the wax parts."

"Then they are not wax all over?" said I.

"No," answered Miss D'Arblay. "They are just dummies; wooden frameworks covered with stuffed canvas, with wax heads, busts and arms and shaped legs. That was just what poor Daddy used to hate about them. He would have liked to model complete figures."

"And as to the business side. Could you dispose of them?"

"Yes, if I could do them satisfactorily. The agent who dealt with my father's work has already written to me asking if I could carry on. I know he will help me so far as he can. He was quite fond of my father."

"And you have nothing else in view?"

"Nothing by which I could earn a real living. For the last year or two I have worked at writing and illuminating – addresses, testimonials and church services when I could get them – and filled in the time writing special window-tickets. But that isn't very remunerative, whereas the wax figures would yield quite a good living. And then," she added, after a pause, "I have the feeling that Daddy would have liked me to carry on his work, and I should like it myself. He taught me quite a lot and I think he meant me to join him when he got old."

As she had evidently made up her mind, and as her decision seemed quite a wise one, I concurred with as much enthusiasm as I could muster.

"I am glad you agree," said she, "and I know Arabella does. So that is settled, subject to my being able to carry out the plan. And now, if we have finished, I should like to show you some of my father's works. The house is full of them and so, even, is the garden. Perhaps we had better go there first before the light fails."

As the treasures of this singularly interesting home were presented, one after another, for my inspection, I began to realize the truth of Miss Boler's statement. Julius D'Arblay had been a remarkably versatile man. He had worked in all sorts of mediums and in all equally well. From the carved stone sundial and the leaden garden figures to the clock-ease decorated with gilded gesso and enriched with delicate bronze plaquettes, all his works were eloquent of masterly skill and a fresh, graceful fancy. It seems to me little short of a tragedy that an artist of his ability should have spent the greater part of his time in fabricating those absurd, posturing effigies that simper and smirk so grotesquely in the enormous windows of Vanity Fair.

I had intended, in compliance with the polite conventions, to make this, my first visit, a rather short one; but a tentative movement to depart only elicited protests and I was easily persuaded to stay until the exigencies of Dr Cornish's practice seemed to call me. When at last I shut the gate of Ivy Cottage behind me and glanced back at the two figures standing in the lighted doorway, I had the feeling of turning away from a house with which, and its inmates, I had been familiar for years.

On my arrival at Mecklenburgh Square I found a note which had been left by hand earlier in the evening. It was from Dr Thorndyke, asking me, if possible, to lunch with him at his chambers on the morrow. I looked over my visiting-list, and finding that Monday would be a light day – most of my days here were light days – I wrote a short letter accepting the invitation and posted it forthwith.

Chapter Seven

Thorndyke Enlarges his Knowledge

"I am glad you were able to come," said Thorndyke, as we took our places at the table. "Your letter was a shade ambiguous. You spoke of discussing the D'Arblay case, but I think you had something more than discussion in your mind."

"You are quite right," I replied. "I had it in my mind to ask if it would be possible for me to retain you – I believe that is the correct expression – to investigate the case, as the police seem to think there is nothing to go on; and if the costs would be likely to be within my means."

"As to the costs," said he, "we can dismiss them. I see no reason to suppose that there would be any costs."

"But your time, sir – " I began.

He laughed derisively. "Do you propose to pay me for indulging in my pet hobby? No, my dear fellow, it is I who should pay you for bringing a most interesting and intriguing case to my notice. So your questions are answered. I shall be delighted to look into this case, and there will be no costs unless we have to pay for some special services. If we do, I will let you know."

I was about to utter a protest, but he continued:

"And now, having disposed of the preliminaries, let us consider the case itself. Your very shrewd and capable inspector believes that the Scotland Yard people will take no active measures unless some new facts turn up. I have no doubt he is right, and I think they are right, too. They can't spend a lot of time – which means public money – on a case in which hardly any data are available and which holds out no promise of any result. But we mustn't forget that we are in the same boat. Our chances of success are infinitesimal. This investigation is a forlorn hope. That, I may say, is what commends it to me; but I want you to understand clearly that failure is what we have to expect."

"I understand that," I answered gloomily, but nevertheless rather disappointed at this pessimistic view. "There seems to be nothing whatever to go upon."

"Oh, it isn't so bad as that," he rejoined. "Let us just run over the data that we have. Our object is to fix the identity of the man who killed Julius D'Arblay. Let us see what we know about him. We will begin with the evidence at the inquest. From that we learned: 1. That he is a man of some education, ingenious, subtle, resourceful. This murder was planned with extraordinary ingenuity and foresight. The body was found in the pond with no tell-tale mark on it but an almost invisible pin-prick in the back. The chances were a thousand to one, or more, against that tiny puncture ever being observed; and if it had not been observed, the verdict would have been 'found drowned' or 'found dead', and the fact of the murder would never have been discovered.

"2. We also learned that he has some knowledge of poisons. The common, vulgar poisoner is reduced to fly-papers, weed-killer or rat-poison – arsenic or strychnine. But this man selects the most suitable of all poisons for his purpose and administers it in the most effective manner – with a hypodermic syringe.

"3. We learned further that he must have had some extraordinarily strong reason for making away with D'Arblay. He made most elaborate plans, he took endless trouble – for instance, it must have been no easy matter to get possession of that quantity of aconitine (unless he were a doctor, which God forbid!). That strong reason – the motive, in fact – is the key of the problem. It is the murderer's one vulnerable point, for it can hardly be beyond discovery; and its discovery must be our principal objective."

I nodded, not without some self-congratulation as I recalled how I had made this very point in my talk with Miss D'Arblay.

"Those," Thorndyke continued, "are the data that the inquest furnished. Now we come to those added by Inspector Follett."

"I don't see that they help us at all," said I. "The ancient coin was a curious find, but it doesn't appear to tell us anything new excepting that this man may have been a collector or a dealer. On the other hand, he may not. It doesn't seem to me that the coin has any significance."

"Doesn't it really?" said Thorndyke, as he refilled my glass. "You are surely overlooking the very curious coincidence that it presents?"

"What coincidence is that?" I asked, in some surprise.

"The coincidence," he replied, "that both the murderer and the victim should be, to a certain extent, connected with a particular form of activity. Here is a man who commits a murder and who at the time of committing it appears to have been in possession of a coin, which is not a current coin but a collector's piece; and behold! the murdered man is a sculptor – a man who, presumably, was capable of making a coin, or at least the working model."

"There is no evidence," I objected, "that D'Arblay was capable of cutting a die. He was not a die-sinker."

"There was no need for him to be," Thorndyke rejoined. "Formerly, the medallist who designed the coin cut the die himself. But that is not the modern practice. Nowadays, the designer makes the model, first in wax and then in plaster, on a comparatively large scale. The model of a shilling may be three inches or more in diameter. The actual die-sinking is done by a copying machine which produces a die of the required size by mechanical reduction. I think there can be no doubt that D'Arblay could have modelled the design for a coin on the usual scale, say three or four inches in diameter."

"Yes," I agreed, "he certainly could, for I have seen some of his small relief work, some little plaquettes, not more than two inches long and most delicately and beautifully modelled. But still I don't see the connexion, otherwise than as a rather odd coincidence."

"There may be nothing more," said he. "There may be nothing in it at all. But odd coincidences should always be noted with very special attention."

"Yes, I realize that. But I can't imagine what significance there could be in the coincidence."

"Well," said Thorndyke, "let us take an imaginary case, just as an illustration. Suppose this man to have been a fraudulent dealer in antiquities; and suppose him to have obtained enlarged photographs of a medal or coin of extreme rarity and of great value, which was in some museum or private collection. Suppose him to have taken the photographs to D'Arblay and commissioned him to model from them a pair of exact replicas in hardened plaster. From those plaster models he could, with a copying machine, produce a pair of dies with which he could strike replicas in the proper metal and of the exact size; and these could be sold for large sums to judiciously chosen collectors."

"I don't believe D'Arblay would have accepted such a commission," I exclaimed indignantly.

"We may assume that he would not, if the fraudulent intent had been known to him. But it would not have been; and there is no reason why he should have refused a commission merely to make a copy. Still, I am not suggesting that anything of the kind really happened. I am simply giving you an illustration of one of the innumerable ways in which a perfectly honest sculptor might be made use of by a fraudulent dealer. In that case, his honesty would be a source of danger to him; for if a really great fraud were perpetrated by means of his work, it would clearly be to the interest of the perpetrator to get rid of him. An honest and unconscious collaborator in a crime is apt to be a dangerous witness if questions arise."

I was a good deal impressed by this demonstration. Here, it seemed to me, was something very like a tangible clue. But at this point Thorndyke again applied a cold douche.

"Still," he said, "we are only dealing with generalities, and rather speculative ones. Our assumptions are subject to all sorts of qualifications. It is possible, for instance, though very improbable, that D'Arblay may have been murdered in error by a perfect stranger; that he may have walked into an ambush prepared for someone else. Again, the coin may not have belonged to the murderer at all, though that is also most improbable. But there are numerous possibilities of error; and we can eliminate them only by following up each suggested clue and seeking verification or disproof. Every new fact that we learn is a multiple gain. For as money makes money, so knowledge begets knowledge."

"That is very true," I answered dejectedly – for it sounded rather like a platitude; "but I don't see any means of following up any of these clues."

"We are going to follow up one of them after lunch, if you have time," said he. As he spoke, he took from the table drawer a paper packet and a jeweller's leather case. "This," he said, handing me the packet, "contains your sealing-wax moulds. You had better take care of them and keep the box with the marked side up to prevent the wax from warping. Here are a pair of casts in hardened plaster – 'fictile ivory,' as it is called – which my assistant, Polton, has made."

He opened the case and passed it to me, when I saw that it was lined with purple velvet and contained what looked like two old ivory replicas of the mysterious coin.

"Mr Polton is quite an artist," I said, regarding them admiringly. "But what are you going to do with these?"

"I had intended to take them round to the British Museum and show them to the Keeper of the Coins and Medals, or one of his colleagues. But I think I will just ask a few questions and hear what he says before I produce the casts. Have you time to come round with me?"

"I shall make time. But what do you want to know about the coin?"

"It is just a matter of verification," he replied. "My books on the British coinage describe the Charles the Second guinea as having a tiny elephant under the bust on the obverse, to show that the gold from which it was minted came from the Guinea Coast."

"Yes," said I. "Well, there is a little elephant under the bust in this coin."

"True," he replied. "But this elephant has a castle on his back and would ordinarily be described as an elephant and castle, to distinguish him from the plain elephant which appeared on some coins. What I want to ascertain is whether there were two different types of guinea. The books make no mention of a second variety."

"Surely they would have referred to it if there had been," said I.

"So I thought," he replied; "but it is better to make sure than to think."

"I suppose it is," I agreed without much conviction, "though I don't see that, even if there were two varieties, that fact would have any bearing on what we want to know."

"Neither do I," he admitted. "But then you can never tell what a fact will prove until you are in possession of the fact. And now, as we seem to have finished, perhaps we had better make our way to the Museum."

The Department of Coins and Medals is associated in my mind with an impassive-looking Chinese person in bronze who presides over the upper landing of the main staircase. In fact, we halted for a moment before him to exchange a final word.

"It will probably be best," said Thorndyke, "to say nothing about this coin, or, indeed, about anything else. We don't want to enter into any explanations."

"No," I agreed. "It is best to keep one's own counsel"; and with this we entered the hall, where Thorndyke led the way to a small door and pressed the electric bell-push. An attendant admitted us, and when we had signed our names in the visitors' book, he ushered us into the keeper's room. As we entered, a keen-faced, middle-aged man who was seated at a table inspected us over his spectacles, and apparently recognizing Thorndyke, rose and held out his hand.

"Quite a long time since I have seen you," he remarked after the preliminary greetings. "I wonder what your quest is this time."

"It is a very simple one," said Thorndyke. "I am going to ask you if you can let me look at a Charles the Second guinea dated 1663."

"Certainly I can," was the reply, accompanied by an inquisitive glance at my friend. "It is not a rarity, you know."

He crossed the room to a large cabinet, and having run his eye over the multitudinous labels, drew out a small, very shallow drawer. With this in his hand, he returned, and picking a coin out of its circular pit, held it out to Thorndyke, who took it from him, holding it delicately by the edges. He looked at it attentively for a few moments, and then silently presented the obverse for my inspection. Naturally my eye at once sought the little elephant under the bust, and there it was, but there was no castle on its back.

"Is this the only type of guinea issued at that date?" Thorndyke asked.

"The only type – with or without the elephant, according to the source of the gold."

"There was no variation or alternative form?"

"No."

"I notice that this coin has a plain elephant under the bust; but I seem to have heard of a guinea, bearing this date, which had an elephant and castle under the bust. You are sure there was no such guinea?"

Our official friend shook his head as he took the coin from Thorndyke and replaced it in its cell. "As sure," he replied, "as one can be of a universal negative." He picked up the drawer and was just moving away towards the cabinet when there came a sudden change in his manner.

"Wait!" he exclaimed, stopping and putting down the drawer. "You are quite right. Only it was not an issue; it was a trial piece, and only a single coin was struck. I will tell you about it. There is a rather curious story hanging to that piece."

"This guinea, as you probably know, was struck from dies cut by John Roettier and was one of the first coined by the mill-and-screw process in place of the old hammer-and-pile method. Now, when Roettier had finished the dies, a trial piece was struck; and in striking that piece, the obverse die cracked right across, but apparently only at the last turn of the screw, for the trial piece was quite perfect. Of course Roettier had to cut a new die; and for some reason he made a slight alteration. The first die had an elephant and castle under the bust. In the second one he changed this to a plain elephant. So your impression was, so far, correct; but the coin, if it still exists, is absolutely unique."

"Is it not known, then, what became of that trial piece?"

"Oh, yes – up to a point. That is the queerest part of the story. For a time it remained in the possession of the Slingsby family – Slingsby was the Master of the Mint when it was struck. Then it passed through the hands of various collectors and finally was bought by an American collector named Van Zellen. Now, Van Zellen was a millionaire and his collection was a typical millionaire's collection. It consisted entirely of things of enormous value which no ordinary man could afford or of unique things of which nobody could possibly have a duplicate. It seems that he was a rather solitary man and that he spent most of his evenings alone in his museum, gloating over his possessions."

"One morning Van Zellen was found dead in the little study attached to the museum. That was about eighteen months ago. There was an empty champagne bottle on the table and a half-emptied glass, which smelt of bitter almonds, and in his pocket was an empty phial labelled Hydrocyanic Acid. At first it was assumed that he had committed suicide; but when, later, the collection was examined, it was found that a considerable part of it was missing. A clean sweep had been made of the gems, jewels and other portable objects of value, and, among other things, this unique trial guinea had vanished. Surely you remember the case?"

"Yes," replied Thorndyke. "I do, now you mention it; but I never heard what was stolen. Do you happen to know what the later developments were?"

"There were none. The identity of the murderer was never discovered, and not a single item of the stolen property has ever been traced. To this day the crime remains an impenetrable mystery – unless you know something about it"; and again our friend cast an inquisitive glance at Thorndyke.

"My practice," the latter replied, "does not extend to the United States. Their own very efficient investigators seem to be able to do all that is necessary. But I am very much obliged to you for having given us so much of your time, to say nothing of this extremely interesting information. I shall make a note of it; for American crime occasionally has its repercussions on this side."

I secretly admired the adroit way in which Thorndyke had evaded the rather pointed question without making any actual mis-statement. But the motive for the evasion was not very obvious to me. I was about to put a question on the subject, but he anticipated it, for, as soon as we were outside, he remarked with a chuckle: "It is just as well that we didn't begin by exhibiting the casts. We could hardly have sworn our friend to secrecy, seeing that the original is undoubtedly stolen property."

"But aren't you going to draw the attention of the police to the fact?"

"I think not," he replied. "They have got the original, and no doubt they have a list of the stolen property. We must assume that they will make use of their knowledge; but if they don't, it may be all the better for us. The police are very discreet; but they do sometimes give the Press more information than I should. And what is told to the Press is told to the criminal."

"And why not?" I asked. "What is the harm of his knowing?"

"My dear Gray!" exclaimed Thorndyke. "You surprise me. Just consider the position. This man aimed at being entirely unsuspected. That failed. But still his identity is unknown, and he is probably confident that it will never be ascertained. Then he is, so far, off his guard. There is no need for him to disappear or go into hiding. But let him know that he is being tracked and he will almost certainly take fresh precautions against discovery. Probably he will slip away beyond our reach. Our aim must be to encourage him in a feeling of perfect security; and that aim commits us to the strictest secrecy. No one must know what cards we hold or that we hold any; or even that we are taking a hand."

"What about Miss D'Arblay?" I asked anxiously. "May I not tell her that you are working on her behalf?"

He looked at me somewhat dubiously. "It would obviously be better not to," he said, "but that might seem a little unfriendly and unsympathetic."

"It would be an immense relief to her to know that you are trying to help her, and I think you could trust her to keep your secrets."

"Very well," he conceded. "But warn her very thoroughly. Remember that our antagonist is hidden from us. Let us remain hidden from him, so far as our activities are concerned."

"I will make her promise absolute secrecy," I agreed; and then, with a slight sense of anti-climax, I added: "But we don't seem to have so very much to conceal. This curious story of the stolen coin is interesting, but it doesn't appear to get us any more forward."

"Doesn't it?" he asked. "Now, I was just congratulating myself on the progress that we had made; on the way in which we are narrowing down the field of inquiry. Let us trace our progress. When you found the body, there was no evidence as to the cause of death; no suspicion of any agent whatever. Then came the inquest, demonstrating the cause of death and bringing into view a person of unknown identity but having certain distinguishing characteristics. Then Follett's discovery added some further characteristics and suggested certain possible motives for the crime. But still there was no hint as to the person's identity or position in life. Now we have good evidence that he is a professional criminal of a dangerous type, that he is connected with another crime and with a quantity of easily identified stolen property. We also know that he was in America about eighteen months ago, and we can easily get exact information as to dates and locality. This man is no longer a mere formless shadow. He is in a definite category of possible persons."

"But," I objected, "the fact that he had the coin in his possession does not prove that he is the man who stole it."

"Not by itself," Thorndyke agreed. "But taken in conjunction with the crime, it is almost conclusive. You appear to be overlooking the striking similarity of the two crimes. Each was a violent murder committed by means of poison; and in each case the poison selected was the most suitable one for the purpose. The one, aconitine, was calculated to escape detection; the other, hydrocyanic acid – the most rapidly acting of all poisons – was calculated to produce almost instant death in a man who was probably struggling and might have raised an alarm. I think we are fairly justified in assuming that the murderer of Van Zellen was the murderer of D'Arblay. If that is so, we have two groups of circumstances to investigate, two tracks by which to follow him; and sooner or later, I feel confident, we shall be able to give him a name. Then, if we have kept our own counsel, and he is unconscious of the pursuit, we shall be able to lay our hands on him. But here we are at the Foundling Hospital. It is time for each of us to get back to the routine of duty."

CHAPTER EIGHT

Simon Bendelow, Deceased

It was near the close of my incumbency of Dr Cornish's practice – indeed, Cornish had returned on the previous evening – that my unsatisfactory attendance on Mr Simon Bendelow came to an end. It had been a wearisome affair. In medical practice, perhaps even more than in most human activities, continuous effort calls for the sustenance of achievement. A patient who cannot be cured or even substantially relieved is of all patients the most depressing. Week after week I had made my fruitless visits, had watched the silent, torpid sufferer grow yet more shrivelled and wasted, speculating even a little impatiently on the possible duration of his long drawn-out passage to the grave. But at last the end came.

"Good morning, Mrs Morris," I said as that grim female opened the door and surveyed me impassively, "and how is our patient today?"

"He isn't our patient any longer," she replied. "He's dead."

"Ha!" I exclaimed. "Well, it had to be, sooner or later. Poor Mr Bendelow! When did he die?"

"Yesterday afternoon, about five," she answered.

"H'm! If you had sent me a note, I could have brought the certificate. However, I can post it to you. Shall I go up and have a look at him?"

"You can if you like," she replied. "But the ordinary certificate won't be enough in his case. He is going to be cremated."

"Oh, indeed," said I, once more unpleasantly conscious of my inexperience. "What sort of certificate is required for cremation?"

"Oh, all sorts of formalities have to be gone through," she answered. "Just come into the drawing-room and I will tell you what has to be done."

She preceded me along the passage and ·I followed meekly, anathematizing myself for my ignorance, and my instructors for having sent me forth crammed with academic knowledge but with the practical business of my profession all to learn.

"Why are you having him cremated?" I asked, as we entered the room and shut the door.

"Because it is one of the provisions of his will," she answered. "I may as well let you see it."

She opened a bureau and took from it a foolscap envelope from which she drew out a folded document. This she first unfolded and then re-folded so that its concluding clauses were visible and laid it on the flap of the bureau. Placing her finger on it, she said: "That is the cremation clause. You had better read it."

I ran my eye over the clause, which read: "I desire that my body shall be cremated and I appoint Sarah Elizabeth Morris the wife of the aforesaid James Morris to be the residuary legatee and sole executrix of this my will." Then followed the attestation clause, underneath which was the shaky but characteristic signature of "Simon Bendelow" and opposite this the signatures of the witnesses, Anne Dewsnep and Martha Bonnington, both described as spinsters and both of a joint address which was hidden by the folding of the document.

"So much for that," said Mrs Morris, returning the will to its envelope; "and now as to the certificate. There is a special form for cremation which has to be signed by two doctors, and one of them must be a hospital doctor or a consultant. So I wrote off at once to Dr Cropper, as he knew the patient, and I have had a telegram from him this morning saying that he will be here this evening at eight o'clock to examine the body and sign the certificate. Can you manage to meet him at that time?"

"Yes," I replied, "fortunately I can, as Dr Cornish is back."

"Very well," said she; "then in that case you needn't go up now. You will be able to make the examination together. Eight o'clock, sharp, remember."

With this she re-conducted me along the passage and – I had almost said ejected me; but she sped the parting guest with a business-like directness that was perhaps accounted for by the presence opposite the door of one of those grim parcels-delivery vans in which undertakers distribute their wares, and from which a rough-looking coffin was at the moment being hoisted out by two men.

The extraordinary promptitude of this proceeding so impressed me that I remarked: "They haven't been long making the coffin."

"They didn't have to make it," she replied. "I ordered it a month ago. It's no use leaving things to the last moment."

I turned away with somewhat mixed feelings. There was certainly a horrible efficiency about this woman. Executrix indeed! Her promptness in carrying out the provisions of the will was positively appalling. She must have written to Cropper before the breath was fairly out of poor Bendelow's body, but her forethought in the matter of the coffin fairly made my flesh creep.

Dr Cornish made no difficulty about taking over the evening consultations, in fact he had intended to do so in any case. Accordingly, after a rather early dinner, I made my way in leisurely fashion back to Hoxton, where, after all, I arrived fully ten minutes too soon. I realized my prematureness when I halted at the corner of Market Street to look at my watch; and as ten additional minutes of Mrs Morris' society offered no allurement, I was about to turn back and fill up the time with a short walk when my attention was arrested by a mast which had just appeared above the wall at the end of the street. With its black-painted truck and halyard blocks and its long tricolour pennant, it looked like the mast of a Dutch schuyt or galliot, but I could hardly believe it possible that such a craft could make its appearance in the heart of London. All agog with curiosity, I hurried up the street and looked over the wall at the canal below; and there, sure enough, she was – a big Dutch sloop, broad-bosomed, massive and mediaeval, just such a craft as one may see in the pictures of old Vandervelde, painted when Charles the Second was king.

I leaned on the low wall and watched her with delighted interest as she crawled forward slowly to her berth, bringing with her, as it seemed, a breath of the distant sea and the echo of the surf murmuring on sandy beaches. I noted appreciatively her old-world air, her antique build, her gay and spotless paint and the muslin curtains in the little windows of her deck-house, and was, in fact, so absorbed in watching her that the late Simon Bendelow had passed completely out of my mind. Suddenly, however, the chiming of a clock recalled me to my present business. With a hasty glance at my watch, I tore myself away reluctantly, darted across the street and gave a vigorous pull at the bell.

Dr Cropper had not yet arrived, but the deceased had not been entirely neglected, for when I had spent some five minutes staring inquisitively about the drawing-room into which Mrs Morris had shown me, that lady returned, accompanied by two other ladies whom she introduced to me somewhat informally by the names of Miss Dewsnep and Miss Bonnington respectively. I recognized the names as those of the two witnesses to the will and inspected them with furtive curiosity, though, indeed, they were quite unremarkable excepting as typical specimens of the genus elderly spinster.

"Poor Mr Bendelow!" murmured Miss Dewsnep, shaking her head and causing an artificial cherry on her bonnet to waggle idiotically. "How beautiful he looks in his coffin!"

She looked at me as if for confirmation, so that I was fain to admit that his beauty in this new setting had not yet been revealed to me.

"So peaceful," she added, with another shake of her head, and Miss Bonnington chimed in with the comment, "Peaceful and restful." Then they both looked at me and I mumbled indistinctly that I had no doubt he did; the fact being that the inmates of coffins are not in general much addicted to boisterous activity.

"Ah!" Miss Dewsnep resumed, "how little did I think when I first saw him, sitting up in bed so cheerful in that nice, sunny room in the house at – "

"Why not?" interrupted Mrs Morris. "Did you think he was going to live for ever?"

"No, Mrs Morris, ma'am," was the dignified reply, "I did not. No such idea ever entered my head. I know too well that we mortals are all born to be gathered in at last as the er – as the – "

"Sparks fly upwards," murmured Miss Bonnington.

"As the corn is gathered in at harvest-time," Miss Dewsnep continued with slight emphasis. "But not to be cast into a burning fiery furnace. When I first saw him in the other house at – "

"I don't see what objection you need have to cremation," interrupted Mrs Morris. "It was his own choice, and a good one, too. Look at those great cemeteries. What sense is there in letting the dead occupy the space that is wanted for the living?"

"Well," said Miss Dewsnep, "I may be old-fashioned, but it does seem to me that a nice quiet funeral with plenty of flowers and a proper, decent grave in a churchyard is the natural end to a human life. That is what I look forward to, myself."

"Then you are not likely to be disappointed," said Mrs Morris; "though I don't quite see what satisfaction you expect to get out of your own funeral."

Miss Dewsnep made no reply, and an interval of dismal silence followed. Mrs Morris was evidently impatient of Dr Cropper's unpunctuality. I could see that she was listening intently for the sound of the bell, as she had been even while the conversation was in progress; indeed I had been dimly conscious all the while of a sense of tension and anxiety on her part. She had seemed to me to watch her two friends with a sort of uneasiness and to give a quite uncalled for attention to their rather trivial utterances.

At length her suspense was relieved by a loud ringing of the bell. She started up and opened the door, but she had barely crossed the threshold when she suddenly turned back and addressed me.

"That will be Dr Cropper. Perhaps you had better come out with me and meet him."

It struck me as an odd suggestion, but I rose without comment and followed her along the passage to the street door, which we reached just as another loud peal of the bell sounded in the house behind us. She flung the door wide open and a small, spectacled man charged in and seized my hand, which he shook with violent cordiality.

"How do you do, Mr Morris?" he exclaimed. "So sorry to keep you waiting, but I was unfortunately detained at a consultation."

Here Mrs Morris sourly intervened to explain who I was; upon which he shook my hand again and expressed his joy at making my acquaintance. He also made polite inquiries as to our hostess' health, which she acknowledged gruffly over her shoulder as she preceded us along the passage; which was now pitch-dark and where Cropper dropped his hat and trod on it, finally bumping his head against the unseen wall in a frantic effort to recover it.

When we emerged into the dimly lighted hall, I observed the two ladies peering inquisitively out of the drawing-room door. But Mrs Morris took no notice of them, leading the way directly up the stairs to the room with which I was already familiar. It was poorly illuminated by a single gas-bracket over the fireplace, but the light was enough to show us a coffin resting on three chairs and beyond it the shadowy figure of a man whom I recognized as Mr Morris.

We crossed the room to the coffin, which was plainly finished with zinc fastenings, in accordance with the regulations of the crematorium authorities, and had let into the top what I first took to be a pane of glass, but which turned out to be a plate of clear celluloid. When we had made our salutations to Mr Morris, Cropper and I looked in through the celluloid window. The yellow, shrunken fact of the dead man, surmounted by the skull-cap, which he had always worn, looked so little changed that he might still have been in the drowsy, torpid state in which I had been accustomed to see him. He had always looked so like a dead man that the final transition was hardly noticeable.

"I suppose," said Morris, "you would like to have the coffin-lid taken off?"

"God bless my soul, yes!" exclaimed Cropper. "What are we here for? We shall want him out of the coffin, too."

"Are you proposing to make a post-mortem?" I asked, observing that Dr Cropper had brought a good-sized handbag. "It seems hardly necessary, as we both know what he died of."

Cropper shook his head. "That won't do," said he. "You mustn't treat a cremation certificate as a mere formality. We have got to certify that we have verified the cause of death. Looking at a body through a window is not verifying the cause of death. We should cut a pretty figure in a court of law if any question arose and we had to admit that we had certified without any examination at all. But we needn't do much, you know. Just get the body out on the bed and a single small incision will settle the nature of the growth. Then everything will be regular and in order. I hope you don't mind, Mrs Morris," he added suavely, turning to that lady.

"You must do what you think necessary," she replied indifferently. "It is no affair of mine"; and with this she went out of the room and shut the door.

While we had been speaking, Mr Morris, who apparently had kept a screwdriver in readiness for the possible contingency, had been neatly extricating the screws and now lifted off the coffin-lid. Then the three of us raised the shrivelled body – it was as light as a child's – and laid it on the bed. I left Cropper to do what he thought necessary, and while he was unpacking his instruments I took the opportunity to have a good look at Mr Morris; for it is a singular fact that in all the weeks of my attendance at this house I had never come into contact with him since that first morning when I had caught a momentary glimpse of him as he looked out over the blind through the glazed shop-door. In the interval his appearance had changed considerably for the better. He was no longer a merely unshaved man; his beard had grown to a respectable length, and, so far as I could judge in the uncertain light, the hare-lip scar was completely concealed by his moustache.

"Let me see," said Cropper, as he polished a scalpel on the palm of his hand, "when did you say Mr Bendelow died?"

"Yesterday afternoon at about five o'clock," replied Mr Morris.

"Did he really?" said Cropper, lifting one of the limp arms and letting it drop on the bed. "Yesterday afternoon! Now, Gray, doesn't that show how careful one should be in giving opinions as to the time that has elapsed since death? If I had been shown this body and asked how long the man had been dead, I should have said three or four days. There isn't the least trace of *rigor mortis* left; and the other appearances – but there it is. You are never safe in giving dogmatic opinions."

"No," I agreed. "I should have said he had been dead more than twenty-four hours. But I suppose there is a good deal of variation."

"There is," he replied. "You can't apply averages to particular cases."

I did not consider it necessary to take any active part in the proceedings. It was his diagnosis and it was for him to verify it. At his request Mr Morris fetched a candle and held it as he was directed; and while these preparations were in progress I looked out of the window, which commanded a partial view of the canal. The moon had now risen and its light fell on the white-painted hull of the Dutch sloop, which had come to rest and made fast alongside a small wharf. It was quite a pleasant picture, strangely at variance with the squalid neighbourhood around. As I looked down on the little vessel, with the ruddy light glowing from the deck-house windows and casting shimmering reflections in the quiet water, the sight seemed to carry me far away from the sordid streets around into the fellowship of the breezy ocean and the far-away shores whence the little craft had sailed; and I determined, as soon as our business was finished, to seek some access to the canal and indulge myself with a quiet stroll in the moonlight along the deserted towing-path.

"Well, Gray," said Cropper, standing up with the scalpel and forceps in his hands, "there it is, if you want to see it. Typical carcinoma. Now we can sign the certificates with a clear conscience. I'll just put in a stitch or two and then we can put him back in his coffin. I suppose you have got the forms?"

"They are downstairs," said Mr Morris. "When we have got him back, I will show you the way down."

This, however, was unnecessary, as there was only one staircase and I was not a stranger. Accordingly, when we had replaced the body, we took our leave of Mr Morris and departed; and glancing back as I passed out of the door, I saw him driving in the screws with the ready skill of a cabinet-maker.

The filling up of the forms was a portentous business which was carried out in the drawing-room under the superintendence of Mrs Morris and was watched with respectful interest by the two spinsters. When it was finished and I had handed the registration certificate to Mrs Morris, Cropper gathered up the forms B and C and slipped them into a long envelope on which the Medical Referee's address was printed.

"I will post this off tonight," said he; "and you will send in Form A, Mrs Morris, when you have filled it in."

"I have sent it off already," she replied.

"Good," said Dr Cropper. "Then that is all; and now I must run away. Can I put you down anywhere, Gray?"

"Thank you, no," I replied. "I thought of taking a walk along the towpath, if you can tell me how to get down to it, Mrs Morris."

"I can't," she replied. "But when Dr Cropper has gone, I will run up and ask my husband. I daresay he knows."

We escorted Cropper along the passage to the door, which he reached without mishap, and having seen him into his brougham, turned back to the hall, where Mrs Morris ascended the stairs and I went into the drawing-room, where the two spinsters appeared to be preparing for departure. In a couple of minutes Mrs Morris returned, and seeing both the ladies standing, said: "You are not going yet, Miss Dewsnep. You must have some refreshment before you go. Besides, I thought you wanted to see Mr Bendelow again."

"So we should," said Miss Dewsnep. "Just a little peep, to see how he looks after – "

"I will take you up in a minute," interrupted Mrs Morris. "When Dr Gray has gone." Then addressing me, she said: "My husband says that you can get down to the towpath through that alley nearly opposite. There is a flight of steps at the end which comes right out on the path."

I thanked her for the direction, and, having bidden farewell to the spinsters, was once more escorted along the passage and finally launched into the outer world.

CHAPTER NINE

A Strange Misadventure

Although I had been in harness but a few weeks, it was with a pleasant sense of freedom that I turned from the door and crossed the road towards the alley. My time was practically my own, for, though I was remaining with Dr Cornish until the end of the week, he was now in charge and my responsibilities were at an end.

The alley was entered by an arched opening so narrow that I had never suspected it of being a public thoroughfare, and I now threaded it with my shoulders almost touching the walls. Whither it finally led I have no idea, for when I reached another arched opening in the left-hand wall and saw that this gave on a flight of stone steps, I descended the latter and found myself on the towpath. At the foot of the steps I stood awhile and looked about me. The moon was nearly full and shone brightly on the opposite side of the canal, but the towpath was in deep shadow, being flanked by a high wall, behind which were the houses of the adjoining streets. Looking back – that is, to my left – I could just make out the bridge and the adjoining buildings, all their unlovely details blotted out by the thin night-haze, which reduced them to mere flat shapes of grey. A little nearer, one or two spots of ruddy light with wavering reflections beneath them marked the cabin windows of the sloop, and her mast, rising above the grey obscurity, was clearly visible against the sky.

Naturally, I turned in that direction, sauntering luxuriously and filling my pipe as I went. Doubtless, by day the place was sordid enough in aspect − though it is hard to vulgarize a navigable waterway − but now, in the moonlit haze, the scene was almost romantic. And it was astonishingly quiet and peaceful. From above, beyond the high wall, the noises of the streets came subdued and distant like sounds from another world; but here there was neither sound nor movement. The towpath was utterly deserted, and the only sign of human life was the glimmer of light from the sloop.

It was delightfully restful. I found myself treading the gravel lightly, not to disturb the grateful silence; and as I strolled along, enjoying my pipe, I let my thoughts ramble idly from one topic to another. Somewhere above me, in that rather mysterious house, Simon Bendelow was lying in his narrow bed, the wasted, yellow face looking out into the darkness through that queer little celluloid window, or perhaps Miss Dewsnep and her friend were even now taking their farewell peep at him. I looked up, but, of course, the house was not visible from the towpath, nor was I now able to guess at its position.

A little farther and the hull of the sloop came clearly into view, and nearly opposite to it, on the towpath, I could see some kind of shed or hut against the wall, with a derrick in front of it overhanging a little quay. When I had nearly reached the shed, I passed a door in the wall, which apparently communicated with some house in one of the streets above. Then I came to the shed, a small wooden building which probably served as a lighterman's office, and I noticed that the derrick swung from one of the corner-posts. But at this moment my attention was attracted by sounds of mild revelry from across the canal. Someone in the sloop's deckhouse had burst into song.

I stepped out on to the little quay and stood at the edge, looking across at the homely curtained windows and wondering what the interior of the deck-house looked like at this moment. Suddenly my car caught an audible creak from behind me. I was in the act of turning to see whence it came when something struck me a heavy, glancing blow on the arm, crashed to the ground and sent me flying over the edge of the quay.

Fortunately the water here was not more than four feet deep, and as I had plunged in feet first and am a good swimmer, I never lost control of myself. In a moment I was standing up with my head and shoulders out of water, not particularly alarmed, though a good deal annoyed and much puzzled as to what had happened. My first care was to recover my hat, which was floating forlornly close by, and the next was to consider how I should get ashore. My left arm was numb from the blow and was evidently useless for climbing. Moreover, the face of the quay was of smooth concrete, as was also the wall below the towpath. But I remembered having passed a pair of boat-steps some fifty yards back and decided to make for them. I had thought of hailing the sloop, but as the droning song still came from the deck-house, it was clear that the Dutchmen had heard nothing, and I did not think it worth while to disturb them. Accordingly I set forth for the steps, walking with no little difficulty over the soft, muddy bottom, keeping close to the side and steadying myself with my right hand, with which I could just reach the edge of the coping.

It seemed a long journey, for one cannot progress very fast over soft mud with the water up to one's armpits; but at last I reached the steps and managed to scramble up on to the towpath. There I stood for a moment or two irresolute. My first impulse was to hurry back as fast as I could and seek the Morrises' hospitality; for I was already chilled to the bone and felt as physically wretched as the proverbial cat in similar circumstances. But I was devoured by curiosity as to what had happened, and, moreover, I believed that I had dropped my stick on the quay. The latter consideration decided me, for it was a favourite stick, and I set out for the quay at a very different pace from that at which I had approached it the first time.

The mystery was solved long before I arrived at the quay; at least it was solved in part. For the derrick, which had overhung the quay, now lay on the ground. Obviously it had fallen – and missed my head only by a matter of inches. But how had it come to fall? Again, obviously, the guy-rope had given way. As it could not have broken, seeing that the derrick was unloaded and the rope must have been strong enough to bear the last load, I was a good deal puzzled as to how the accident could have befallen. Nor was I much less puzzled when I had made my inspection. The rope was, of course, unbroken and its "fall" – the part below the pulley-blocks – passed into the shed through a window-like hole. This I could see as I approached, and also that a door in the end of the shed nearest to me was ajar. Opening it, I plunged into the dark interior, and partly by touch and partly by the faint glimmer that came in at the window, I was able to make out the state of affairs. Just below the hole through which the rope entered was a large cleat, on which the fall must have been belayed. But the cleat was vacant, the rope hung down from the hole and its end lay in an untidy raffle on the floor. It looked as if it had been cast off the cleat; but as there had apparently been no one in the shed, the only possible supposition was that the rope had been badly secured, that it had gradually worked loose and had at last slipped off the cleat. But it was difficult to understand how it had slipped right off.

I found my stick lying at the edge of the quay and close by it my pipe. Having recovered these treasures, I set off to retrace my steps along the towpath, sped on my way by a jovial chorus from the sloop. A very few minutes brought me to the steps, which I ascended two at a time, and then, having traversed the alley, I came out sheepishly into Market Street. To my relief, I saw a light in Mr Morris' shop and could even make out a moving figure in the background. I hurried across, and, opening the glazed door, entered the shop, at the back of which Mr Morris was seated at a bench filing some small object which was fixed in a vice. He looked round at me with no great cordiality, but suddenly observing my condition, he dropped his file on the bench and exclaimed,

"Good Lord, Doctor! What on earth have you been doing?"

"Nothing on earth," I replied with a feeble grin, "but something in the water. I've been into the canal."

"But what for?" he demanded.

"Oh, I didn't go in intentionally," I replied; and then I gave him a sketch of the incident, as short as I could make it, for my teeth were chattering and explanations were chilly work. However, he rose nobly to the occasion.

"You'll catch your death of cold!" he exclaimed, starting up. "Come in here and slip off your things at once while I go for some blankets."

He led me into a little den behind the shop, and, having lighted a gas fire, went out by a back door. I lost no time in peeling off my dripping clothes, and by the time that he returned I was in the state in which I ought to have been when I took my plunge.

"Here you are," said he. "Put on this dressing-gown and wrap yourself in the blankets. We'll draw this chair up to the fire and then you will be all right for the present."

I followed his directions, pouring out my thanks as well as my chattering teeth would let me.

"Oh, that's all right," said he. "If you will empty your pockets, the missus can put some of the things through the wringer and then they'll soon dry. There happens to be a good fire in the kitchen; some advance cooking on account of the funeral. You can dry your hat and boots here. If anyone comes to the shop, you might just press that electric bellpush."

When he had gone, I drew the Windsor armchair close to the fire and made myself as comfortable as I could, dividing my attention between my hat and my boots, which called for careful roasting, and the contents of the room. The latter appeared to be a sort of store for the reserve stock-in-trade and certainly this was a most amazing collection. I could not see a single article for which I would have given sixpence. The array on the shelves suggested that the shop had been stocked with the sweepings of all the stalls in Market Street, with those of Shoreditch High Street thrown in. As I ran my eye along the ranks of dial-less clocks, cracked fiddles, stopperless decanters and tattered theological volumes, I found myself speculating profoundly on how Mr Morris made a livelihood. He professed to be a "dealer in antiques" and there was assuredly no question as to the antiquity of the goods in this room. But there is little pecuniary value in the kind of antiquity that is unearthed from a dust-bin.

It was really rather mysterious. Mr Morris was a somewhat superior man and he did not appear to be poor. Yet this shop did not seem capable of yielding an income that would have been acceptable to a rag-picker. And during the whole of the time in which I sat warming myself, there was not a single visitor to the shop. However, it was no concern of mine; and I had just reached this sage conclusion when Mr Morris returned with my clothes.

"There," he said, "they are very creased and disreputable but they are quite dry. They would have had to be cleaned and pressed in any case."

With this he went out into the shop and resumed his filing while I put on the stiff and crumpled garments. When I was dressed, I followed him and thanked him effusively for his kind offices, leaving also a grateful message for his wife. He took my thanks rather stolidly, and having wished me "good night", picked up his file and fell to work again.

I decided to walk home; principally, I think, to avoid exhibiting myself in a public vehicle. But my self-consciousness soon wore off, and when, in the neighbourhood of Clerkenwell, I perceived Dr Usher on the opposite side of the street, I crossed the road and touched his arm. He looked round quickly, and recognizing me, shook hands cordially.

"What are you doing on my beat at this time of night?" he asked. "You are not still at Cornish's, are you?"

"Yes," I answered, "but not for long. I have just made my last visit and signed the death certificate."

"Good man," said he. "Very methodical. Nothing like finishing a case up neatly. They didn't invite you to the funeral, I suppose?"

"No," I replied, "and I shouldn't have gone if they had."

"Quite right," he agreed. "Funerals are rather outside medical practice. But you have to go sometimes. Policy, you know. I had to go to one a couple of days ago. Beastly nuisance it was. Chappie would insist on putting me down at my own door in the mourning coach. Meant well, of course, but it was very awkward. All the neighbours came to their shop-doors and grinned as I got out. Felt an awful fool; couldn't grin back, you see. Had to keep up the farce to the end."

"I don't see that it was exactly a farce," I objected.

"That is because you weren't there," he retorted. "It was the silliest exhibition you ever saw. Just think of it! The parson who ran the show had actually got a lot of schoolchildren to stand round the grave and sing a blooming hymn: something about gathering at the river – I expect you know the confounded doggerel."

"Well, why not?" I protested. "I daresay the friends of the deceased liked it."

"No doubt," said he. "I expect they put the parson up to it. But it was sickening to hear those kids bleating that stuff. How did they know where he was? – an old rip with malignant disease of the pancreas, too!"

"Really, Usher," I exclaimed, laughing at his quaint cynicism, "you are unreasonable. There are no pathological disqualification's for the better land, I hope."

"I suppose not," he agreed with a grin. "Don't have to show a clean bill of health before they let you in. But it was a trying business, you must admit. I hate cant of that sort; and yet one had to pull a long face and join in the beastly chorus."

The picture that his last words suggested was too much for my gravity. I laughed long and joyously. However, Usher was not offended; indeed I suspected that he appreciated the humour of the situation as much as I did. But he had trained himself to an outward solemnity of manner that was doubtless a valuable asset in his particular class of practice and he walked at my side with unmoved gravity, taking an occasional quick, critical look at me.

When we came to the parting of our ways, he once more shook my hand warmly and delivered a little farewell speech.

"You've never been to see me, Gray. Haven't had time, I suppose. But when you are free you might look me up one evening to have a smoke and a glass and talk over old times. There's always a bit of grub going, you know."

I promised to drop in before long, and he then added: "I gave you one or two tips when I saw you last. Now I'm going to give you another. Never neglect your appearance. It's a great mistake. Treat yourself with respect and the world will respect you. No need to be a dandy. But just keep an eye on your tailor and your laundress; especially your laundress. Clean collars don't cost much, and they pay; and so does a trousers-press. People expect a doctor to be well turned out. Now, you mustn't think me impertinent. We are old pals and I want you to get on. So long, old chap. Look me up as soon as you can"; and without giving me the opportunity to reply, he turned about and bustled off, swinging his umbrella and offering, perhaps, a not very impressive illustration of his own excellent precepts. But his words served as a reminder which caused me to pursue the remainder of my journey by way of side-streets neither too well lighted nor too much frequented.

As I let myself in with my key and closed the street-door, Cornish stepped out of the dining-room.

"I thought you were lost, Gray," said he. "Where the deuce have you been all this time?" Then, as I came into the light of the hall-lamp, he exclaimed.

"And what in the name of Fortune have you been up to?"

"I have had a wetting," I explained. "I'll tell you all about it presently."

"Dr Thorndyke is in the dining-room," said he; "came in a few minutes ago to see you." He seized me by the arm and ran me into the room, where I found Thorndyke methodically filling his pipe. He looked up as I entered and regarded me with raised eyebrows.

"Why, my dear fellow, you've been in the water!" he exclaimed. "But yet your clothes are not wet. What has been happening to you?"

"If you can wait a few minutes," I replied, "while I wash and change, I will relate my adventures. But perhaps you haven't time."

"I want to hear all about it," he replied, "so run along and be as quick as you can."

I bustled up to my room, and having washed and executed a lightning change, came down to the dining-room, where I found Cornish in the act of setting out decanters and glasses.

"I've told Dr Thorndyke what took you to Hoxton," said he, "and he wants a full account of everything that happened. He is always suspicious of cremation cases, as you know from his lectures."

"Yes, I remember his warnings," said I. "But this was a perfectly commonplace, straightforward affair."

"Did you go for your swim before or after the examination?" Thorndyke asked.

"Oh, after," I replied.

"Then let us hear about the examination first," said he.

On this I plunged into a detailed account of all that had befallen since my arrival at Market Street, to which Thorndyke listened, not only patiently but with the closest attention and even cross-examined me to elicit further details. Everything seemed to interest him, from the construction of the coffin to the contents of Mr Morris' shop. When I had finished, Cornish remarked:

"Well, it is a queer affair. I don't understand that rope at all. Ropes don't uncleat themselves. They may slip, but they don't come right off the cleat. It looks more as if some mischievous fool had cast it off for a joke."

"But there was no one there," said I. "The shed was empty when I examined it and there was not a soul in sight on the towpath."

"Could you see the shed when you were in the water?" Thorndyke asked.

"No. My head was below the level of the towpath. But if anyone had run out and made off. I must have seen him on the path when I came out. He couldn't have got out of sight in the time. Besides, it is incredible that even a fool should play such a trick as that."

"It is," he agreed. "But every explanation seems incredible. The only plain fact is that it happened.

"It is a queer business altogether; and not the least queer feature in the case is your friend Morris. Hoxton is an unlikely place for a dealer in antiques, unless he should happen to deal in other things as well – things, I mean, of ambiguous ownership."

"Just what I was thinking," said Cornish. "Sounds uncommonly like a fence. However, that is no business of ours."

"No," agreed Thorndyke, rising and knocking out his pipe. "And now I must be going. Do you care to walk with me to the bottom of Doughty Street, Gray?"

I assented at once, suspecting that he had something to say to me that he did not wish to say before Cornish. And so it turned out; for as soon as we were outside he said:

"What I really called about was this: it seems that we have done the police an injustice. They were more on the spot than we gave them credit for. I have learned – and this is in the strictest confidence – that they took that coin round to the British Museum for the expert's report. Then a very curious fact came to light. That coin is not the original which was stolen. It is an electrotype in gold, made in two halves very neatly soldered together and carefully worked on the milled edge to hide the join. That is extremely important in several respects. In the first place it suggests an explanation of the otherwise incredible circumstance that it was being carried loose in the waistcoat pocket. It had probably been recently obtained from the electrotyper. That suggests the question, is it possible that D'Arblay might have been that electrotyper? Did he ever work the electrotype process? We must ascertain whether he did."

"There is no need," said I. "It is known to me as a fact that he did. The little plaquettes that I took for castings are electrotypes, made by himself. He worked the process quite a lot and was very skilful in finishing. For instance, he did a small bust of his daughter in two parts and brazed them together."

"Then, you see, Gray," said Thorndyke, "that advances us considerably. We now have a plausible suggestion as to the motive and a new field of investigation. Let us suppose that this man employed D'Arblay to make electrotype copies of certain unique objects with the intention of disposing of them to collectors. The originals, being stolen property, would be almost impossible to dispose of with safety, but a copy would not necessarily incriminate the owner. But when D'Arblay had made the copies, he would be a dangerous person, for he would know who had the originals. Here, to a man whom we know to be a callous murderer, would be a sufficient reason for making away with D'Arblay."

"But do you think that D'Arblay would have undertaken such a decidedly fishy job? It seems hardly like him."

"Why not?" demanded Thorndyke. "There was nothing suspicious about the transaction. The man who wanted the copies was the owner of the originals, and D'Arblay would not know or suspect that they were stolen."

"That is true," I admitted. "But you were speaking of a new field of investigation."

"Yes. If a number of copies of different objects have been made, there is a fair chance that some of them have been disposed of. If they have and can be traced, they will give us a start along a new line which may bring us in sight of the man himself. Do you ever see Miss D'Arblay now?"

"Oh, yes," I replied. "I am quite one of the family at Highgate. I have been there every Sunday lately."

"Have you!" he exclaimed with a smile. "You are a pretty locum tenens. However, if you are quite at home there you can make a few discreet inquiries. Find out, if you can, whether any electros had been made recently and, if so, what they were and who was the client. Will you do that?"

I agreed readily, only too glad to take an active part in the investigation; and having by this time reached the end of Doughty Street, I took leave of Thorndyke and made my way back to Cornish's house.

CHAPTER TEN

Marion's Peril

The mist, which had been gathering since the early afternoon, began to thicken ominously as I approached Abbey Road, Hornsey, from Crouch End station, causing me to quicken my pace so that I might make my destination before the fog closed in; for this was my first visit to Marion D'Arblay's studio and the neighbourhood was strange to me. And in fact I was none too soon; for hardly had I set my hand on the quaint bronze knocker above the plate inscribed "Mr J D'Arblay", when the adjoining houses grew pale and shadowy and then vanished altogether.

My elaborate knock – in keeping with the distinguished knocker – was followed by soft, quick footsteps, the sound whereof set my heart ticking in double-quick time; the door opened and there stood Miss D'Arblay, garbed in a most alluring blue smock or pinafore, with sleeves rolled up to the elbow, with a smile of friendly welcome on her comely face and looking so sweet and charming that I yearned then and there to take her in my arms and kiss her. This, however, being inadmissible, I shook her hand warmly and was forthwith conducted through the outer lobby into the main studio, where I stood looking about me with amused surprise. She looked at me inquiringly as I emitted an audible chuckle.

"It is a queer-looking place," said I; "something between a miracle-shrine hung with votive offerings from sufferers who have been cured of sore heads and arms and legs and a meat emporium in a cannibal district."

"It is nothing of the kind!" she exclaimed, indignantly. "I don't mind the votive offerings, but I reject the cannibal meat-market as a gross and libellous fiction. But I suppose it does look rather queer to a stranger."

"To a what?" I demanded fiercely.

"Oh, I only meant a stranger to the place, of course, and you know I did. So you needn't be cantankerous."

She glanced smilingly round the studio and for the first time, apparently, the oddity of its appearances dawned on her, for she laughed softly and then turned a mischievous eye on me as I gaped about me like a bumpkin at a fair. The studio was a very large and lofty room or hall with a partially glazed roof and a single large window just below the skylight. The walls were fitted partly with rows of large shelves and the remainder with ranks of pegs. From the latter hung row after row of casts of arms, hands, legs and faces – especially faces – while the shelves supported a weird succession of heads, busts and a few half-length, but armless figures. The general effect was very strange and uncanny, and what made it more so was the fact that all the heads presented perfectly smooth, bare craniums.

"Are artists' models usually bald?" I inquired, as I noted this latter phenomenon.

"Now you are being foolish," she replied – "wilfully and deliberately foolish. You know very well that all these heads have got to be fitted with wigs; and you couldn't fit a wig to a head that already had a fine covering of plaster curls. But I must admit that it rather detracts from the beauty of a girl's head if you represent it without hair. The models used to hate it when they were shown with heads like old gentlemen's, and so did poor Daddy; in fact he usually rendered the hair in the clay, just sketchily, for the sake of the model's feelings and his own and took it off afterwards with a wire tool. But there is the kettle boiling over. I must make the tea."

While this ceremony was being performed, I strolled round the studio and inspected the casts, more particularly the heads and faces. Of these latter the majority were obviously modelled, but I noticed quite a number with closed eyes, having very much the appearance of death-masks. When we had taken our places at the little table near the great gas-ring, I inquired what they were.

"They do look rather cadaverous, don't they?" she said as she poured out the tea; "but they are not death-masks. They are casts from living faces, mostly from the faces of models, but my father always used to take a cast from anyone who would let him. They are quite useful to work from, though, of course, the eyes have to be put in from another cast or from life."

"It must be rather an unpleasant operation," I said, "having the plaster poured all over the face. How does the victim manage to breathe?"

"The usual plan is to put little quills or tubes into the nostrils. But my father could keep the nostrils free without any tubes. He was a very skilful moulder; and then he always used the best plaster, which sets very quickly so that it only took a few minutes."

"And how are you getting on; and what were you doing when I came in?"

"I am getting on quite well," she replied. "My work has been passed as satisfactory and I have three new commissions. When you came in I was just getting ready to make a mould for a head and shoulders. After tea I shall go on with it and you shall help me. But tell me about yourself. You have finished with Dr Cornish, haven't you?"

"Yes, I am a gentleman at large for the time being; but that won't do. I shall have to look out for another job."

"I hope it will be a London job," she said. "Arabella and I would feel quite lonely if you went away, even for a week or two. We both look forward so much to our little family gathering on Sunday afternoon."

"You don't look forward to it as much as I do," I said warmly. "It is difficult for me to realize that there was ever a time when you were not a part of my life. And yet we are quite new friends."

"Yes," she said; "only a few weeks old. But I have the same feeling. I seem to have known you for years; and as for Arabella, she speaks of you as if she had nursed you from infancy. You have a very insinuating way with you."

"Oh, don't spoil it by calling me insinuating!" I protested.

"No, I won't," she replied. "It was the wrong word. I meant sympathetic. You have the gift of entering into other people's troubles and feeling them as if they were your own; which is a very precious gift – to the other people."

"Your troubles are my own," said I, "since I have the privilege to be your friend. But I have been a happier man since I shared them."

"It is very nice of you to say that," she murmured with a quick glance at me and just a faint heightening of colour; and then for a while neither of us spoke.

"Have you seen Dr Thorndyke lately?" she asked, when she had refilled our cups, and thereby, as it were, punctuated our silence.

"Yes," I answered. "I saw him only a night or two ago. And that reminds me that I was commissioned to make some inquiries. Can you tell me if your father ever did any electrotype work for outsiders?"

"I don't know," she answered. "He used latterly to electrotype most of his own work instead of sending it to the bronze-founders, but it is hardly likely that he would do electros for outsiders. There are firms who do nothing else, and I know that, when he was busy, he used to send his own work to them. But why do you ask?"

I related to her what Thorndyke had told me and pointed out the importance of ascertaining the facts, which she saw at once.

"As soon as we have finished tea," she said, "we will go and look over the cupboard where the electro moulds were kept – that is, the permanent ones. The gelatine moulds for works in the round couldn't be kept. They were melted down again. But the waterproofed-plaster moulds were stored away in this cupboard, and the gutta-percha ones too until they were wanted to soften down to make new moulds. And even if the moulds were destroyed, Father usually kept a cast."

"Would you be able to tell by looking through the cupboard?" I asked.

"Yes. I should know a strange mould, of course, as I saw all the original work that he did. Have we finished? Then let us go and settle the question now."

She produced a bunch of keys from her pocket and crossed the studio to a large, tall cupboard in a corner. Selecting a key, she inserted it and was trying vainly to turn it when the door came open. She looked at it in surprise and then turned to me with a somewhat puzzled expression.

"This is really very curious," she said. "When I came here this morning I found the outer door unlocked. Naturally I thought I must have forgotten to lock it, though that would have been an extraordinary oversight. And now I find this door unlocked. But I distinctly remember locking it before going away last night, when I had put back the box of modelling wax. What do you make of that?"

"It looks as if someone had entered the studio last night with false keys or by picking the lock. But why should they? Perhaps the cupboard will tell. You will know if it has been disturbed."

She ran her eyes along the shelves and said at once: "It has been. The things are all in disorder and one of the moulds is broken. We had better take them all out and see if anything is missing – so far as I can judge, that is, for the moulds were just as my father left them."

We dragged a small work-table to the cupboard and emptied the shelves one by one. She examined each mould as we took it out, and I jotted down a rough list at her dictation. When we had been through the whole collection and rearranged the moulds on the shelves – they were mostly plaques and medallions – she slowly read through the list and reflected for a few moments. At length she said:

"I don't miss anything that I can remember. But the question is, were there any moulds or casts that I did not know about? I am thinking of Dr Thorndyke's question. If there were any, they have gone, so that question cannot he answered."

We looked at one another gravely and in both our minds was the same unspoken question: "Who was it that had entered the studio last night?"

We had just closed the cupboard and were moving away when my eye caught a small object half-hidden in the darkness under the cupboard itself – the bottom of which was raised by low feet about an inch and a half from the floor. I knelt down and passed my hand into the shallow space and was just able to hook it out. It proved to be a fragment of a small plaster mould, saturated with wax and black-leaded on the inside. Miss D'Arblay stooped over it eagerly and exclaimed: "I don't know that one. What a pity it is such a small piece. But it is certainly part of a coin."

"It is part of *the* coin," said I. "There can be no doubt of that. I examined the cast that Mr Polton made and I recognize this as the same. There is the lower part of the bust, the letters CA – the first two letters of Carolus – and the tiny elephant and castle. That is conclusive. This is the mould from which that electrotype was made. But I had better hand it to Dr Thorndyke to compare with the cast that he has."

I carefully bestowed the fragment in my tobacco-pouch, as the safest place for the time being, and meanwhile Miss D'Arblay looked fixedly at me with a very singular expression.

"You realize," she said in a hushed voice, "what this means. *He* was in here last night."

I nodded. The same conclusion had instantly occurred to me, and a very uncomfortable one it was. There was something very sinister and horrid in the thought of that murderous villain quietly letting himself into this studio and ransacking its hiding-places in the dead of the night. So unpleasantly suggestive was it that, for a time, neither of us spoke a word, but stood looking blankly at one another in silent dismay. And in the midst of the tense silence there came a knock at the door.

We both started as if we had been struck. Then Miss D'Arblay, recovering herself quickly, said, "I had better go," and hurried down the studio to the lobby.

I listened nervously, for I was a little unstrung. I heard her go into the lobby and open the outer door. I heard a low voice, apparently asking a question; the outer door closed and then came a sudden scuffling sound and a piercing shriek. With a shout of alarm, I raced down the studio, knocking over a chair as I ran, and darted into the lobby just as the outer door slammed.

For a moment I hesitated. Miss D'Arblay had shrunk into a corner and stood in the semi-darkness with both her hands pressed tightly to her breast. But she called out excitedly, "Follow him! I am not hurt"; and on this I wrenched open the door and stepped out.

But the first glance showed me that pursuit was hopeless. The fog had now become so dense that I could hardly see my own feet. I dared not leave the threshold for fear of not being able to find my way back. Then she would be alone – and *he* was probably lurking close by even now.

I stood irresolutely, stock-still, listening intently. The silence was profound. All the natural noises of a populous neighbourhood seemed to be smothered by the dense blanket of dark yellow vapour. Not a sound came to my ear; no stealthy foot-fall, no rustle of movement. Nothing but stark silence.

Uneasily I crept back until the open doorway showed as a dim rectangle of shadow; crept back and peered fearfully into the darkness of the lobby. She was still standing in the corner – an upright smudge of deeper darkness in the obscurity. But even as I looked the shadowy figure collapsed and slid noiselessly to the floor.

In an instant the pursuit was forgotten and I darted into the lobby, shutting the outer door behind me, and dropped on my knees at her side. Where she had fallen a streak of light came in from the studio, and the sight that it revealed turned me sick with terror. The whole front of her smock, from the breast downwards, was saturated with blood; both her hands were crimson and gory, and her face was dead-white to the lips.

For an instant I was paralysed with horror. I could see no movement of breathing, and the white face with its parted lips and half-closed eyes was as the face of the dead. But when I dared to search for the wound, I was a little reassured; for, closely as I scrutinized it, the gory smock showed no sign of a cut excepting on the bloodstained right sleeve. And now I noticed a deep gash on the left hand, which was still bleeding freely, and was probably the source of the blood which had soaked the smock. There seemed to be no vital wound.

With a deep breath of relief, I hastily tore my handkerchief into strips and applied the improvised bandage tightly enough to control the bleeding. Then with the scissors from my pocket-case, which I now carried from habit, I laid open the bloodstained sleeve. The wound on the arm, just above the elbow was quite shallow; a glancing wound which tailed off upwards into a scratch. A turn of the remaining strip of bandage secured it for the time being, and this done, I once more explored the front of the smock, pulling its folds tightly apart in search of the dreaded cut. But there was none; and now, the bleeding being controlled, it was safe to take measures of restoration. Tenderly – and not without effort – I lifted her and carried her into the studio, where was a shabby but roomy couch, on which poor D'Arblay had been accustomed to rest when he stayed for the night. On this I laid her, and fetching some water and a towel, dabbed her face and neck. Presently she opened her eyes and heaved a deep sigh, looking at me with a troubled, bewildered expression and evidently only half-conscious. Suddenly her eye caught the great bloodstain on her smock and her expression grew wild and terrified. For a few moments she gazed at me with eyes full of horror; then, as the memory of her dreadful experience rushed back on her, she uttered a little cry and burst into tears, moaning and sobbing almost hysterically.

I rested her head on my shoulder, and tried to comfort her; and she, poor girl, weak and shaken by the awful shock, clung to me, trembling, and wept passionately with her face buried in my breast. As for me, I was almost ready to weep, too, if only from sheer relief and revulsion from my late terrors.

"Marion darling!" I murmured into her ear as I stroked her damp hair. "Poor dear little woman! It was horrible. But you mustn't cry any more now. Try to forget it, dearest."

She shook her head passionately. "I can never do that," she sobbed. "It will haunt me as long as I live. Oh! I and I am so frightened, even now. What a coward I am!"

"Indeed you are not!" I exclaimed. "You are just weak from loss of blood. Why did you let me leave you, Marion?"

"I didn't think I was hurt, and I wasn't particularly frightened then; and I hoped that if you followed him, he might be caught. Did you see him?"

"No. There is a thick fog outside. I didn't dare to leave the threshold. Were you able to see what he was like?"

She shuddered and choked down a sob. "He is a dreadful-looking man," she said; "I loathed him at the first glance – a beetle-browed, hook-nosed wretch with a face like that of some horrible bird of prey. But I couldn't see him very distinctly, for it is rather dark in the lobby and he wore a wide-brimmed hat, pulled down over his brows."

"Would you know him again? And can you give a description of him that would be of use to the police?"

"I am sure I should know him again," she said with a shudder. "It was a face that one could never forget. A hideous face! The face of a demon! I can see it now and it will haunt me, sleeping and waking, until I die."

Her words ended with a catch of the breath and she looked piteously into my face with wide, terrified eyes. I took her trembling hand and once more drew her head to my shoulder.

"You mustn't think that, dear," said I. "You are all unstrung now, but these terrors will pass. Try to tell me quietly just what this man was like. What was his height for instance?"

"He was not very tall. Not much taller than me. And he was rather slightly built."

"Could you see whether he was dark or fair?"

"He was rather dark. I could see a shock of hair sticking out from under his hat and he had a moustache with turned-up ends and a beard – a rather short beard."

"And now as to his face. You say he had a hooked nose?"

"Yes; a great, high-bridged nose like the beak of some horrible bird. And his eyes seemed to be deep-set under heavy brows with bushy eyebrows. The face was rather thin with high cheek-bones – a fierce, scowling, repulsive face."

"And the voice? Should you know that again?"

"I don't know," she answered. "He spoke in quite a low tone, rather indistinctly. And he said only a few words – something about having come to make some inquiries about the cost of a wax model. Then he stepped into the lobby and shut the outer door, and immediately, without another word, he seized my right arm and struck at me. But I saw the knife in his hand and, as I called out, I snatched at it with my left hand, so that it missed my body and I felt it cut my right arm. Then I got hold of his wrist. But he had heard you coming and wrenched himself free. The next moment he had opened the door and rushed out, shutting it behind him."

She paused and then added in a shaking voice: "If you had not been here – if I had been alone – "

"We won't think of that, Marion. You were not alone; and you will never be again in this place. I shall see to that."

At this she gave a little sigh of satisfaction, and looked into my face with the pallid ghost of a smile.

"Then I shan't be frightened any more," she murmured; and closing her eyes she lay for a while, breathing quietly as if asleep. She looked very delicate and frail with her waxen cheeks and the dark shadows under her eyes, but still I noted a faint tinge of colour stealing back into her lips. I gazed down at her with fond anxiety, as a mother might look at a sleeping child that had just passed the crisis of a dangerous illness. Of the bare chance that had snatched her from imminent death I would not allow myself to think. The horror of that moment was too fresh for the thought to be endurable. Instead I began to occupy myself with the practical question as to how she was to be got home. It was a long way to North Grove – some two miles, I reckoned – too far for her to walk in her present weak state; and there was the fog. Unless it lifted it would be impossible for her to find her way; and I could give her no help, as I was a stranger to this locality. Nor was it by any means safe; for our enemy might still be lurking near, waiting for the opportunity that the fog would offer.

I was still turning over these difficulties when she opened her eyes and looked up at me a little shyly.

"I'm afraid I've been rather a baby," she said, "but I am much better now. Hadn't I better get up?"

"No," I answered. "Lie quiet and rest. I am trying to think how you are to be got home. Didn't you say something about a caretaker?"

"Yes; a woman in the little house next door, which really belongs to the studio. Daddy used to leave the key with her at night so that she could clean up. But I just fetch her in when I want her help. Why do you ask?"

"Do you think she could get a cab for us?"

"I am afraid not. There is no cab-stand anywhere near here. But I think I could walk, unless the fog is too thick. Shall we go and see what it is like?"

"I will go," said I, rising. But she clung to my arm.

"You are not to go alone," she said, in sudden alarm. "*He* may be there still."

I thought it best to humour her and accordingly helped her to rise. For a few moments she seemed rather unsteady on her feet, but soon she was able to walk, supported by my arm, to the studio door, which I opened, and through which wreaths of vapour drifted in. But the fog was perceptibly thinner; and even as I was looking across the road at the now faintly visible houses, two spots of dull yellow light appeared up the road and my ear caught the muffled sound of wheels. Gradually the lights grew brighter and at length there stole out of the fog the shadowy form of a cab with a man leading the horse at a slow walk. Here seemed a chance to escape from our dilemma.

"Go in and shut the door while I speak to the cabman," said I. "He may be able to take us. I shall give four knocks when I come back."

She was unwilling to let me go, but I gently pushed her in and shut the door and then advanced to meet the cab. A few words set my anxieties at rest, for it appeared that the cabman had to set down a fare a little way along the street and was very willing to take a return fare on suitable terms. As any terms would have been suitable to me under the circumstances, the cabman was able to make a good bargain and we parted with mutual satisfaction and a cordial *au revoir*. Then I steered back along the fence to the studio door, on which I struck four distinct knocks and announced myself vocally by name. Immediately the door opened and a hand drew me in by the sleeve.

"I am so glad you have come back," she whispered. "It was horrid to be alone in the lobby even for a few minutes. What did the cabman say?"

I told her the joyful tidings and we at once made ready for our departure. In a minute or two the welcome glare of the cab-lamps reappeared, and when I had locked up the studio and pocketed the key I helped her into the rather ramshackle vehicle.

I don't mind admitting that the cabman's charges were extortionate; but I grudged him never a penny. It was probably the slowest journey that I had ever made, but yet the funereal pace was all too swift. Half-ashamed as I was to admit it to myself, this horrible adventure was bearing sweet fruit to me in the unquestioned intimacy that had been born in the troubled hour.

Little enough was said; but I sat happily by her side, holding her uninjured hand in mine (on the pretence of keeping it warm), blissfully conscious that our sympathy and friendship had grown to something sweeter and more precious.

"What are we to say to Arabella?" I asked. "I suppose she will have to be told?"

"Of course she will," replied Marion; "you shall tell her. But," she added in a lower tone, "you needn't tell her everything – I mean what a baby I was and how you had to comfort and soothe me. She is as brave as a lion and she thinks I am, too. So you needn't undeceive her too much."

"I needn't undeceive her at all," said I, "because you are"; and we were still arguing this weighty question when the cab drew up at Ivy Cottage. I sent the cabman off rejoicing, and then escorted Marion up the path to the door, where Miss Boler was waiting, having apparently heard the cab arrive.

"Thank goodness!" she exclaimed. "I was wondering how on earth you would manage to get home." Then she suddenly observed Marion's bandaged hand and uttered an exclamation of alarm.

"Miss Marion has cut her hand rather badly," I explained. "We won't talk about it just now. I will tell you everything presently when you have put her to bed. Now I want some stuff to make dressings and bandages."

Miss Boler looked at me suspiciously, but made no comment. With extraordinary promptitude she produced a supply of linen, warm water and other necessaries, and then stood by to watch the operation and give assistance.

"It is a nasty wound," I said as I removed the extemporized dressing, "but not so bad as I feared. There will be no lasting injury."

I put on the permanent dressing and then exposed the wound on the arm, at the sight of which Miss Boler's eyebrows went up. But she made no remark; and when a dressing had been put on this, too, she took charge of the patient to conduct her up to the bedroom.

"I shall come up and see that she is all right before I go," said I; "and meanwhile, no questions, Arabella."

She cast a significant look at me over her shoulder and departed with her arm about the patient's waist. The rites and ceremonies above-stairs were briefer than I had expected – perhaps the promised explanations had accelerated matters. At any rate, in a very few minutes Miss Boler bustled into the room and said: "You can go up now, but don't stop to gossip. I am bursting with curiosity."

Thereupon, I ascended to my lady's chamber, which I entered as diffidently and reverentially as though such visits were not the commonplace of my professional life. As I approached the bed, she heaved a little sigh of content and murmured:

"What a fortunate girl I am! To be petted and cared for and pampered in this way! Arabella is a perfect angel; and you, Dr Gray – "

"Oh, Marion!" I protested. "Not Dr Gray."

"Well, then, Stephen," she corrected with a faint blush.

"That is better. And what am I?"

"Never mind," she replied, very pink and smiling. "I expect you know. If you don't, ask Arabella when you go down."

"I expect she will do most of the asking," said I. "And I have strict orders not to stop to gossip, so let me see the bandages and then I must go."

I made my inspection, without undue hurry, and having seen that all was well, I took her hand.

"You are to stay here until I have seen you tomorrow morning; and you are to be a good girl and try not to think of unpleasant things."

"Yes; I will do everything that you tell me."

"Then I can go away happy. Goodnight Marion."

"Good night, Stephen."

I pressed her hand and felt her fingers close on mine. Then I turned away and, with only a moment's pause at the door for a last look at the sweet, smiling face, descended the stairs to confront the formidable Arabella.

Of my cautious statement and her keen cross-examination I will say nothing. I made the proceedings as short as was decent, for I wanted, if possible, to take counsel with Thorndyke. On my explaining this, the brevity of my account was condoned, and even my refusal of food.

"But remember, Arabella," I said as she escorted me to the gate, "she has had a very severe shock. The less you say to her about the affair for the present, the quicker will be her recovery."

With this warning I set forth through the rapidly thinning fog to catch the first conveyance that I could find to bear me southward.

CHAPTER ELEVEN

Arms and the Man

The fog had thinned to a mere haze when the porter admitted me at the Inner Temple Gate, so that, as I passed the Cloisters and looked through into Pump Court, I could see the lighted windows of the residents' chambers at the far end. The sight of them encouraged me to hope that the chambers in King's Bench Walk might throw out a similar hopeful gleam. Nor was I disappointed; and the warm glow from the windows of number 5A sent me tripping up the stairs profoundly relieved though a trifle abashed at the untimely hour of my visit.

The door was opened by Thorndyke himself, who instantly cut short my apologies.

"Nonsense, Gray!" he exclaimed, shaking my hand. "It is no interruption at all. On the contrary: how beautiful upon the staircase are the feet of him that bringeth – well, what sort of tidings?"

"Not good, I am afraid, sir."

"Well, let us have them. Come and sit by the fire." He drew up an easy-chair, and having installed me in it and taken a critical look at me, invited me to proceed. I accordingly proceeded bluntly to inform him that an attempt had been made to murder Miss D'Arblay.

"Ha!" he exclaimed. "These are bad tidings indeed! I hope she is not injured in any way."

I reassured him on this point and gave him the details as to the patient's condition, and he then asked:

"When did the attempt occur and how did you hear of it?"

"It happened this evening and I was present."

"You were present!" he repeated, gazing at me in the utmost astonishment. "And what became of the assailant?"

"He vanished into the fog," I replied.

"Ah, yes. The fog. I had forgotten that. But now let us drop this question and answer method. Give me a narrative from the beginning with the events in their proper sequence. And omit nothing, no matter how trivial."

I took him at his word – up to a certain point. I described my arrival at the studio, the search in the cupboard, the sinister interruption, the attack and the unavailing attempt at pursuit. As to what befell thereafter I gave him a substantially complete account – with certain reservations – up to my departure from Ivy Cottage.

"Then you never saw the man at all?"

"No; but Miss D'Arblay did"; and here I gave him such details of the man's appearance as I had been able to gather from Marion.

"It is quite a vivid description," he said as he wrote down the details; "and now shall we have a look at that piece of the mould?"

I disinterred it from my tobacco-pouch and handed it to him. He glanced at it and then went to a cabinet, from a drawer in which he produced the little case containing Polton's casts of the guinea and a box which he placed on the table and opened.

From it he took a lump of moulding-wax and a bottle of powdered French chalk. Pinching off a piece of the wax, he rolled it into a ball, dusted it lightly with the chalk powder and pressed it with his thumb into the mould. It came away on his thumb bearing a perfect impression of the inside of the mould.

"That settles it," said he, taking the obverse cast from the case and laying it on the table beside the wax "squeeze". "The squeeze and the cast are identical. There is now no possible doubt that the electrotype guinea that was found in the pond was made by Julius D'Arblay. Probably it had been delivered by him to the murderer on the very evening of his death. So we are undoubtedly dealing with that same man. It is a most alarming situation."

"It would be alarming if it were any other man," I remarked.

"No doubt," he agreed. "But there is something very special about this man. He is a criminal of a type that is almost unknown here, but is not uncommon in South European and Slav countries. You find him, too, in the United States, principally among the foreign-born or alien population. He is not a normal human being. He is an inveterate murderer, to whom a human life does not count at all. And this type of man continually grows more and more dangerous, for two reasons: first, the murder habit becomes more confirmed with each crime; second, there is virtually no penalty for the succeeding murders, for the first one entails the death-sentence and fifty murders can involve no more. This man killed Van Zellen as a mere incident of a robbery. Then he appears to have killed D'Arblay to secure his own safety, and he is now attempting to kill Miss D'Arblay, apparently for the same reason. And he will kill you and he will kill me if our existence is inconvenient or dangerous to him. We must bear that in mind and take the necessary measures."

"I can't imagine," said I, "what motive he can have for wanting to kill Miss D'Arblay."

"Probably he believes that she knows something that would be dangerous to him – something connected with those moulds, or perhaps something else. We are rather in the dark. We don't know for certain what it was he came to look for when he entered the studio, or whether or not he found what he wanted. But to return to the danger. It is obvious that he knows the Abbey Road district well, for he found his way to the studio in the fog. He may be living close by. There is no reason why he should not be. His identity is quite unknown."

"That is a horrid thought!" I exclaimed.

"It is," he agreed; "but it is the assumption that we have to act upon. We must not leave a loophole unwatched. He mustn't get another chance."

"No," I concurred warmly; "he certainly must not — if we can help it. But it is an awful position. We carry that poor girl's life in our hands, and there is always the possibility that we may be caught off our guard, just for a moment."

He nodded gravely. "You are quite right, Gray. An awful responsibility rests on us. I am very unhappy about this poor young lady. Of course, there is the other side — but at present we are concerned with Miss D'Arblay's safety."

"What other side is there?" I demanded.

"I mean," he replied, "that if we can hold out, this man is going to deliver himself into our hands."

"What makes you think that?" I asked eagerly.

"I recognize a familiar phenomenon," he replied. "My large experience and extensive study of crimes against the person have shown me that in the overwhelming majority of cases of obscure crime the discovery has been brought about by the criminal's own efforts to make himself safe. He is constantly trying to hide his tracks — and making fresh ones. Now, this man is one of those criminals who won't let well alone. He kills Van Zellen and disappears, leaving no trace. He seems to be quite safe. But he is not satisfied. He can't keep quiet. He kills D'Arblay; he enters the studio, he tries to kill Miss D'Arblay: all to make himself more safe. And every time he moves, he tells us something fresh about himself. If we can only wait and watch, we shall have him."

"What has he told us about himself this time?" I asked.

"We won't go into that now, Gray. We have other business on hand. But you know all that I know as to the facts. If you will turn over those facts at your leisure, you will find that they yield some very curious and striking inferences."

I was about to press the question when the door opened and Mr Polton appeared on the threshold. Observing me, he crinkled benevolently and then, in answer to Thorndyke's inquiring glance, said: "I thought I had better remind you, sir, that you have not had any supper."

"Dear me, Polton," Thorndyke exclaimed, "now you mention it, I believe you are right. And I suspect that Dr Gray is in the same case. So we place ourselves in your hands. Supper and pistols are what we want."

"Pistols, sir!" exclaimed Polton, opening his eyes to an unusual extent and looking at us suspiciously.

"Don't be alarmed, Polton," Thorndyke chuckled. "It isn't a duel. I just want you to go over our stock of pistols and ammunition."

At this I thought I detected a belligerent gleam in Polton's eye, but even as I looked, he was gone. Not for long, however. In a couple of minutes he was back with a large hand-bag, which he placed on the table and again retired. Thorndyke opened the bag and took out quite a considerable assortment of weapons – single pistols, revolvers and automatics – which he laid out on the table, each with its box of appropriate cartridges.

"I hate fire-arms!" he exclaimed as he viewed the collection distastefully. "They are dangerous things; and when it comes to business they are scurvy weapons. Any poltroon can pull a trigger. But we must put ourselves on equal terms with our opponent, who is certain to be provided. Which will you have? I recommend this Baby Browning for portability. Have you had any practice?"

"Only target practice. But I am a fair shot with a revolver. I have never used an automatic."

"We will go over the mechanism after supper," said he. "Meanwhile, I hear the approach of Polton and am conscious of a voracious interest in what he is bringing. When did you feed last?"

"I had tea at the studio about half past four."

"My poor Gray!" he exclaimed, "you must be starving. I ought to have asked you sooner. However, here comes relief." He opened a folding table by the fire just as Polton entered with the tray, on which I was gratified to observe a good-sized dishcover and a claret-jug. Polton rapidly laid the little table and then, whisking off the cover, retired with a triumphant crinkle.

"You have a regular kitchen upstairs, I presume," said I as we took our seats at the table, "as well as a laboratory? And a pretty good cook, too, to judge by the results."

Thorndyke chuckled. "The kitchen and the laboratory are one," he replied, "and Polton is the cook. An uncommonly good cook, as you suggest, but his methods are weird. These cutlets were probably grilled in the cupel furnace, but I have known him to do a steak with the brazing-jet. There is nothing conventional about Polton. But whatever he does, he does to a finish; which is fortunate, because I thought of calling in his aid in our present difficulty."

I looked at him inquiringly and he continued: "If Miss D'Arblay is to go on with her work, which she ought to, as it is her livelihood, she must be guarded constantly. I had considered applying to Inspector Follett, and we may have to later; but for the present it will be better for us to keep our own counsel and play our own hand. We have two objects in view. First – and paramount – is the necessity of securing Miss D'Arblay's safety. But, second, we want to lay our hands on this man, not to frighten him away, as we might do if we put the police on his track. When once we have him, her safety is secured forever; whereas if he were merely scared away he would be an abiding menace. We have got to catch him, and at present he is catchable. Secure in his unknown identity, he is lurking within reach, ready to strike, but also ready to be pounced upon when we are ready to pounce. Let us keep him confident of his safety while we are gathering up the clues."

"Hm! yes," I assented, without much enthusiasm. "What is it that you propose to do?"

"Somebody," he replied, "must keep watch over Miss D'Arblay from the moment when she leaves her house until she returns to it. How much time – if any – can you give up to this duty?"

"My whole time," I answered promptly. "I shall let everything else go."

"Then," said he, "I propose that you and Polton relieve one another on duty. It will be better than for you to be there all the time."

I saw what he meant and agreed at once. The conventions must be respected as far as possible.

"But," I suggested, "isn't Polton rather a lightweight — if it should come to a scrap, I mean?"

"Don't undervalue small men, even physically," he replied. "They are commonly better built than big men and more enduring and energetic. Polton is remarkably strong and he has the pluck of a bulldog. But we must see how he is placed as regards work."

The question was put to him and the position of affairs explained when he came down to clear the table; whereupon it appeared (from his own account) that he was absolutely without occupation of any kind and pining for something to do. Thorndyke laughed incredulously but did not contest this outrageous and barefaced untruth, merely remarking:

"I am afraid it will be rather an idle time for you."

"Oh, no, it won't, sir," Polton assured him emphatically. "I've always wanted to learn something about sculptor's moulding and wax-casting, but I've never had a chance. Now I shall have. And that opportunity isn't going to be wasted."

Thorndyke regarded his assistant with a twinkling eye. "So it was mere self-seeking that made you so enthusiastic," said he. "But you are quite a good moulder already."

"Not a sculptor's moulder, sir," replied Polton; "and I know nothing about wax-work. But I shall, before I have been there many days."

"I am sure you will," said Thorndyke. "Miss D'Arblay will have an apprentice and journeyman in one. You will be able to give her quite a lot of help; which will be valuable just now while her hand is disabled. When do you think she will be able to go back to work, Gray?"

"I can't say. Not tomorrow certainly. Shall I send you a report when I have seen her?"

"Do," he replied; "or better still, come in tomorrow evening and give me the news. So, Polton, we shan't want you for another day or so."

"Ah!" said Polton, "then I shall be able to finish that recording-clock before I go"; upon which Thorndyke and I laughed aloud, and Polton, his mendacity thus unmasked, retired with the tray, crinkling but unabashed.

The short remainder of the evening – or rather of the night – was spent in the study of the mechanism and mode of use of automatic pistols. When I finally bestowed the "Baby", fully loaded, in my hip-pocket and rose to go, Thorndyke sped me on my way with a few words of warning and advice.

"Be constantly on your guard, Gray. You are going to make a bitter enemy of a man who knows no scruples; indeed, you have done so already, and something tells me that he is aware of it. Avoid all solitary or unfrequented places. Keep to main thorough-fares and well-lighted streets and maintain a vigilant look-out for any suspicious appearances. You have said truly that we carry Miss D'Arblay's life in our hands. But to preserve her life we must preserve our own; which we should probably prefer to do in any case. Don't get jumpy – I don't much think you will; but keep your attention alert and your weather eyelid lifting."

With these encouraging words and a hearty handshake, he let me out and stood watching me as I descended the stairs.

CHAPTER TWELVE
A Dramatic Discovery

About eleven o'clock in the forenoon of the third day after the terrible events of that unforgettable night of the great fog, Marion and I drew up on our bicycles opposite the studio door. She was now outwardly quite recovered, excepting as to her left hand, but I noticed that, as I inserted the key into the door, she cast a quick, nervous glance up and down the road; and as we passed through the lobby, she looked down for one moment at the great bloodstain on the floor and then hastily averted her face.

"Now," I said, assuming a brisk, cheerful tone, "we must get to work. Mr Polton will be here in half an hour and we must be ready to put his nose on the grindstone at once."

"Then your nose will have to go on first," she replied with a smile, "and so will mine, with two raw apprentices to teach and an important job waiting to be done. But, dear me! what a lot of trouble I am giving!"

"Nothing of the kind, Marion," I exclaimed; "you are a public benefactor. Polton is delighted at the chance to come here and enlarge his experience, and as for me – "

"Well? As for you?" She looked at me half shyly, half-mischievously. "Go on. You've stopped at the most interesting point."

"I think I had better not," said I. "We don't want the forewoman to get too uppish."

She laughed softly, and when I had helped her out of her overcoat and rolled up the sleeve of her one serviceable arm, I went out to the lobby to stow away the bicycles and lock the outer door. When I returned, she had got out from the cupboard a large box of flaked gelatine and a massive spouted bucket which she was filling at the sink.

"Hadn't you better explain to me what we are going to do?" I asked.

"Oh, explanations are of no use," she replied. "You just do as I tell you and then you will know all about it. This isn't a school; it's a workshop. When we have got the gelatine in to soak, I will show you how to make a plaster case."

"It seems to me," I retorted, "that my instructress has graduated in the academy of Squeers. 'W–i–n–d–e–r, winder; now go and clean one.' Isn't that the method?"

"Apprentices are not allowed to waste time in wrangling," she rejoined severely. "Go and put on one of Daddy's blouses and I will set you to work."

This practical method of instruction justified itself abundantly. The reasons for each process emerged at once as soon as the process was completed. And it was withal a pleasant method, for there is no comradeship so sympathetic as the comradeship of work, nor any which begets so wholesome and friendly an intimacy. But though there were playful and frivolous interludes – as when the forewoman's working hand became encrusted with clay and had to be cleansed with a sponge by the apprentice – we worked to such purpose that by the time Mr Polton was due, the plaster bust (of which a wax replica had to be made) was firmly fixed on the work-table on a clay foundation and surrounded by a carefully levelled platform of clay, in which it was embedded to half its thickness. I had just finished smoothing the surface when there came a knock at the outer door; on which Marion started violently and clutched my arm. But she recovered in a moment and exclaimed in a tone of vexation:

"How silly I am! Of course it is Mr Polton."

It was. I found him on the threshold in rapt contemplation of the knocker and looking rather like an archdeacon on tour. He greeted me with a friendly crinkle, and I then conducted him into the studio and presented him to Marion, who shook his hand warmly and thanked him so profusely for coming to her aid that he was quite abashed. However, he did not waste time in compliments, but, producing an apron from his hand-bag, took off his coat, donned the apron, rolled up his sleeves and beamed inquiringly at the bust.

"We are going to make a plaster case for the gelatine mould, Mr Polton," Marion explained, and proceeded to a few preliminary directions, to which the new apprentice listened with respectful attention. But she had hardly finished when he fell to work with a quiet, unhurried facility that filled me with envy. He seemed to know where to find everything. He discovered the waste paper with which to cover the model to prevent the clay from sticking to it, he pounced on the clay-bin at the first shot, and when he had built up the shape for the case, found the plaster-bin, mixing-bowl and spoon as if he had been born and bred in the workshop, stopping only for a moment to test the condition of the gelatine in the bucket.

"Mr Polton," Marion said after watching him for a while, "you are an impostor – a dreadful impostor. You pretend to come here as an improver, but you really know all about gelatine moulding; now, don't you?"

Polton admitted apologetically that he "had done a little in that way". "But," he added, in extenuation, "I have never done any work in wax. And talking of wax, the doctor will be here presently."

"Dr Thorndyke?" Marion asked.

"Yes, miss. He had some business in Holloway, so he thought he would come on here to make your acquaintance and take a look at the premises."

"All the same, Mr Polton," said I, "I don't quite see the connexion between Dr Thorndyke and wax."

He crinkled with a slightly embarrassed air and explained that he must have been thinking of something that the doctor had said to him; but his explanations were cut short by a knock at the door.

"That is his knock," said Polton; and he and I together proceeded to open the door, when I inducted the distinguished visitor into the studio and presented him to the presiding goddess. I noticed that each of them inspected the other with some curiosity and that the first impressions appeared to be mutually satisfactory, though Marion was at first a little overawed by Thorndyke's impressive personality.

"You mustn't let me interrupt your work," the latter said, when the preliminary politenesses had been exchanged. "I have just come to fill in Dr Gray's outline sketches with details of my own observing. I wanted to see you — to convert a name into an actual person, to see the studio for the same reason, and to get as precise a description as possible of the man whom we are trying to identify. Will it distress you to recall his appearance?"

She had turned a little pale at the mention of her late assailant, but she answered stoutly enough: "Not at all; besides, it is necessary."

"Thank you," said he; "then I will read out the description that I had from Dr Gray and we will see if you can add anything to it."

He produced a note-book from which he read out the particulars that I had given him, at the conclusion of which he looked at her inquiringly.

"I think that is all that I remember," she said. "There was very little light and I really only glanced at him."

Thorndyke looked at her reflectively. "It is a fairly full description," said he. "Perhaps the nose is a little sketchy. You speak of a hooked nose with a high bridge. Was it a curved nose of the Jewish type, or a squarer Roman nose?"

"It was rather square in profile; a Wellington nose, but with a rather broad base. Like a vulture's beak, and very large."

"Was it actually a hook-nose — I mean, had it a drooping tip?"

"Yes; the tip projected downwards and it was rather sharp – not bulbous."

"And the chin? Should you call it a pronounced or a retreating chin?"

"Oh, it was quite a projecting chin, rather of the Wellington type."

Thorndyke reflected once more; then, having jotted down the answers to his questions, he closed the book and returned it to his pocket.

"It is a great thing to have a trained eye," he remarked. "In your one glance you saw more than an ordinary person would have noted in a leisurely inspection in a good light. You have no doubt that you would know this man again if you should meet him?"

"Not the slightest," she replied with a shudder. "I can see him now, if I shut my eyes."

"Well," he rejoined, with a smile, "I wouldn't recall that unpleasant vision too often, if I were you. And now, may I, without disturbing you further, just take a look round the premises?"

"But, of course, Dr Thorndyke," she replied. "Do exactly what you please."

With this permission he drew away; and stood for some moments letting a very reflective eye travel round the interior; and meanwhile I watched him curiously and wondered what he had really come for. His first proceeding was to walk slowly round the studio and examine closely, one by one, all the casts which hung on pegs. Next, in the same systematic manner, he inspected all the shelves, mounting a chair to examine the upper ones. It was after scrutinizing one of the latter that he turned towards Marion and asked:

"Have you moved these casts lately, Miss D'Arblay?"

"No," she replied; "so far as I know, they have not been touched for months."

"Someone has moved them within the last day or two," said he. "Apparently the nocturnal explorer went over the shelves as well as the cupboard."

"I wonder why?" said Marion. "There were no moulds on the shelves."

Thorndyke made no rejoinder, but as he stood on the chair he once more ran his eye round the studio. Suddenly he stepped down from the chair, picked it up, carried it over to the tall cupboard and once more mounted it. His stature enabled him easily to look over the cornice on to the top of the cupboard and it was evident that something there had attracted his attention.

"Here is a derelict of some sort," he announced, which certainly has not been moved for some months." As he spoke, he reached over the cornice into the enclosed space and lifted out an excessively grimy plaster mask, from which he blew the thick coating of dust, and then stood for a while looking at it thoughtfully.

"A striking face, this," he remarked, "but not attractive. It rather suggests a Russian or Polish Jew. Do you recognize the person, Miss D'Arblay?"

He stepped down from the chair and handed the mask to Marion, who had advanced to look at it and who now held it in her hand, regarding it with a frown of perplexity.

"This is very curious," she said. "I thought I knew all the casts that have been made here. But I have never seen this one before, and I don't know the face. I wonder who he was. It doesn't look like an English face, but I should hardly have taken it for the face of a Jew, with that rather small and nearly straight nose."

"The East-European Jews are not a very pure breed," said Thorndyke. "You will see many a face of that type in Whitechapel High Street and the Jewish quarters hard by."

At this point, deserting the work-table, I came and looked over Marion's shoulder at the mask which she was holding at arm's length. And then I got a surprise of the most singular kind, for I recognized the face at a glance.

"What is it, Gray?" asked Thorndyke, who had apparently observed my astonishment.

"This is a most extraordinary coincidence!" I exclaimed. "Do you remember my speaking to you about a certain Mr Morris?"

"The dealer in antiques?" he queried.

"Yes. Well, this is his face."

He regarded me for some moments with a strangely intent expression. Then he asked: "When you say that this is Morris' face, do you mean that it resembles his face or that you identify it positively?"

"I identify it positively. I can swear to the identity. It isn't a face that one would forget. And if any doubt were possible, there is this hare-lip scar, which you can see quite plainly on the cast."

"Yes, I noticed that. And Morris has a hare-lip scar, has he?"

"Yes; and in the same position and of the same character. I think you can take it as a fact that this cast was undoubtedly taken from Morris' face."

"Which," said Thorndyke, "is a really important fact and one that is worth looking into."

"In what way is it important?" I asked.

"In this respect," he answered. "This man, Morris, is unknown to Miss D'Arblay; but he was not unknown to her father. Here we have evidence that Mr D'Arblay had dealings with people of whom his daughter had no knowledge. The circumstances of the murder made it clear that there must be such people; but here we have proof of their existence and we can give to one of them 'a local habitation and a name'. And you will notice that this particular person is a dealer in curios and possibly in more questionable things. There is just a hint that he may have had some rather queer acquaintances."

"He seemed to have had rather a fancy for plaster masks," I remarked. "I remember that he had one in his shop window."

"Did your father make many life- or death-masks as commissions, Miss D'Arblay?" Thorndyke asked.

"Only one or two, so far as I know," she replied. "There is very little demand for portrait masks nowadays. Photography has superseded them."

"That is what I should have supposed," said he. "This would be just a chance commission. However, as it establishes the fact that this man Morris was in some way connected with your father, I think I should like to have a record of his appearance. May I take this mask away with me to get a photograph of it made? I will take great care of it and let you have it back safely."

"Certainly," replied Marion; "but why not keep it, if it is of any interest to you? I have no use for it."

"That is very good of you," said he, "and if you will give me some rag and paper to pack it in, I will take myself off and leave you to finish your work in peace."

Marion took the cast from him and, having procured some rag and paper, began very carefully to wrap it up. While she was thus engaged, Thorndyke stood letting his eye travel once more round the studio.

"I see," he remarked, "that you have quite a number of masks moulded from life or death. Do I understand that they were not commissions?"

"Very few of them were," Marion replied. "Most of them were taken from professional models, but some from acquaintances whom my father bribed with the gift of a duplicate mask."

"But why did he make them? They could not have been used for producing wax faces for the show figures; for you could hardly turn a shopwindow into a wax-work exhibition with lifelike portraits of real persons."

"No," Marion agreed; "that wouldn't do at all. These masks were principally used for reference as to details of features when my father was modelling a head in clay. But he did sometimes make moulds for the wax from these masks, only he obliterated the likeness, so that the wax face was not a portrait."

"By working on the wax, I suppose?"

"Yes; or more usually by altering the mask before making the mould. It is quite easy to alter a face. Let me show you."

She lifted one of the masks from its peg and laid it on the table.

"You see," she said, "that this is the face of a young girl – one of my father's models. It is a round, smooth, smiling face with a very short, weak chin and a projecting upper lip. We can change all that in a moment."

She took up a lump of clay, and pinching off a pellet, laid it on the right cheek-bone and spread it out. Having treated the other side in the same manner, she rolled an elongated pellet with which she built up the lower lip. Then, with a larger pellet, she enlarged the chin downwards and forwards, and having added a small touch to each of the eyebrows, she dipped a sponge in thick clay-water, or "slip," and dabbed the mask all over to bring it to a uniform colour.

"There," she said, "it is very rough, but you see what I mean."

The result was truly astonishing. The weak, chubby, girlish face had been changed by these few touches into the strong, coarse face of a middle-aged woman.

"It really is amazing!" I exclaimed. "It is a perfectly different face. I wouldn't have believed that such a thing was possible."

"It is a most striking and interesting demonstration," said Thorndyke. "But yet I don't know that we need be so surprised. If we consider that of all the millions of persons in this island alone, each one has a face which is different from any other and yet that all those faces are made up of the same anatomical parts, we realize that the differences which distinguish one face from another must be excessively subtle and minute."

"We do," agreed Marion, "especially when we are modelling a portrait bust and the likeness won't come, although every part appears to be correct and all the measurements seem to agree. A true likeness is an extraordinarily subtle and exact piece of work."

"So I have always thought," said Thorndyke. "But I mustn't delay you any longer. May I have my precious parcel?"

Marion hastily put the finishing touches to the not very presentable bundle and handed it to him with a smile and a bow. He then took his leave of her and I escorted him to the door, where he paused for a moment as we shook hands.

"You are bearing my advice in mind, I hope, Gray," he said.

"As to keeping clear of unfrequented places? Yes, I have been very careful in that respect, and I never go abroad without the pistol. It is in my hip-pocket now. But I have seen no sign of anything to justify so much caution. I doubt if our friend is even aware of my existence, and in any case, I don't see that he has anything against me, excepting as Miss D'Arblay's watch-dog."

"Don't be too sure, Gray," he rejoined earnestly. "There may be certain little matters that you have overlooked. At any rate, don't relax your caution. Give all unfrequented places a wide berth and keep a bright look-out."

With this final warning, he turned away and strode off down the road, while I re-entered the studio just in time to see Polton mix the first bowl of plaster, as Marion, having washed the clay from the transformed mask, dried it and rehung it on its peg.

CHAPTER THIRTEEN

A Narrow Escape

The statement that I had made to Thorndyke was perfectly true in substance; but it was hardly as significant in fact as the words implied. I had, it is true, in my journeyings abroad, restricted myself to well-beaten thoroughfares. But then I had had no occasion to do otherwise. Until Polton's arrival on the scene my time had been wholly taken up in keeping a watch on Marion; and so it would have continued if I had followed my own inclination. But at the end of the first day's work she intervened resolutely.

"I am perfectly ashamed," she said, "to occupy the time of two men, both of whom have their own affairs to attend to, though I can't tell you how grateful I am to you for sacrificing yourselves."

"We are acting under the doctor's orders, miss," said Polton, thereby, in his opinion, closing the subject.

"You mean Dr Thorndyke's?" said Marion, not realizing – or not choosing to realize – that, to Polton, there was no other doctor in the world who counted.

"Yes, miss. The doctor's orders must be carried out."

"Of course they must," she agreed warmly, "since he has been so very good as to take all this trouble about my safety. But there is no need for both of you to he here together. Couldn't you arrange to take turns on duty – alternate days or a half-day – eh? I hate the thought that I am wasting the whole of both your times."

I did not look on the suggestion with favour, for I was reluctant to yield up to any man – even to Polton – the privilege of watching over the safety of one who was so infinitely dear to me. Nor was Polton much less unwilling to agree, for he loathed to leave a piece of work uncompleted. However, Marion refused to accept our denials (as is the way of women), and the end of it was that Polton and I had to arrange our duties in half-day shifts, changing over at the end of each week, the first spell allotting the mornings to me and the latter half of the day – with the duty of seeing Marion home – to him.

Thus, during each of the following six working days, I found myself with the entire afternoon and evening free. The former I usually spent at the hospital, but in the evenings, feeling too unsettled for study, I occupied myself very pleasantly with long walks through the inexhaustible streets, extending my knowledge of the town and making systematic explorations of such distant regions as Mile End, Kingsland, Dalston, Wapping and the Borough.

One evening I bethought me of my promise to look in on Usher. I did not find myself yearning for his society, but a promise is a promise. Accordingly, when I had finished my solitary dinner, I set forth from my lodgings in Camden Square and made a bee-line for Clerkenwell; so far, that is to say, as was possible, while keeping to the wider streets. For in this respect, I followed Thorndyke's instructions to the letter, though, as to the other matter – that of keeping a bright look-out – I was less attentive, my mind being much more occupied with thoughts of Marion (who would, just now, be on her way home under Polton's escort) than with any considerations of my own personal safety. Indeed, to tell the truth, I was inclined to be more than a little sceptical as to the need for these extraordinary precautions.

I found Usher in the act of bowing out the last of the "evening consultations" and was welcomed by him with enthusiasm.

"Delighted to see you, old chap!" he exclaimed, shaking my hand warmly. "It is good of you to drop in on an old fossil like me.

Didn't much think you would. I suppose you don't often come this way?"

"No," I replied. "It is rather off my beat. I've finished with Hoxton – for the present, at any rate."

"So have I," said Usher, "since poor old Crile went off to the better land."

"Crile?" I repeated. "Who was he?"

"Don't you remember my telling you about his funeral, when they had those Sunday-school kids yowling hymns round the grave? That was Mr Crile – Christian name, Jonathan."

"I remember; but I didn't realize that he was a Hoxton aristocrat."

"Well, he was. Fifty-two Field Street was his earthly abode. I used to remember it by the number of weeks in the year. And glad enough I was when he hopped off his perch, for his confounded landlady, a Mrs Pepper, would insist on fixing the times for my visits, and deuced inconvenient times, too. Between four and six on Tuesdays and Fridays. I hate patients who turn your visits into appointments. Upsets your whole visiting-list."

"It seems to be the fashion in Hoxton," I remarked. "I had to make my visits at appointed times, too. It would have been frightfully inconvenient if I had been busy. Is it often done?"

"They will always do it if you let 'em. Of course it is a convenience to a woman who doesn't keep a servant, to know what time the doctor is going to call; but it doesn't do to give way to 'em."

I assented to this excellent principle, noting, however, that he seemed to have "given way to 'em" all the same.

As we had been talking, we had gradually drifted from the surgery up a flight of stairs to a shabby, cosy little room on the first floor, where a cheerful fire was burning and a copper kettle on a trivet purred contentedly and breathed forth little clouds of steam. Usher inducted me into a large easychair, the depressed seat of which suggested its customary use by an elephant of sedentary habits, and produced from a cupboard a spirit-decanter, a high-shouldered Dutch gin-bottle, a sugar-basin and a couple of tumblers and sugar-crushers.

"Whisky or Hollands?" he demanded; and as curiosity led me to select the latter, he commented: "That's right, Gray. Good stuff, Hollands. Touches up the cubical epithelium – what! I am rather partial to a drop of Hollands."

It was no empty profession. The initial dose made me open my eyes; and that was only a beginning. In a twinkling, as it seemed, his tumbler was empty and the collaboration of the bottle and the copper kettle was repeated. And so it went on for nearly an hour, until I began to grow quite uneasy, though without any visible cause, so far as Usher was concerned. He did not turn a hair (he hadn't very many to turn for that matter, but I speak figuratively). The only effect that I could observe was an increasing fluency of speech with a tendency to discursiveness; and I must admit that his conversation was highly entertaining. But his evident intention to "make a night of it" set me planning to make my escape without appearing to slight his hospitality. How I should have managed it, unaided by the direct interposition of Providence, I cannot guess; for his conversation had now taken the form of an interminable sentence punctuated by indistinguishable commas; but in the midst of this steadily-flowing stream of eloquence the outer silence was rent by the sudden jangling of a bell.

Usher stopped short, stared at me solemnly, deliberately emptied his tumbler and stood up.

"Night bell, ol' chappie," he explained. "Got to go out. But don't you disturb yourself. Back in a few minutes. Soon polish 'em off."

"I'll walk round with you as far as your patient's house," said I, "and then I shall have to get home. It is past ten and I have a longish walk to Camden Square."

He was disposed to argue the point, but another violent jangling cut his protests short and sent him hurrying down the stairs with me close at his heels. A couple of minutes later we were out in the street, following in the wake of a hurrying figure; and, looking at Usher as he walked sedately at my side, with his top-hat, his whiskers and his inevitable umbrella, I had the feeling that all those jorums of Hollands had been consumed in vain. In appearance, in manner, in speech and in gait he was just his normal self, with never a hint of any change from the *status quo ante bellum.*

Our course led us into the purlieus of St John Street Road, where we presently turned into a narrow, winding and curiously desolate little street, along which we proceeded for a few hundred yards, when our "fore-runner" halted at a door into which he inserted a latch-key. When we arrived at the open door, inside which a shadowy figure was lurking, Usher stopped and held out his hand.

"Good night, old chap," he said. "Sorry you can't come back with me. If you keep straight on and turn to the left at the cross-roads, you will come out presently into the King's Cross Road. Then you'll know your way. So long."

He turned into the dark passage, the door was closed and I went on my way.

The little meandering street was singularly silent and deserted; and its windings cut off the light from the scanty street-lamps, so that stretches of it were in almost total darkness. As I strode forward the echoes of my foot-falls resounded with hollow reverberations which smote my ear – and ought to have smitten my conscience – causing me to wonder, with grim amusement, what Thorndyke would have said if he could have seen me thus setting his instructions at defiance. Indeed, I was so far sensible of the impropriety of my being in such a place at such an hour that I was about to turn to take a look back along the street; but at the very moment that I halted within a few feet of a street-lamp, something struck the brim of my hat with a sharp, weighty blow like the stroke of a hammer, and I heard a dull thud from the lamp-post.

In an instant I spun round, mighty fierce, whipping out my pistol, cocking it and pointing it down the street as I raced back towards the spot from whence the missile had appeared to come. There was not a soul in sight nor any sound of movement, and the shallow doorways seemed to offer no possible hiding-place. But some thirty yards back I came suddenly on a narrow opening like an empty doorway but actually the entrance to a covered alley not more than three feet wide and as dark as a pocket. This was evidently the ambush (which I had passed, like a fool, without observing it), and I halted beside it, with my pistol still pointed, listening intently and considering what I had better do. My first impulse had been to charge into the alley, but a moment's reflection showed the futility of such a proceeding. Probably my assailant had made off by some well-known outlet; but in any case it would be sheer insanity for me to plunge into that pitch-dark passage. For if he were still lurking there, he would be invisible to me, whereas I should be a clear silhouette against the dim light of the street. Moreover, I had seen no one and I could not shoot at any chance stranger whom I might find there. Reluctantly, I recognized that there was nothing for it but to retreat cautiously and be more careful in future.

My retirement would have looked an odd proceeding to an observer, if there had been one; for I had to retreat crabwise in order that I might keep the entrance of the alley covered with my pistol and yet see where I was going. When I reached the lamp-post, I scanned the area of lighted ground beneath it, and, almost at the first glance, perceived an object like a largish marble lying in the road. It proved, when I picked it up, to be a leaden ball, like an old-fashioned musket-ball, with one flattened side, which had prevented it from rolling away from the spot where it had fallen. I dropped it into my pocket and resumed my masterly retreat until, at length, the cross-roads came into view. Then I quickened my pace, and as I reached the corner, put away my pistol after slipping in the safety-catch.

Once more out in the lighted and frequented main streets, my thoughts were free to turn over this extraordinary experience. But I did not allow them to divert me from a very careful look-out. All my scepticism was gone now. I realized that Thorndyke had not been making mere vague guesses, but that he had clearly foreseen that something of this kind would probably happen. That was, to me, the most perplexing feature of this incomprehensible affair.

I turned it over in my mind again and again and could make nothing of it. I could see no adequate reason why this man should want to make away with me. True, I was Marion's protector; but that – even if he were aware of it – did not seem an adequate reason. Indeed, I could not see why he was seeking to make away with her – nor, even was it clear to me that there had been a reasonable motive for murdering her father. But as to myself, I seemed to be out of the picture altogether. The man had nothing to fear from me or to gain by my death.

That was how it appeared to me; and yet I saw plainly that I must be mistaken. There must he something behind all this – something that was unknown to me but was known to Thorndyke. What could it be? I found myself unable to make any sort of guess. In the end, I decided to call on Thorndyke the following evening, report the incident and see if I could get any enlightenment from him.

The first part of this programme I carried out successfully enough, but the second presented more difficulties.

Thorndyke was not a very communicative man, and a perfectly impossible one to pump. What he chose to tell, he told freely; and beyond that, no amount of ingenuity could extract the faintest shadow of a hint.

"I am afraid I am disturbing you, sir," I said in some alarm, as I noted a portentous heap of documents on the table.

"No," he replied. "I have nearly finished, and I shall treat you as a friend and keep you waiting while I do the little that is left." He turned to his papers and took up his pen, but paused to cast one of his quick, penetrating glances at me.

"Has anything fresh happened?" he asked.

"Our unknown friend has had a pot at me," I answered. "That is all."

He laid down his pen and, leaning back in his chair, demanded particulars. I gave him an account of what had happened on the preceding night, and taking the leaden ball from my pocket, laid it on the table. He picked it up, examined it curiously and then placed it on the letter-balance.

"Just over half an ounce," he said. "It is a mercy it missed your head. With that weight and the velocity indicated by the flattening, it would have dropped you insensible with a fractured skull."

"And then he would have come along and put the finishing touches, I suppose. But I wonder how he shot the thing. Could he have used an air-gun?"

Thorndyke shook his head. "An air-gun that would discharge a ball of that weight would make quite a loud report, and you say you heard nothing. You are quite sure of that, by the way?"

"Perfectly. The place was as silent as the grave."

"Then he must have used a catapult; and an uncommonly efficient weapon it is in skilful hands, and as portable as a pistol. You mustn't give him another chance, Gray."

"I am not going to if I can help it. But what the deuce does the fellow want to pot at me for? It is a most mysterious thing. Do you understand what it is all about, sir?"

"I do not," he replied. "My knowledge of the facts of this case is nearly all second-hand knowledge, derived from you. You know all that I know and probably more."

"That is all very well, sir," said I; "but you foresaw that this was likely to happen. I didn't. Therefore you must know more about the case than I do."

He chuckled softly. "You are confusing knowledge and inference," said he. "We had the same facts, but our inferences were not the same. It is just a matter of experience. You haven't squeezed out of the facts as much as they are capable of yielding. Come, now, Gray; while I am finishing my work, you shall look over my notes of this case, and then you should take a sort of bird's-eye view of the whole case and see if anything new occurs to you. And you must add to those notes that this man has been at the enormous trouble of stalking you continuously, that he shadowed you to Usher's, that he waited patiently for you to come out, that he followed you most skilfully and took instant advantage of the first opportunity that you gave him. You might also note that he did not elect to overtake you and make a direct attack on you as he did on Miss D'Arblay. Note those facts and consider what their significance may be. And now just go through this little dossier. It won't take you many minutes."

He took out of a drawer a small portfolio, on the cover of which was written "J D'Arblay, decd.," and, passing it to me, returned to his documents. I opened it and found it to contain a number of separate abstracts, each duly headed with its descriptive title, and an envelope marked "Photographs". Glancing over the abstracts, I saw that they dealt respectively with J D'Arblay, the Inquest, the Van Zellen Case, Miss D'Arblay, Dr Gray and Mr Morris; the last containing, somewhat to my surprise, all the details that I had given Thorndyke respecting that rather mysterious person together with an account of my dealings with him and cross-references to the abstract bearing my name. It was all very complete and methodical, but none of the abstracts contained any information that was new to me. If this represented all the facts that were known to Thorndyke, then he was no better informed than I was. But he had evidently got a great deal more out of the information than I had.

Returning the abstracts with some disappointment to the portfolio, I turned to the photographs; and then I got a very thorough surprise. There were only three, and the first two were of no great interest, one representing the two casts of the guinea and the other the plaster mask of Morris. But the third fairly took away my breath. It was a very bad photograph, apparently an enlargement from a rather poor snap-shot portrait; but, bad as it was, it gave a very vivid presentment of one of the most evil-looking faces that I have ever looked on: a lean, bearded face with high cheek-bones, with heavy, frowning brows that overhung deep-shadowed, hollow eye-sockets and an almost grotesquely large nose, thin, curved and sharp, that jutted out like a great predatory beak.

I stared at the photograph in speechless amazement. At the first glance I had been struck by the perfect way in which this crude portrait realized Marion's description of the man who had tried to murder her. But that was not all. There was another resemblance which I now perceived with even more astonishment; indeed it was so incredible that the perception of it reduced me to something like stupefaction. I sat for fully a minute with the portrait in my hand and my thoughts surging confusedly in a vain effort to grasp the meaning of this extraordinary likeness; then, happening to glance up at Thorndyke, I found him quietly regarding me with undisguised interest.

"Well," he said, as he caught my eye.

"Who is he?" I demanded, holding up the photograph.

"That is what I want to know," he replied. "The photograph came to me without any description. The identity of the subject is unknown. Who do you think he is?"

"To begin with," I answered, "he exactly corresponds in appearance with Miss D'Arblay's description of her would-be murderer. Don't you think so?"

"I do," he replied. "The correspondence seems complete in every detail, so far as I can judge. That was why I secured the photograph. But the actual resemblance will have to be settled by her. I suggest that you take the portrait and let her see it; but you had better not show it to her pointedly for identification. It would be better to put it in some place where she will see it without previous suggestion or preparation. But you said just now 'to begin with'. Was there anything else that struck you about this photograph?"

"Yes," I answered, "there was a most amazing thing. You remember my telling you about the patient I attended in Morris' house?"

"The man who died of gastric cancer and was eventually cremated?"

"Yes. His name was Bendelow. Well, this photograph might have been a portrait of Bendelow, taken with a beard and moustache before the disease got hold of him. Excepting for the emaciation and the beard — Bendelow was clean-shaved — I should think it would be quite an excellent likeness of him."

Thorndyke made no immediate reply or comment, but sat quite still, looking at me with a very singular expression. I could see that he was thinking rapidly and intensely, but I suspected that his thoughts were in a good deal less confusion than mine had been.

"It is," he remarked at length, "as you say, a most amazing affair. The face is no ordinary face. It would be difficult to mistake it, and one would have to go far to find another with which it could be confused. Still, one must not forget the possibility of a chance resemblance. Nature doesn't take out letters–patent even for a human face. But I will ask you, Gray, to write down and send to me all that you know about the late Mr Bendelow, including all the details of your attendance on him, dead and alive."

"I will," said I, "though it is difficult to imagine what connexion he could have had with the D'Arblay case."

"It seems incredible that he could have had any," Thorndyke agreed. "But at present we are collecting facts, and we must note everything impartially. It is a fatal mistake to select your facts in accordance with the apparent probabilities. By the way, if Bendelow was like this photograph, he must have corresponded pretty exactly with Miss D'Arblay's very complete and lucid description. I wonder why you did not realize that at the time."

"That is what I have been wondering. But I suppose it was the beard and the absence of any kind of association between Bendelow and the D'Arblays."

"Probably," he agreed. "A beard and moustache alter very greatly even a striking face like this. Incidentally, it illustrates the superiority of a picture over a verbal description for purposes of identification. No mere description will enable you to visualize correctly a face which you have never seen. I shall be curious to hear what Miss D'Arblay has to say about this photograph."

"I will let you know without delay," said I; and then, as he seemed to have completed his work and put the documents aside, I made a final effort to extract some definite information from him.

"It is evident," I said, "that the body of facts in your notes has conveyed a good deal more to you than it has to me."

"Probably," he agreed. "If it had not, I should seem to have profited little by years of professional practice."

"Then," I said persuasively, "may I ask if you have formed a really satisfactory theory as to who this man is and why he murdered D'Arblay?"

Thorndyke reflected for a few moments and then replied: "My position, Gray, is this: I have arrived at a very definite theory as to the motive of the murder, and a most extraordinary motive it is. But there are one or two points that I do not understand. There are some links missing from the chain of evidence. So with the identity of the man. We know pretty certainly that he is the murderer of Van Zellen and we know what he is like to look at; but we can't give him a name and a definite personality. There are links missing there, too. But I have great hopes of finding those missing links. If I find them, I shall have a complete case against this man and I shall forthwith set the law in motion. I can't tell you more than that at present; but I repeat that you are in possession of all the facts and that if you think over all that has happened and ask yourself what it can mean, though you will not arrive at a complete solution any more than I have, you will at least begin to see the light."

This was all that I could get out of him, and as it was now growing late I presently rose to take my departure. He walked with me as far as the Middle Temple Gate and stood outside the wicket watching me as I strode away westward.

CHAPTER FOURTEEN
The Haunted Man

When I arrived at the studio on the following afternoon I found the door open and Polton waiting just inside with his hat and overcoat on and his bag in his hand.

"I am glad you are punctual, sir," he said, with his benevolent smile. "I wanted to get back to the chambers in good time today. It won't matter tomorrow, which is fortunate, as you may be late."

"Why may I be late tomorrow?" I asked.

"I have a message for you from the doctor," he replied. "It is about what you were discussing last night. He told me to tell you that he is expecting a visit from an officer of the Criminal Investigation Department and he would like you to he present, if it would be convenient. About half past ten, sir."

"I will certainly be there," said I.

"Thank you, sir," said he. "And the doctor told me to warn you, in case you should arrive after the officer, not to make any comment on anything that may he said, or to seem to know anything about the subject of the interview."

"This is very mysterious, Polton," I remarked.

"Why, not particularly, sir," he replied. "You see, the officer is coming to give certain information, but he will try to get some for himself if he can. But he won't get anything out of the doctor; and the only way for you to prevent his pumping you is to say nothing and appear to know nothing."

I laughed at his ingenuous wiliness. "Why," I exclaimed, "you are as bad as the doctor, Polton. A regular Machiavelli,"

"I never heard of him," said Polton, "but most Scotchmen are pretty close. Oh, and there is another little matter that I wanted to speak to you about – on my own account this time. I gathered from the doctor, in confidence, that someone has been following you about. Now sir, don't you think it would be very useful to be able to see behind you without turning your head?"

"By jove!" I exclaimed. "It would indeed! Capital! I never thought of it. I will have a supplementary eye fixed in the back of my head without delay."

Polton crinkled deprecatingly. "No need for that, sir," said he. "I have invented quite a lot of different appliances for enabling you to see behind you – reflecting spectacles and walking-sticks with prisms in the handle and so on. But for use at night I think this will answer your purpose best."

He produced from his pocket an object somewhat like a watchmaker's eye-glass, and having fixed it in his eye to show me how it worked, handed it to me with the request that I would try it. I did so and was considerably surprised at the efficiency of the appliance; for it gave me a perfectly clear view of the street almost directly behind me.

"I am very much obliged to you, Polton," I said enthusiastically. "This is a most valuable gift, especially under the present circumstances."

He was profoundly gratified. "I think you will find it useful, sir," he said. "The doctor uses these things sometimes, and so do I if the occasion arises. You see, sir, if you are being shadowed, it is a fatal thing to turn round and look behind you. You never get a chance of seeing what the stalker is like, and you put him on his guard."

I saw this clearly enough and once more thanked him for his timely gift. Then, having shaken his hand and sped him on his way, I entered the lobby and shut the outer door, at the same time transferring Thorndyke's photograph from my letter-case to my jacket-pocket. When I passed through into the studio, I found

Marion putting the finishing touches to a plaster case. She greeted me with a smile as I entered and then plunged her hand once more into the bowl of rapidly thickening plaster; whereupon I took the opportunity to lay the photograph on a side bench, as I walked towards the table on which she was working.

"Good afternoon, Marion," said I.

"Good afternoon, Stephen," she responded, adding, "I can't shake hands until I have washed," and held out her emplastered hands in evidence.

"That will be too late," said I, and as she looked up at me inquiringly, I stooped and kissed her.

"You are very resourceful," she remarked with a smile and a warm blush, as she scooped up another handful of plaster; and then, as if to cover her slight confusion, she asked: "What was all that solemn pow-wow about with Mr Polton? And why did he wait for you at the door in that suspicious manner? Had he some secret message for you?"

"I don't know whether it was intended to be secret," I answered; "but it isn't going to be so far as you are concerned"; and I repeated to her the substance of Thorndyke's message, to which she listened with an eagerness that rather surprised me, until her further inquiries explained it.

"This sounds rather encouraging," she said; "as if Dr Thorndyke had been making some progress in his investigations. I wonder if he has. Do you think he really knows much more than we do?"

"I am sure he does," I replied; "but how much more, I cannot guess. He is extraordinarily close. But I have a feeling that the end is not so very far off. He seems to be quite hopeful of laying his hand on this villain."

"Oh! I hope you are right, Stephen," she exclaimed. "I have been getting so anxious. There has seemed to be no end to this dead-lock. And yet it can't go on indefinitely."

"What do you mean, Marion?" I asked.

"I mean," she answered, "that you can't go on wasting your time here and letting your career go. Of course, it is delightful to have you here. I don't dare to think what the place will be like without you. But it makes me wretched to think how much you are sacrificing for me."

"I am not really sacrificing anything," said I. "On the contrary, I am spending my time most profitably in the pursuit of knowledge and most happily in a sweet companionship which I wouldn't exchange for anything in the world."

"It is very nice of you to say that," she said, "but still, I shall be very relieved when the danger is over and you are free."

"Free!" I exclaimed. "I don't want to be free. When my apprenticeship has run out I am coming on as journeyman. And now I had better get my blouse on and start work."

I went to the further end of the studio, and taking the blouse down from its peg, proceeded to exchange it for my coat. Suddenly I was startled by a sharp cry, and turning round, beheld Marion stooping over the photograph with an expression of the utmost horror.

"Where did this come from?" she demanded, turning a white, terror-stricken face on me.

"I put it there, Marion," I answered somewhat sheepishly, hurrying to her side. "But what is the matter? Do you know the man?"

"Do I know him?" she repeated. "Of course I do. It is he – the man who came here that night."

"Are you quite sure?" I asked. "Are you certain that it is not just a chance resemblance?"

She shook her head emphatically. "It is he, Stephen. I can swear to him. It is no mere resemblance. It is a likeness, and a perfect one, though it is such a bad photograph. But where did you get it? And why didn't you show it to me when you came in?"

I told her how I came by it and explained Thorndyke's instructions.

"Then," she said, "Dr Thorndyke knows who the man is."

"He says he doesn't, and he was very close and rather obscure as to how the photograph came into his possession."

"It is very mysterious," said she, with another terrified glance at the photograph. Then suddenly she snatched it up and, with averted face, held it out to me. "Put it away, Stephen," she entreated. "I can't bear the sight of that horrible face. It brings back afresh all the terrors of that awful night."

I hastily returned the photograph to my letter-case, and taking her arm, led her back to the work-table. "Now," I said, "let us forget it and get on with our work"; and I proceeded to turn the case over and fix it in the new position with lumps of clay. For a little while she watched me in silence, and I could see by her pallor that she was still suffering from the shock of that unexpected encounter. But presently she picked up a scraper and joined me in trimming up the edges of the case, cutting out the "key-ways" and making ready for the second half; and by degrees her colour came back and the interest of the work banished her terrors.

We were, in fact, extremely industrious. We not only finished the case – it was an arm from the shoulder which was to be made – cut the pouring-holes and varnished the inside with knotting, but we filled one half with the melted gelatine which was to form the actual mould in which the wax would be cast. This brought the day's work to an end, for nothing more, could be done until the gelatine had set – a matter of at least twelve hours.

"It is too late to begin anything fresh," said Marion. "You had better come and have supper with me and Arabella."

I agreed readily enough to this proposal, and when we had tidied up in readiness for the morning's work, we set forth at a brisk pace – for it was a cold evening – towards Highgate, gossiping cheerfully as we went. By the time we reached Ivy Cottage eight o'clock was striking and "the village" was beginning to settle down for the night. The premature quiet reminded me that the adjacent town would presently be settling down, too, and that I should do well to start for home before the streets had become too deserted.

Nevertheless, so pleasantly did the time slip away in the cosy sitting-room with my two companions that it was close upon half past ten when I rose to take my departure. Marion escorted me to the door, and as I stood in the hall buttoning up my overcoat she said:

"You needn't worry if you are detained tomorrow. We shall be making the wax cast of the bust and I am certain Mr Polton won't leave the studio until it is finished, whether you are there or not. He is perfectly mad on wax-work. He wormed all the secrets of the trade out of me the very first time we were alone and he is extraordinarily quick at learning. But I can't imagine what use the knowledge will be to him."

"Perhaps he thinks of starting an opposition establishment," I suggested, "or he may have an eye to a partnership. But if he has, he will have a competitor, and one with a prior claim. Good night, dear child. Save some of the wax-work for me tomorrow."

She promised to restrain Polton's enthusiasm as far as possible and, wishing me "good night", held out her hand, but submitted without demur to being kissed; and I took my departure in high spirits, more engrossed with the pleasant leave-taking than with the necessity of keeping a bright look-out.

I was nearing the bottom of the High Street when the prevailing quiet recalled me to the grim realities of my position, and I was on the point of stopping to take a look round when I bethought me of Polton's appliance and also of that cunning artificer's advice not to put a possible "stalker" on his guard. I accordingly felt in my pocket, and having found the appliance, carefully fixed it in my eye without altering my pace. The first result was a collision with a lamp-post, which served to remind me of the necessity of keeping both eyes open. The instrument was, in fact, not very easy to use while walking and it took me a minute or two to learn how to manage it. Presently, however, I found myself able to divide my attention between the pathway in front and the view behind, and then it was that I became aware of a man following me at a distance of about a hundred yards. Of course, there was nothing remarkable or suspicious in this, for it was a main thoroughfare and by no means deserted at this comparatively early hour. Nevertheless, I kept the man in view, noting that he wore a cloth cap and a monkey-jacket, that he carried no stick or umbrella and that when I slightly slackened my pace he did not seem to overtake me. As this suggested that he was accommodating his pace to mine, I decided to put the matter to the test by giving him an opportunity to pass me at the next side-turning.

At this moment the Roman Catholic church came into view and I recalled that at its side a narrow lane – Dartmouth Park Hill – ran down steeply between high fences towards Kentish Town. Instantly I decided to turn into the lane – which bent sharply to the left behind the church – walk a few yards down it and then return slowly. If my follower were a harmless stranger, he would then have passed on down Highgate Hill, whereas if he were stalking me I should meet him at the entrance to the lane and could then see what he was like.

But I was not very well satisfied with this plan, for the obvious manœuvre would show him that he was suspected; and as I approached the church, a better plan suggested itself. On one side by the entrance to the lane were some low railings and a gate with large brick piers. In a moment I had vaulted over the railings and taken up a position behind one of the piers, where I stood motionless, listening intently. Very soon I caught the sound of distinctly rapid footsteps; which suddenly grew louder as my follower came opposite the entrance to the lane, and louder still as, without a moment's hesitation, he turned into it.

From my hiding-place in the deep shadow of the pier, I could safely peep out into the wide space at the entrance of the lane; and as this space was well lighted by a lamp I was able to get an excellent view of my follower. And very much puzzled I was therewith. Naturally I had expected to recognize the man whose photograph I had in my pocket. But this was quite a different type of man. It is true that he was shortish and rather slightly built and that he had a beard: but there the resemblance ended. His face, which I could see plainly by the lamp-light, so far from being of an aquiline or vulturine cast, was rather of the blunt and bibulous type. The short, though rather bulbous nose made up in colour what it lacked in size, and its florid tint extended into the cheek on either side in the form of what dermatologists call *acne rosacea*.

I say that his appearance puzzled me; but it was not his appearance alone. For the latter showed that he was a stranger to me and suggested that he was going down the lane on his lawful occasions; but his movements did not support that suggestion. He had turned into the lane and passed my hiding-place at a very quick walk. But just as he reached the sharp turn he slackened his pace, stepping lightly, and then stopped for a moment, listening intently and peering forward into the darkness of the lane. At length he started again and disappeared round the corner, and by the sound of his retreating footsteps I could tell that he was once more putting on the pace.

I listened until these sounds had nearly died away and was just about to emerge from my shelter when I became aware of footsteps approaching from the opposite direction, and as I did not choose to be seen in the act of climbing the railings, I decided to remain *perdu* until this person had passed. These footsteps, too, had a distinctly hurried sound, a fact which I noted with some surprise; but I was a good deal more surprised when the new-comer turned sharply into the entrance, walked swiftly past my ambush, and then, as he approached the corner, suddenly slowed down, advancing cautiously on tip-toe, and finally halted to listen and stare into the obscurity of the lane.

I peered out at this new arrival with an amazement that I cannot describe. Like the first man, he was a complete stranger to me: a tallish, athletic-looking man of about thirty-five, not ill-looking and having something of a military air; fair-complexioned with a sandy moustache but otherwise clean-shaved, and dressed in a suit of thick tweed with no overcoat. I could see these details clearly by the light of the lamp; and even as I was noting them, he disappeared round the corner and I could hear him walking quickly but lightly down the lane.

As soon as he was gone I looked out from my hiding-place and listened attentively. There was no one in sight nor could I hear anyone approaching. I accordingly came forth and, quickly climbing over the railings, stood for a few moments irresolute. The obviously reasonable thing to do was to make off down Highgate Hill as fast as I could and take the first conveyance that I could get homeward. But the appearance of that second man had inflamed me with curiosity. What was he here for? Was he shadowing me or was he in pursuit of the other man? Either supposition was incredible, but one of them must be true. The end of it was that curiosity got the better of discretion and I, too, started down the lane, walking as fast as I could and treading as lightly as circumstances permitted.

The second man was some considerable distance ahead, for his footsteps came to me but faintly, and I did not seem to be gaining on him; and I took it that his speed was a fair measure of that of the man in front. Keeping thus within hearing of my quarry, I sped on, turning over the amazing situation in my bewildered mind. The first man was a mystery to me, though apparently not to Thorndyke. Who could he be, and why on earth was he taking this prodigious amount of trouble to get rid of a harmless person like myself? For there could be no mistake as to the magnitude of the efforts that he was making. He must have waited outside the studio; followed Marion and me to her home and there kept a patient vigil of over two hours, waiting for me to come out. It was a stupendous labour. And what was it all about? I could not form the most shadowy guess; while as to the other man, the very thought of him reduced me to a state of hopeless bewilderment.

As my reflections petered out to this rather nebulous conclusion, I halted for a moment to listen for the footsteps ahead. They were still audible, though they sounded somewhat farther away. But now I caught the sound of other footsteps, approaching from behind. Someone else was coming down the lane. Of course, there was nothing surprising in that circumstance, for, after all, this was a public thoroughfare, little frequented as it was, especially after dark. Nevertheless, something in the character of those footsteps put me on the *qui vive*. For this man, too, was walking quickly – very quickly – and with a certain stealthiness, as if he had rubber-soled boots and, like the rest of us, were making as little noise as possible.

I walked on at my previous rapid pace, keeping my ears cocked now both fore and aft; and as I went, my mind surged with wild speculation. Could it be that I had yet another follower? The thing was becoming grotesque. My bewilderment began to mingle with a spice of grim amusement; but still I listened, not without anxiety, to those footsteps from behind, which seemed to be growing rapidly more distinct. Whoever this newcomer might be, he was no mean walker, for he was overtaking me apace; and this fact gave a pretty broad hint as to his size and strength.

I looked back from time to time, but without stopping or slackening my pace, trying to pierce the deep obscurity of the narrow, closed-in lane. But it was a dark winter's night, and the high fences shut out even the glimmer from the murky sky. It was not until the approaching foot-falls sounded quite near that I was able, at length, to make out a smear of deeper darkness on the general obscurity. Then I drew out my pistol and, withdrawing the safety-catch, put my hand, grasping it, into my overcoat pocket. Having thus made ready for possible contingencies, I watched the black shape emerge from the darkness until it developed into a tall, portly man, bearing down on me with long, swinging strides, when I halted and drew back against the fence to let him pass.

But he had no intention of passing. As he came up to me, he, too, halted, and, looking into my face with undissembled curiosity, he addressed me in a brusque though not uncivil tone.

"Now, sir, I must ask you to explain what is going on."

"What do you mean?" I demanded.

"I'll tell you," he replied. "I saw you, a little time ago, climb over the railings and hide behind a gate-post. Then I saw a man come up in a deuce of a hurry, and turn into the lane. I saw him stop and listen for a moment and then bustle off down the hill. Close on this fellow's heels comes another man, also in a devil of a hurry. *He* turns into the lane too, and suddenly he pulls up and creeps forward on tiptoe like a cat on hot bricks. *He* stops and listens, too; and then off he goes down the lane like a lamplighter. Then out you come from behind the gatepost, over the railings you climb, and then *you* creep up to the corner and listen, and then off *you* go, down the hill like another lamplighter. Now, sir, what's it all about?"

"I assume," said I, repressing a strong tendency to giggle, "that you have some authority for making these inquiries?"

"I have, sir," he replied. "I am a police officer on plain-clothes duty. I happened to be at the corner of Hornsey Lane when I saw you coming down the High Street walking in a queer sort of way as if you couldn't see where you were going. So I drew back into the shadow and had a look at you. Then I saw you nip into the lane and climb over the railings, so I waited to see what was going to happen next. And then those other two came along. Well, now, I ask you again, sir, what's going on? What is it all about?"

"The fact is," I said a little sheepishly, "I thought the first man was following me, so I hid just to see what he was up to."

"What about the second man?"

"I don't know anything about him."

"What do you know about the first man?"

"Nothing, except that he certainly was following me."

"Why should he be following you?"

"I can't imagine. He is a stranger to me and so is the other man."

"Hm!" said the officer, regarding me with a distrustful eye. "Dam funny affair. I think you had better walk up to the station with me and give us a few particulars about yourself."

"I will with pleasure," said I. "But I am not altogether a stranger there. Inspector Follett knows me quite well. My name is Gray – Dr Gray."

The officer did not reply for a few moments. He seemed to be listening to something. And now my ear caught the sound of footsteps approaching hurriedly from down the lane. As they drew near, my friend peered into the darkness and muttered in an undertone:

"Will that be one of 'em coming back?" He listened again for a moment or two and then, resuming his inquiries, said aloud: "You say Inspector Follett knows you. Well, perhaps you had better come and see Inspector Follett."

As he finished speaking, he again listened intently, and his mouth opened slightly. I suspect my own did, too. For the footsteps had ceased. There was now a dead silence in the lane.

"That chap has stopped to listen," my new friend remarked in a low voice. "We had better see what his game is. Come along, sir"; and with this he strode off at a pace that taxed my powers to keep up with him.

But at the very moment that he started, the footsteps became audible again, only now they were obviously retreating; and straining my ears I caught the faint sound of other and more distant foot-falls, also retreating, so far as I could judge, and in the same hurried fashion.

For a couple of minutes the officer swung along like a professional pedestrian and I struggled on just behind him, perspiring freely and wishing that I could shed my overcoat. Still, despite our efforts, there was no sign of our gaining on the men ahead. My friend evidently realized this, for he presently growled over his shoulder: "This won't do," and forthwith broke into a run.

Instantly this acceleration communicated itself to the men in front. The rhythm of both sets of foot-falls showed that our fore-runners were literally justifying that description of them; and as both had necessarily given up any attempt to move silently, the sounds of their retreat were borne to us quite distinctly. And from those sounds, the unsatisfactory conclusion emerged that they were drawing ahead pretty rapidly. My friend the officer was, as I have said, an uncommonly fine walker. But he was no runner. His figure was against him. He was fully six feet in height and he had a "presence". He could have walked me off my legs; but when it came to running I found myself ambling behind him with such ease that I was able to get out my pistol and, after replacing the safety-catch, stow the weapon in my hip-pocket out of harm's way.

However, if my friend was no sprinter he was certainly a stayer, for he lumbered on doggedly until the lane entered the new neighbourhood of Dartmouth Park; and here it was that the next act opened. We had just passed the end of the first of the streets when I saw a surprisingly agile policeman dart out from a shady corner and follow on in our wake in proper Lilliebridge style. I immediately put on a spurt and shot past my companion, and a few moments later, sounds of objurgation arose from behind. I stopped at once and turned back just in time to hear an apologetic voice exclaim:

"I'm sure I beg your pardon, Mr Plonk. I didn't reckernize you in the dark."

"No, of course you wouldn't," replied the plainclothes officer. "Did you see two men run past here just now?"

"I did," answered the constable; "one after the other, and both running as if the devil was after them. I was half-way up the street, but I popped down to have a look at them, and when I got to the corner I heard you coming. So I just kept out of sight and waited for you."

"Quite right too," said Mr Plonk. "Well, I don't see or hear anything of those chaps now."

"No," agreed the constable, "and you are not likely to. There's a regular maze of new streets about here. You can take it that they've got clear away."

"Yes, I'm afraid they have," said Plonk. "Well, it can't be helped and there's nothing much in it. Good night, constable."

He moved off briskly, not wishing, apparently, to discuss the affair, and in a few minutes we came to the wide cross-roads. Here he halted and looked me over by the light of a street-lamp. Apparently the result was satisfactory, for he said: "It's hardly worth while to take you all the way back to the station at this time of night. Where do you live?" I told him Camden Square and offered a card in corroboration.

"Then you are pretty close to home," said he, inspecting my card. "Very well, doctor. I'll speak to Inspector Follett about this affair, and if you have any further trouble of this sort you had better let us know. And you had better let us have a description of the men in any case."

I promised to send him the particulars on the following day, and we then parted with mutual good wishes, he making his way towards Holloway Road and I setting my face homeward by way of the Brecknock Road and keeping an uncommonly sharp look-out as I went.

CHAPTER FIFTEEN

Thorndyke Proposes a New Move

On the following morning, in order to make sure of arriving before the detective officer, I presented myself at King's Bench Walk a good half-hour before I was due. The door was opened by Thorndyke himself, and as we shook hands, he said: "I am glad you have come early, Gray. No doubt Polton explained the programme to you, but I should like to make our position quite clear. The officer who is coming here presently is Detective-Superintendent Miller of the Criminal Investigation Department. He is quite an old friend and he is coming at my request to give me certain information. But, of course, he is a detective officer, with his own duties to his department, and an exceedingly shrewd, capable man. Naturally, if he can pick up any crumbs of information from us, he will; and I don't want him to learn more, at present, than I choose to tell him."

"Why do you want to keep him in the dark?" I asked.

"Because," he replied, "we are doing quite well, and I want to get the case complete before I call in the police. If I were to tell him all I know and all I think, he might get too busy and scare our man away before we have enough evidence to justify an arrest. As soon as the investigation is finished and we have such evidence as will secure a conviction, I shall turn the case over to him; meanwhile, we keep our own counsel. Your rôle this morning will be that of listener. Whatever happens, make no comment. Act as if you knew nothing that is not of public knowledge."

I promised to follow his directions to the letter, though I could not get rid of the feeling that all this secrecy was somewhat futile. Then I began to tell him of my experiences of the previous night, to which he listened at first with grave interest, but with growing amusement as the story developed. When I came to the final chase and the pursuing policeman, he leaned back in his chair and laughed heartily.

"Why," he exclaimed, wiping his eyes, "it was a regular procession! It only wanted a string of sausages and a harlequin to bring it up to pantomime form."

"Yes," I admitted with a grin, "it was a ludicrous affair. But it was a mighty mysterious affair too. You see, neither of the men was the man I had expected. There must be more people in this business than we had supposed. Have you any idea who these men can be?"

"It isn't much use making vague guesses," he replied. "The important point to note is that this incident, farcical as it turned out, might easily have taken a tragical turn; and the moral is that, for the present, you can't be too careful in keeping out of harm's way."

It was obvious to me that he was evading my question; that those two sinister strangers were not the mystery to him that they were to me, and I was about to return to the charge with a more definitely pointed question when an elaborate flourish on the little brass knocker of the inner door announced a visitor.

The tall, military-looking man whom Thorndyke admitted was evidently the superintendent, as I gathered from the mutual greetings. He looked rather hard at me until Thorndyke introduced me, which he did with characteristic reticence.

"This is Dr Gray, Miller; you may remember his name. It was he who discovered the body of Mr D'Arblay."

"Yes, I remember," said the superintendent, shaking my hand unemotionally and still looking at me with a slightly dubious air.

"He is a good deal interested in the case," Thorndyke continued, "not only professionally, but as a friend of the family – since the catastrophe."

"I see," said the superintendent, taking a final inquisitive look at me and obviously wondering why the deuce I was there. "Well, there is nothing of a very secret nature in what I have to tell you, and I suppose you can rely on Dr Gray to keep his own counsel and ours."

"Certainly," replied Thorndyke, "He quite understands that our talk is confidential, even if it is not secret."

The officer nodded, and having been inducted into an easy-chair, by the side of which a decanter, a siphon and a box of cigars had been placed, settled himself comfortably, lit a cigar, mixed himself a modest refresher and drew from his pocket a bundle of papers secured with red tape.

"You asked me, Doctor," he began, "to get you all particulars up to date of the Van Zellen case. Well, I can do that without difficulty, as the case – or at least what is left of it – is in my hands. The circumstances of the actual crime I think you know already, so I will take up the story from that point."

"Van Zellen, as you know, was found dead in his room, poisoned with prussic acid, and a quantity of very valuable portable property was missing. It was not clear whether the murderer had let himself in with false keys or whether Van Zellen had let him in; but the place hadn't been broken into. The job had been done with remarkable skill, so that not a trace of the murderer was left. Consequently, all that was left for the police to do was to consider whether they knew of anyone whose methods agreed with those of this murderer."

"Well, they did know of such a person, but they had nothing against him but suspicion. He had never been convicted of any serious crime, though he had been in chokee once or twice for receiving. But there had been a number of cases of robbery with murder – or rather murder with robbery; for this man seemed to have committed the murder as a preliminary precaution – and they were all of this kind: a solitary crime, very skilfully carried out by means of poison. There was never any trace of the criminal; but gradually the suspicions of the police settled down on a rather mysterious individual of the name of Bendelow – Simon Bendelow. Consequently, when the Van Zellen crime came to light, they were inclined to put it on this man Bendelow, and they began making fresh inquiries about him. But presently it transpired that someone had seen a man, on the morning of the crime, coming away from the neighbourhood of Van Zellen's house just about the time when the murder must have been committed."

"Was there anything to connect him with the crime?" Thorndyke asked.

"Well, there was the time – the small hours of the morning – and the man was carrying a good-sized handbag which seemed to be pretty heavy and which would have held the stuff that was missing. But the most important point was the man's appearance. He was described as a smallish man, cleanshaved, with a big hooked nose and very heavy eyebrows set close down over his eyes.

"Now, this put Bendelow out of it as the principal suspect, because the description didn't fit him at all" (here I caught Thorndyke's eye for an instant and was warned afresh, and not unnecessarily, to make no comment); "but," continued the superintendent, "it didn't put him out altogether. For the man whom the description did fit – and it fitted him to a T – was a fellow named Crile – Jonathan Crile – who was a pal of Bendelow's and was known to have worked with him as a confederate in the receiving business and had been in prison once or twice. So the police started to make inquiries about Crile, and before long they were able to run him to earth. But that didn't do them much good; for it turned out that Crile wasn't in New York at all. He was in Philadelphia; and it was clearly proved that he had been there on the day of the murder, on the day before and the day after. So they seemed to have drawn a blank; but they were still a bit suspicious of Mr Crile, who seems to have been as downy a bird as his friend Bendelow, and of the other chappie, too. But they hadn't a crumb of evidence against either.

"So there the matter stuck. A complete deadlock. There was nothing to be done; for you can't arrest a man on mere suspicion with not a single fact to support it. But the police kept their eye on both gents, so far as they could, and presently they got a chance. Bendelow made a slip – or at any rate they said he did. It was a little trumpery affair, something in the receiving line, and of no importance at all. Probably a faked charge, too. But they thought that if they could get him arrested they might be able to squeeze something out of him – the police in America can do things that we aren't allowed to. So they tried to pounce on him. But Mr Bendelow was a slippery customer and he got wind of their intentions just in time. When they got into his rooms they found that he had left – in a deuce of a hurry, too, and only a few minutes before they arrived. They searched the place, but found nothing incriminating, and they tried to get on Bendelow's track, but they didn't succeed. He had managed to get clear away, and Crile seemed to have disappeared, too.

"Well, that seemed to be the end of the affair. Both of these crooks had made off without leaving a trace, and the police – having no evidence – didn't worry any more about them. And so things went on for about a year, until the Van Zellen case had been given up and nearly forgotten. Then something happened quite recently that gave the police a fresh start.

"It appears that there was a fire in the house in which Bendelow's rooms were and a good deal of damage was done, so that they had to do some rebuilding; and in the course of the repairs the builder's men found, hidden under the floor-boards, a small parcel containing part of the Van Zellen swag. There was nothing of real value; just coins and medals and seal-rings and truck of that kind. But the things were all identified by means of Van Zellen's catalogue, and, of course, the finding of them in what had been Bendelow's rooms put the murder pretty clearly on to him.

"On this, as you can guess, the police and the detective agencies got busy. They searched high and low for the missing man, but for a long time they could pick up no traces of him At last they discovered that he and Crile had taken a passage, nearly a year ago, on a tramp-steamer bound for England. Thereupon they sent a very smart, experienced detective over to work at the case in conjunction with our own detective department.

"But we didn't have much to do with it. The American — Wilson was his name — had all the particulars, with the prison photographs and fingerprints of both the men, and he made most of the inquiries himself. However, there were two things that we did for him. We handed over to him the Van Zellen guinea and the particulars of the D'Arblay murder; and we were able to inform him that his friend Bendelow was dead."

"How did you find that out?" Thorndyke asked.

"Oh, quite by chance. One of our men happened to be at Somerset House looking up some details of a will when in the list of wills he came across the name of Simon Bendelow, which he had heard from Wilson himself. He at once got out the will, copied out the address of the executrix and the names and addresses of the witnesses and handed them over to Wilson, who was mightily taken aback, as you may suppose. However, he wasn't taking anything for granted. He set off instantly to look up the executrix — a Mrs Morris. But there he got another disappointment; for the Morrises had gone away and no one knew where they had gone."

"I take it," said Thorndyke, "that probate of the will had been granted."

"Yes; everything in that way had been finished up. Well, on this, Wilson set off in search of the witnesses, and he had better luck this time. They were two elderly spinsters who lived together in a house in Turnpike Lane, Hornsey. They didn't know much about Bendelow, for they had only made his acquaintance after he had taken to his bed. They were introduced to him by his friend and landlady, Mrs Morris, who used to take them up to his room to talk to him and cheer him up a bit. However, they knew all about his death, for they had seen him in his coffin and they followed him to the Ilford Crematorium."

"Ha!" said Thorndyke. "So he was cremated."

"Yes," chuckled the superintendent with a sly look at Thorndyke. "I thought that would make you prick up your ears, Doctor. Yes, there were no half-measures for Mr Bendelow. He had gone literally to ashes. But it was all right, you know. There couldn't have been any hanky-panky. These two ladies had not only seen him in his coffin; they actually had a last look at him through a little celluloid window in the coffin-lid, just before the coffin was passed through into the cremation furnace."

"And there was no doubt as to his identity?"

"None whatever. Wilson showed the old ladies his photograph and they recognized him instantly; picked his photograph out of a dozen others."

"Where was Bendelow living when they made his acquaintance?"

"Not far from their house: in Abbey Road, Hornsey. But the Morrises moved afterwards to Market Street, Hoxton, and that is where he died and where the will was signed."

"I suppose Wilson ascertained the cause of death?"

"Oh, yes. The old ladies told him that. But he went to Somerset House and got a copy of the death certificate. I haven't got that, as he took it back with him; but the cause of death was cancer of the pylorus – that's some part of the gizzard, I believe, but you'll know all about it. At any rate, there was no doubt on the subject, as the two doctors made a *post-mortem* before they signed the death-certificate. It was all perfectly plain and straightforward.

"Well, so much for Mr Bendelow. When Wilson had done with him, he turned his attention to Crile. And then he really did get a proper shake-up. When he was at Somerset House, looking up Bendelow's death-certificate, it occurred to him just to run his eye down the list and make sure that Crile was still in the land of the living. And there, to his astonishment, he found Crile's name. He was dead, too! And not only was he dead: he, also, had died of cancer – it was the pancreas this time; another part of the gizzard – and he had died at Hoxton, too, and he had died just four days before Bendelow. The thing was ridiculous. It looked like a conspiracy. But here again everything was plain and above-board. Wilson got a copy of the certificate and called on the doctor who had signed it, a man named Usher. Of course, Dr Usher remembered all about the case as it had occurred quite recently. There was not a shadow of doubt that Crile was dead. Usher had helped to put him in his coffin and had attended at his funeral; and he, too, had no difficulty in picking out Crile's photograph, and he had no doubt at all as to what Crile died of. So there it was. Queer as it was, there was no denying the plain facts. Those two crooks had slipped through the fingers of the law, so far as it was possible to see.

"But I must admit that I was not quite satisfied; the circumstances were so remarkably odd. I told Wilson so, and I advised him to look further into the matter. I reminded him of the D'Arblay murder and the finding of that guinea, but he said that the murder was our affair; that the men he had come to look for were dead and that was all that concerned him. So back he went to New York, taking with him the death-certificates and the two photographs with the certificates of recognition on the backs of them. But he left the notes of the case with me, on the chance that they might be useful to me, and the two sets of fingerprints, which certainly don't seem likely to be of much use under the circumstances."

"You never know," said Thorndyke, with an enigmatical smile.

The superintendent gave him a quick, inquisitive look and agreed. "No, you don't; especially when you are dealing with Dr John Thorndyke." He pulled out his watch and, staring at it anxiously, exclaimed: "What a confounded nuisance! I've got an appointment at the Law Courts in five minutes. It is quite a small matter. Won't take me more than half an hour. May I come back when I have finished? I should like to hear what you think of this extraordinary story."

"Come back, by all means," said Thorndyke, "and I will turn over the facts in my mind while you are gone. Probably some suggestion may present itself in the interval."

He let the officer out, and when the hurried footsteps had died away on the stairs, he closed the door and turned to me with a smile.

"Well, Gray," he said, "what do you think of that? Isn't it a very pretty puzzle for a medical jurist?"

"It is a hopeless tangle to me," I replied. "My brain is in a whirl. You can't dispute the facts and yet you can't believe them. I don't know what to make of the affair."

"You note the fact that, whoever may be dead, there is somebody alive – very much alive; and that that somebody is the murderer of Julius D'Arblay."

"Yes, I realize that. But obviously he can't be either Crile or Bendelow. The question is, who is he?"

"You note the link between him and the Van Zellen murder – I mean the electrotype guinea?"

"Yes; there is evidently some connexion, but I can't imagine what it can be. By the way, you noticed that the American police had got muddled about the personal appearance of these two men. The description of that man who was seen coming away from Van Zellen's house, and who was said to be quite unlike Bendelow, actually fitted him perfectly. They had evidently made a mistake of some kind."

"Yes, I noticed that. But the description may have fitted Crile better. We must get into touch with this man Usher. I wonder if he will be the Usher who used to attend at St Margaret's."

"He is; and I am in touch with him already. In fact, he was telling me about this very patient, Jonathan Crile."

"Indeed! Can you remember the substance of what he told you?"

"I think so. It wasn't very thrilling;" and here I gave him, as well as I could remember them, the details with which Usher had entertained me of his attendance on the late Jonathan Crile, his dealings with the landlady, Mrs Pepper, and the incidents of the funeral, including Usher's triumphant return in the mourning-coach. It seemed a dull and trivial story, but Thorndyke listened to it with the keenest interest, and when I had finished, he asked:

"He didn't happen to mention where Crile lived, I suppose?"

"Yes, curiously enough, he did. The address, I remember, was 52 Field Street, Hoxton."

"Ha!" said Thorndyke. "You are a mine of information, Gray."

He rose, and taking down from the bookshelves Philip's Atlas of London, opened it and pored over one of the maps. Then, replacing the atlas, he got out his notes of the D'Arblay case and searched for a particular entry. It was evidently quite a short one, for when he had found it he gave it but a single glance and closed the portfolio. Then, returning to the bookshelves, he took out the Post Office Directory and opened it at the "streets" section. Here, also, his search was but a short one, though it appeared to be concerned with two separate items; for having examined one, he turned to a different part of the section to find the other. Finally he closed the unwieldy volume, and having replaced it on the shelf, turned and once more looked at me inquiringly.

"Reflecting on what Miller has told us," he said, "does anything suggest itself to you? Any sort of hypothesis as to what the real facts may be?"

"Nothing whatever," I replied. "The confusion that was already in my mind is only the worse confounded. But that is not your case, I take it?"

"Not entirely," he admitted. "The fact is that I had already formed a hypothesis as to the motives and circumstances which lay behind the murder of Julius D'Arblay and I find this new matter not inconsistent with it. But that hypothesis may, nevertheless, turn out to be quite wrong when we put it to the test of further investigation."

"You have some further investigation in view, then?"

"Yes. I am going to make a proposal to Superintendent Miller – and here he comes, before his time; by which I judge that he, also, is keen on the solution of this puzzle."

Thorndyke's opinion seemed to be justified, for the superintendent entered all agog and opened the subject at once.

"Well, Doctor, I suppose you have been thinking over Wilson's story? How does it strike you? Have you come to any conclusion?"

"Yes," replied Thorndyke. "I have come to the conclusion that I can't accept that story at its face value as representing the actual facts."

Miller laughed with an air of mingled amusement and vexation. "That is just my position," said he. "The story seems incredible, but yet you can't raise any objection. The evidence in support of it is absolutely conclusive at every point. There isn't a single weak spot in it – at least I haven't found one. Perhaps you have?" And here he looked at Thorndyke with eager inquiry in his eyes.

"I won't say that," Thorndyke replied. "But I put it to you, Miller, that the alleged facts that are offered are too abnormal to be entertained. We cannot accept that string of coincidences. It must be obvious to you that there is a fallacy somewhere and that the actual facts are not what they seem."

"Yes, I feel that myself," rejoined Miller. "But what are we to do? How are we to find the flaw in the evidence, if there is one? Can you see where to look for it? I believe you can."

"I think there, is one point which ought to be verified," said Thorndyke. "The identification of Crile doesn't strike me as perfectly convincing."

"How does his case differ from Bendelow's?" Miller demanded.

"In two respects," was the reply. "First, Bendelow was identified by two persons who had known him well for some time and who gave a circumstantial account of his illness, his death and the disposal of his body; and second, Bendelow's remains have been cremated and are therefore, presumably, beyond our reach for purposes of identification."

"Well," Miller objected, "Crile isn't so very accessible, being some few feet under ground."

"Still, he is there; and he has been buried only a few weeks. It would be possible to exhume the body and settle the question of his identity once for all."

"Then you are not satisfied with Dr Usher's identification?"

"No. Usher saw him only after a long, wasting illness, which must have altered his appearance very greatly; whereas the photograph was taken when Crile was in his normal health. It couldn't have been so very like Usher's patient."

"That's true," said Miller; "and I remember that Usher wasn't so very positive, according to Wilson. But he agreed that it seemed to be the same man; and all the other facts seemed to point to the certainty that it was really Crile. Still, you are not satisfied? It's a pity Wilson took the photograph back with him."

"The photograph is of no consequence," said Thorndyke. "You have the fingerprints – properly authenticated fingerprints, actually taken from the man in the presence of witnesses. After this short time it will be possible to get perfectly recognisable fingerprints from the body, and those fingerprints will settle the identity of Usher's patient beyond any possible doubt."

The superintendent scratched his chin thoughtfully.

"It's a bit of a job to get an exhumation order," said he. "Before I raise the question with the Commissioner, I should like to have a rather more definite opinion from you. Do you seriously doubt that the man in that coffin is Jonathan Crile?"

"It is my opinion," replied Thorndyke, "of course, I may be wrong, but it is my considered opinion that the Crile who is in that coffin is not the Crile whose fingerprints are in your possession."

"Very well, Doctor," said Miller, rising and picking up his hat, "that is good enough for me. I won't ask you for your reasons, because I know you won't give them. But I have known you long enough to feel sure that you wouldn't give a definite opinion like that unless you had got something pretty solid to go on. And I don't think we shall have any difficulty about the exhumation order after what you have said."

With this the superintendent took his leave, and very shortly afterwards Thorndyke carried me off to lunch at his club before dismissing me to take up my duties at the studio.

CHAPTER SIXTEEN

A Surprise for the Superintendent

It appeared that Thorndyke was correct in his estimate of the superintendent's state of mind, for that officer managed to dispose in a very short time of the formalities necessary for the obtaining of an exhumation licence from the Home Office. It was less than a week after the interview that I have recorded when I received a note from Thorndyke asking me to join him and Miller at King's Bench Walk on the following morning at the unholy hour of half past six. He offered to put me up for the night at his chambers, but I declined this hospitality, not wishing to trouble him unnecessarily; and after a perfunctory breakfast by gaslight, a ride on an early tram and a walk through the dim, lamp-lit streets, I entered the Temple just as the subdued notes of an invisible clock-bell announced a quarter past six. On my arrival at Thorndyke's chambers, I observed a roomy hired carriage drawn up at the entry, and ascending the stairs, found "the Doctor" and Miller ready to start, each provided with a good-sized handbag.

"This is a queer sort of function," I remarked, as we took our way down the stairs – "a sort of funeral the wrong way about."

"Yes," Thorndyke agreed; "it is what Lewis Carroll would have called an unfuneral – and very appropriately too. I didn't give you any particulars in my note, but you understand the object of this expedition?"

"I assume that we are going to resurrect the late Jonathan Crile," I replied. "It isn't very clear to me what I have to do with the business, as I never knew Mr Crile, though I am delighted to have this rather uncommon experience. But I should have thought that Usher would be the proper person to accompany you."

"So the superintendent thought," said Thorndyke, "and quite rightly; so I have arranged to pick up Usher and take him with us. He will be able to identify the body as that of his late patient, and you and I will help the superintendent to take the fingerprints."

"I am taking your word for it, Doctor," said Miller, "that the fingerprints will be recognizable; and that they will be the wrong ones."

"I don't guarantee that," Thorndyke replied; "but still, I shall be surprised if you get the right ones."

Miller nodded with an air of satisfaction, and nothing more was said on the subject until we drew up before Dr Usher's surgery. That discreet practitioner was already waiting at the open door and at once took his place in the carriage, watched curiously by observers from adjacent windows.

"This is a rum go," he remarked, diffusing a vinous aroma into the atmosphere of the carriage. "I really did think I had paid my last visit to Mr Crile. But there's no such thing as certainty in this world." He chuckled softly and continued: "A bit different this journey from the last. No hat-bands this time and no Sunday-school children. Lord! when I think of those kids piping round the open grave, and that our dear departed brother was wanted by the police so badly that they are actually going to dig him up, it makes me smile – it does indeed."

In effect, it made him cackle; and as Miller had not heard the account of the funeral, it was repeated for his benefit in great detail. Then the anecdotal ball was set rolling in a fresh direction by one or two questions from Thorndyke, with the result that the entire history of Usher's attendance on the deceased, including the misdeeds of Mrs Pepper, was retailed with such a wealth of circumstance that the narration lasted until we stopped at the cemetery gate.

Our arrival was not unexpected, for, as we got out of the carriage, two gentlemen approached the entrance and one of them unlocked a gate to admit us. He appeared to be the official in charge of the cemetery, while the other, to whom he introduced us, was no less a person than Dr Garroll, the Medical Officer of Health.

"The Home Office licence," the latter explained, "directs that the removal shall be carried out under my supervision and to my satisfaction – very necessary in a populous neighbourhood like this."

"Very necessary," Thorndyke agreed gravely.

"I have provided a supply of fresh ground-lime, according to the directions," Dr Garroll continued; and as a further precaution, I have brought with me a large formalin spray. That, I think, would satisfy all sanitary requirements."

"It certainly should be sufficient," Thorndyke agreed, "to meet the requirements of the present case. Has the excavation been commenced yet?"

"Oh, yes," replied the cemetery official. "It was started quite early and has been carried down nearly to the full depth; but I thought that the coffin had better not be uncovered until you arrived. I have had a canvas screen put up round the grave so that the proceedings may be quite private. We can send the labourers outside before we unscrew the coffin lid. You said, Superintendent, that you were anxious to avoid any kind of publicity; and I have warned the men to say nothing to anyone about the affair."

"Quite right," said Miller. "We don't want this to get into the papers, in case – well, in any case."

"Exactly, sir," agreed the official, who was evidently bursting with curiosity himself. "Exactly. Here is the screen. If you will step inside, the excavation can be proceeded with."

We passed inside the screen, where we found four men reposefully contemplating a coil of stout rope, a basket, attached to another rope, and a couple of spades. The grave yawned in the middle of the enclosure, flanked on one side by the mound of newly dug earth and on the other by a tub of lime and a Winchester quart bottle fitted with a spray nozzle and large rubber bellows.

"You can get on with the digging now," said the official; whereupon one of the men was let down into the grave, together with a spade and the basket, and fell to work briskly. Then Dr Garroll directed one of the other men to sprinkle in a little lime; which he did, with a pleased smile and so little discretion that the man below was seen to stop digging, and after looking up indignantly, take off his cap, shake it violently and ostentatiously dust his shoulders with it.

When about a dozen basketfuls of earth had been hoisted up, a hollow, woody sound accompanying the thrusts of the spade announced that the coffin had been reached. Thereupon more lime was sprinkled in, and Dr Garroll, picking up the formalin bottle, sprayed vigorously into the cavity until a plaintive voice from below − accompanied by an unnaturally loud sneeze − was heard to declare that "he'd 'ave brought his umbrella if he'd knowed he was goin' to be squirted at." A few minutes' more work exposed the coffin and enabled us to read the confirmatory inscription on the plate. Then the rope slings were let down and with some difficulty worked into position by the excavator below; who, when he had completed his task, climbed to the surface and grasped one end of a sling in readiness to haul on it.

"It's a good deal easier letting 'em down than hoisting 'em up," Usher remarked, as a final shower of lime descended and the men began to haul; "but poor old Crile oughtn't to take much lifting. There was nothing of him but skin and bone."

However this might be, it took the united efforts of the four men to draw the coffin up to the surface and slew it round clear of the yawning grave. But at last this was accomplished and it was lifted, for convenience of inspection, on to one of the mounds of newly dug earth.

"Now," said the presiding official, "you men had better go outside and wait down at the end of the path until you are wanted again" – an order that was received with evident disfavour and complied with rather sulkily. As soon as they were gone, our friend produced a couple of screwdrivers, with which he and Miller proceeded in a very workmanlike manner to extract the screws, while Dr Garroll enveloped them in a cloud of spray and Thorndyke, Usher and I stood apart to keep out of range. It was not a long process; indeed, it came to an end sooner than I had expected, for the first intimation that I received of its completion was a loud exclamation (consisting of the single word "Snakes!") in the voice of Superintendent Miller. I turned quickly and saw that officer standing with the raised coffin-lid in his hand, staring into the interior with a look of perfectly indescribable amazement. Instantly I rushed forward and looked into the coffin; and then I was no less amazed. For in place of the mortal remains of the late Jonathan Crile was a portly sack oozing sawdust from a hole in its side, through which coyly peeped a length of thick lead pipe.

For a sensible time we all stood in breathless silence gazing down at that incredible sack. Suddenly Miller looked up eagerly at Thorndyke, whose sphinx-like countenance showed the faintest shadow of a smile.

"You knew this coffin was empty, Doctor," said he.

Thorndyke shook his head. "If I had known," he replied, "I should have told you."

"Well, you suspected that it was empty?"

"Yes," Thorndyke admitted; "I don't deny that."

"I wonder why you did and why it never occurred to me."

"It did not occur to you, perhaps, because you were not in possession of certain suggestive facts which are known to me. Still, if you consider that the circumstances surrounding the alleged deaths of these two men were so incredible as to make us both feel certain that there was some fallacy or deception in regard to the apparent facts, you will see that this was a very obvious possibility. Two men were alleged to have died, and one of them was certainly cremated. It followed that either the other man had died, as alleged, or that his funeral was a mock funeral. There was no other alternative. You must admit that, Miller."

"I do, I do," the superintendent replied ruefully.

"It is always like this. Your explanations are so obvious when you have given them, and yet no one thinks of them but yourself. All the same, this isn't so very obvious, even now. There are some extraordinary discrepancies that have yet to be explained. But we can discuss them on the way back. The question now is, what is to be done with this coffin?"

"The first thing to be done," replied Thorndyke, "is to screw on the lid. Then we can leave the cemetery authorities to deal with it. But those men must be sworn to absolute secrecy. That is vitally important, for if this exhumation should get reported in the press, we should probably lose the whole advantage of this discovery."

"Yes, by Jove!" the superintendent agreed emphatically. "It would be a disaster. At present the late Mr Crile is at large, perfectly happy and secure and entirely off his guard. We can just follow him up at our leisure and take him unawares. But if he got wind of this, he would be out of reach in a twinkling – that is, if he is alive, which I suppose – " And here the superintendent suddenly paused, with knitted brows.

"Exactly," said Thorndyke. "The advantage of surprise is with us and we must keep it at all costs. You realize the position," he added, addressing the cemetery official and the Medical Officer.

"Perfectly," the latter replied – a little glumly, I thought, "and you may rely on us both to do everything that we can to keep the affair secret."

With this we all emerged from the screen and walked back slowly towards the gate; and as we went, I strove vainly to get my ideas into some kind of order. But the more I considered the astonishing event which had just happened, the more incomprehensible did it appear. And yet I saw plainly that it could not really be incomprehensible since Thorndyke had actually arrived at its probability in advance. The glaring discrepancies and inconsistencies which chased one another through my mind could not be real. They must be susceptible of reconciliation with the observed facts. But by no effort was I able to reconcile them.

Nor, evidently, was I alone the subject of these difficulties and bewilderments. The superintendent walked with corrugated brows and an air of profound cogitation, and even Usher — when he could detach his thoughts from the juvenile choir at the funeral — was obviously puzzled. In fact it was he who opened the discussion as the carriage moved off.

"This job," he observed with conviction, "is what the sporting men would call a fair knock-out. I can't make head nor tail of it. You talk of the late Mr Crile being at large and perfectly happy. But the late Mr Crile died of cancer of the pancreas. I attended him in his illness. There was no doubt about the cancer, though I wouldn't swear to the pancreas. But he died of cancer all right. I saw him dead, and what is more, I helped to put him into that coffin. What do you say to that, Dr Thorndyke?"

"What is there to say?" was the elusive reply. "You are a competent observer and your facts are beyond dispute. But inasmuch as Mr Crile was not in that coffin when we opened it, the unavoidable inference is that after you had put him in, somebody else must have taken him out."

"Yes, that is clear enough," rejoined Usher. "But what has become of him? The man was dead; that I am ready to swear to. But where is he?"

"Yes," said Miller. "That is what is bothering me. There has evidently been some hanky-panky. But I can't follow it. It isn't as though we were dealing with a supposititious body. There was a real dead man. That isn't disputed — at least, I take it that it isn't."

"It certainly is not disputed by me," said Thorndyke.

"Then what the deuce became of him? And why, in the name of blazes, was he taken out of the coffin? That's what I want to know. Can you tell me, Doctor? But there! What is the good of asking you? Of course you know all about it! You always do. But it is the same old story. You have got the ace of trumps up your sleeve, but you won't bring it out until it is time to take the trick. Now, isn't that the position, Doctor?"

Thorndyke's impassive face softened with a faint, inscrutable smile.

"We hold a promising hand, Miller," he replied quietly; "but if the ace is there, it is you who will have the satisfaction of playing it. And I hope to see you put it down quite soon."

Miller grunted. "Very well," said he. "I can see that I am not going to get any more out of you than that; so I must wait for you to develop your plans. Meanwhile I am going to ask Dr Usher for a signed statement."

"Yes, that is very necessary," said Thorndyke. "You two had better go on together and set down Gray and me in the Kingsland Road, where he and I have some other business to transact."

I glanced at him quickly as he made this astonishing statement, for we had no business there, or anywhere else that I knew of. But I said nothing. My recent training had not been in vain.

A few minutes later, near to Dalston Junction, he stopped the carriage, and having made our adieux, we got out. Then Thorndyke strode off down the Kingsland Road, but presently struck off westward through a bewildering maze of seedy suburban streets and shabby squares in which I was as completely lost as if I had been dropped into the midst of the Sahara.

"What is the nature of the business that we are going to transact?" I ventured to ask as we turned yet another corner.

"In the first place," he replied, "I wanted to hear what conclusions you had reached in view of this discovery at the cemetery."

"Well, that won't take long," I said, with a grin. "They can be summed up in half a dozen words: I have come to the conclusion that I am a fool."

He laughed good-humouredly. "There is no harm in thinking that," he said, "provided you are not right – which you are not. But did that empty coffin suggest no new ideas to you?"

"On the contrary," I replied, "it scattered the few ideas that I had. I am in the same condition as Superintendent Miller – an inextricable muddle."

"But," he objected, "you are not in the same position as the superintendent. If he knew all that you and I know, he wouldn't be in a muddle at all. What is your difficulty?"

"Primarily the discrepancies about this man Crile. There seems to be no possible doubt that he died. But apparently he was never buried; and you and Miller seem to believe that he is still alive. Further, I don't see what business Crile is of ours at all."

"You will see that presently," said he, "and meanwhile you must not confuse Miller's beliefs with mine. However," he added as we crossed a bridge over a canal – presumably the Regent's Canal – "we will adjourn the discussion for the moment. Do you know what street that is ahead of us?"

"No," I answered; "I have never been here before, so far as I know."

"That is Field Street," said he.

"The street that the late Mr Crile lived in?"

"Yes," he answered; and as we passed on into the street from the foot of the bridge, he added, pointing to a house on our left hand, "And that is the residence of the late Mr Crile – empty, and to let, as you observe."

As we walked past I looked curiously at the house with its shabby front and its blank, sightless windows, its desolate condition emphasized by the bills which announced it; but I made no remark until we came to the bottom of the street, when I recognized the cross-roads as the one along which I used to pass on my way to the Morrises' house. I mentioned the fact to Thorndyke, and he replied: "Yes. That is where we are going now. We are going to take a look over the premises. That house also is empty, and I have got a permit from the agent to view it and have been entrusted with the keys."

In a few minutes we turned into the familiar little thoroughfare, and as we took our way past its multitudinous stalls and barrows I speculated on the object of this exploration. But it was futile to ask questions, seeing that I had but to wait a matter of minutes for the answer to declare itself. Soon we reached the house and halted for a moment to look through the glazed door into the empty shop. Then Thorndyke inserted the key into the side-door and pushed it open.

There is always something a little melancholy in the sight of an empty house which one has known in its occupied state. Nothing, indeed, could be more cheerless than the Morris household; yet it was with a certain feeling of depression that I looked down the long passage (where Cropper had bumped his head in the dark) and heard the clang of the closing door. This was a dead house – a mere empty shell. The feeble life that I had known in it was no more. So I reflected as I walked slowly down the passage at Thorndyke's side, recalling the ungracious personalities of Mrs Morris and her husband and the pathetic figure of poor Mr Bendelow.

When from the passage we came out into the hall, the sense of desolation was intensified; for here not only the bare floor and vacant walls proclaimed the untenanted state of the house. The big curtain that had closed in the end of the hall and to a great extent furnished it was gone, leaving the place very naked and chill. Incidentally, its disappearance revealed a feature of whose existence I had been unaware.

"Why," I exclaimed, "they had a second streetdoor. I never saw that. It was hidden by a curtain. But it can't open into Market Street."

"It doesn't," replied Thorndyke. "It opens on Field Street."

"On Field Street!" I repeated in surprise. "I wonder why they didn't let me in that way. It is really the front of the house."

"I think," answered Thorndyke, "that if you open the door and look out, you will understand why you were admitted at the back."

I unbolted the door and, opening it, stepped out on the wide threshold and looked up and down the street. Thorndyke was right. The thoroughfare was undoubtedly Field Street, down which, we had passed only a few minutes ago, and close by, on the right hand, was the canal bridge. Strongly impressed with the oddity of the affair, I turned to re-enter, and as I turned I glanced up at the number on the door. As my eye lighted on it I uttered a cry of astonishment. For the number was fifty-two!

"But this is amazing!" I exclaimed, re-entering the hall – where Thorndyke stood watching me with quiet amusement – and shutting the door. "It seems that Usher and I were actually visiting at the same house!"

"Evidently," said he.

"But it almost looks as if we were visiting the same patient!"

"There can be practically no doubt that you were," he agreed. "It was on that assumption that I induced Miller to apply for the exhumation order; and the empty coffin seems to confirm it completely."

I was thunderstruck; not only by the incredible thing that had happened, but by Thorndyke's uncanny knowledge of all the circumstances.

"Then," I said, after a pause, "if Usher and I were attending the same man, we were both attending Bendelow."

"That is certainly what the appearances suggest," he agreed.

"It was undoubtedly Bendelow who was cremated," said I.

"All the circumstances seem to point to that conclusion," he admitted, "unless you can think of any that point in the opposite direction."

"I cannot," I replied. "Everything points in the same direction. The dead man was seen and identified as Bendelow by those two ladies, Miss Dewsnep and Miss Bonnington; and they not only saw him here, but they actually saw him in his coffin just before it was passed through into the crematorium. And there is no doubt that they knew Bendelow by sight, for you remember that they recognized the photograph of him that the American detective showed them."

"Yes," he admitted, "that is so. But their identification is a point that requires further investigation. And it is a vitally important point. I have my own hypothesis as to what took place, but that hypothesis will have to be tested; and that test will be what the logicians would call the Experimentum Crucis. It will settle one way or the other whether my theory of this case is correct. If my hypothesis as to their identification is true, there will be nothing left to investigate. The case will be complete and ready to turn over to Miller."

I listened to this statement in complete bewilderment. Thorndyke's reference to "the case'," conveyed nothing definite to me. It was all so involved that I had almost lost count of the subjects of our investigation.

"When you speak of 'the case,'" said I, "what case are you referring to?"

"My dear Gray!" he protested. "Do you not realize that we are trying to discover who murdered Julius D'Arblay?"

"I thought you were," I answered; "but I can't connect this new mystery with his death in any way."

"Never mind," said he. "When the case is completed, we will have a general elucidation. Meanwhile there is something else that I have to show you before we go. It is through this side-door."

He led me out into a large neglected garden and along a wide path that was all overgrown with weeds.

As we went, I tried to collect and arrange my confused ideas, and suddenly a new discrepancy occurred to me. I proceeded to propound it.

"By the way, you are not forgetting that the two alleged deaths were some days apart? I saw Bendelow dead on a Monday. He had died on the preceding afternoon. But Crile's funeral had already taken place a day or two previously."

"I see no difficulty in that," Thorndyke replied. "Crile's funeral occurred, as I have ascertained, on a Saturday. You saw Bendelow alive for the last time on Thursday morning. Usher was sent for and saw Crile dead on Thursday evening, he having evidently died – with or without assistance – soon after you left. Of course, the date of death given to you was false; and you mention in your notes of the case that both you and Cropper were surprised at the condition of the body. The previous funeral offers no difficulty, seeing that we know that the coffin was empty. This is what I thought you might be interested to see."

He pointed to a flight of stone steps, at the bottom of which was a wooden gate set in the wall that enclosed the garden. I looked at the steps – a little vacantly, I am afraid – and inquired what there was about them that I was expected to find of interest.

"Perhaps," he replied, "you will see better if we open the gate."

We descended the steps and he inserted a key into the gate, drawing my attention to the fact that the lock had been oiled at no very distant date and was in quite good condition. Then he threw the gate open and we both stepped out on to the tow-path of the canal. I looked about me in considerable surprise, for we were within a few yards of the hut with the derrick and the little wharf from which I had been flung into the canal.

"I remember this gate," said I – "in fact, I think I mentioned it to you in my account of my adventure here. But I little imagined that it belonged to the Morrises' house. It would have been a short way in, if I had known. But I expect it was locked at the time."

"I expect it was," Thorndyke agreed; and thereupon turned and re-entered. We passed once more down the long passage, and came out into Market Street, when Thorndyke locked the door and pocketed the key.

"That is an extraordinary arrangement," I remarked; "one house having two frontages on separate streets."

"It is not a very uncommon one," Thorndyke replied. "You see how it comes about. A house fronting on one street has a long back garden extending to another street which is not yet fully built on. As the new street fills up, a shop is built at the end of the garden. A small house may be built in connexion with it and cut off from the garden or the shop may be connected with the original house, as in this instance. But in either case, the shop belongs to the new street and has its own number. What are you going to do now?"

"I am going straight on to the studio," I replied.

"You had better come and have an early lunch with me first," said he. "There is no occasion to hurry. Polton is there and you won't easily get rid of him, for I understand that Miss D'Arblay is doing the finishing work on a wax bust."

"I ought to see that, too," said I.

He looked at me with a mischievous smile. "I expect you will have plenty of opportunities in the future," said he, "whereas Polton must make hay while the sun shines. And, by the way, he may have something to tell you. I have instructed him to make arrangements with those two ladies, Miss Dewsnep and her friend, to go into the question of their identification of Bendelow. I want you to be present at the interview, but I have left him to fix the date. Possibly he has made the arrangement by now. You had better ask him."

At this moment an eligible omnibus making its appearance, we both climbed on board and were conveyed to King's Cross, where we alighted and lunched at a modest restaurant, thereafter separating to go our respective ways north and south.

CHAPTER SEVENTEEN
A Chapter of Surprises

In answer to my knock, the studio door was opened by Polton; and as I met his eyes for a moment I was conscious of something unusual in his appearance. I had scanty opportunity to examine him, for he seemed to be in a hurry, bustling away after a few hasty words of apology and returning whence he had come. Following close on his heels, I saw what was the occasion of his hurry. He was engaged with a brush and a pot of melted wax in painting a layer of the latter on the insides of the moulds of a pair of arms, while Marion, seated on a high stool, was working at a wax bust, which was placed on a revolving modelling-stand, obliterating the seams and other irregularities with a steel tool which she heated from time to time at a small spirit-lamp.

When I had made my salutations, I offered my help to Polton, which he declined – without looking up from his work – saying that he wanted to carry the job through by himself. I sympathized with this natural desire, but it left me without occupation; for the work which Marion was doing was essentially a one-person job, and in any case was far beyond the capabilities of either of the apprentices. For a minute or two I stood idly looking on at Polton's proceedings, but noticing that my presence seemed to worry him, I presently moved away – again with a vague impression that there was something unusual in his appearance – and drawing up another high stool beside Marion's, settled myself to take a lesson in the delicate and difficult technique of surface finishing.

We were all very silent. My two companions were engrossed by their respective occupations and I must needs refrain from distracting them by untimely conversation; so I sat, well content to watch the magical tool stealing caressingly over the wax surface, causing the disfiguring seams to vanish miraculously into an unbroken contour. But my own attention was somewhat divided; for even as I watched the growing perfection of the bust there would float into my mind now and again an idle speculation as to the change in Polton's appearance. What could it be? It was something that seemed to have altered, to some extent, his facial expression. It couldn't be that he had shaved off his moustache or whiskers, for he had none to shave. Could he have parted his hair in a new way? It seemed hardly sufficient to account for the change; and looking round at him cautiously, I could detect nothing unfamiliar about his hair.

At this point he picked up his wax-pot and carried it away to the farther end of the studio, to exchange it for another which was heating in a water-bath. I took the opportunity to lean towards Marion and ask in a whisper:

"Have you noticed anything unusual about Polton?"

She nodded emphatically and cast a furtive glance over her shoulder in his direction.

"What is it?" I asked in the same low tone.

She took another precautionary glance and then, leaning towards me with an expression of exaggerated mystery, whispered: "He has cut his eyelashes off."

I gazed at her in amazement, and was about to put a further question, but she held up a warning fore-finger and turned again to her work. However, my curiosity was now at boiling-point. As soon as Polton returned to his bench, I slipped off my stool and sauntered over to it on the pretence of seeing how his wax cast was progressing.

Marion's report was perfectly correct. His eyelids were as bare of lashes as those of a marble bust. And this was not all. Now that I came to look at him critically, his eyebrows had a distinctly moth-eaten appearance. He had been doing something to them, too.

It was an amazing affair. For one moment I was on the point of demanding an explanation, but good sense and good manners conquered the inquisitive impulse in time. Returning to my stool I cast an inquiring glance at Marion, from whom, however, I got no enlightenment but such as I could gather from a most alluring dimple that hovered about the corner of her mouth and that speedily diverted my thoughts into other channels.

My two companions continued for some time to work silently, leaving me to my meditations – which concerned themselves alternately with Polton's eyelashes and the dimple aforesaid. Suddenly Marion turned to me and asked:

"Has Mr Polton told you that we are all to have a holiday tomorrow?"

"No," I answered; "but Dr Thorndyke mentioned that Mr Polton might have something to tell us. Why are we all to have a holiday?"

"Why, you see, sir," said Polton, standing up and forgetting all about his eyelashes, "the Doctor instructed me to make an appointment with those two ladies, Miss Dewsnep and Miss Bonnington, to come to our chambers on a matter of identification. I have made the appointment for ten o'clock tomorrow morning; and as the Doctor wants you to be present at the interview and wants me to be in attendance, and we can't leave Miss D'Arblay here alone, we have arranged to shut up the studio for tomorrow."

"Yes," said Marion; "and Arabella and I are going to spend the morning looking at the shops in Regent Street, and then we are coming to lunch with you and Dr Thorndyke. It will be quite a red-letter day."

"I don't quite see what these ladies are coming to the chambers for," said I.

"You will see, all in good time, sir," replied Polton; and as if to head me off from any further questions, he added: "I forgot to ask how your little party went off this morning."

"It went off with a bang," I answered. "We got the coffin up all right, but Mr Fox wasn't at home. The coffin was empty."

"I rather think that was what the Doctor expected," said Polton.

Marion looked at me with eager curiosity. "This sounds rather thrilling," she said. "May one ask who it was that you expected to find in that coffin?"

"My impression is," I replied, "that the missing tenant was a person who bore a strong resemblance to that photograph that I showed you."

"Oh, dear!" she exclaimed. "What a pity! I wish that coffin hadn't been empty. But, of course, it could hardly have been occupied, under the circumstances. I suppose I mustn't ask for fuller details?"

"I don't imagine that there is any secret about the affair, so far as you are concerned," I answered; "but I would rather that you had the details from Dr Thorndyke, or at least with his express authority. He is conducting the investigations, and what I know has been imparted to me in confidence."

This view was warmly endorsed by Polton (who had by now either forgotten his eyelashes or abandoned concealment as hopeless). The subject was accordingly dropped and the two workers resumed their occupations. When Polton had painted a complete skin of wax over the interior of both pairs of moulds, I helped him to put the latter together and fasten them with cords. Then into each completed mould we poured enough melted wax to fill it, and after a few seconds poured it out again, leaving a solid layer to thicken the skin and unite the two halves of the wax cast. This finished Polton's job, and shortly afterwards he took his departure. Nor did we remain very much longer, for the final stages of the surface finishing were too subtle to be carried out by artificial light and had to be postponed until daylight was available.

As we walked homewards we discussed the situation so far as was possible without infringing Thorndyke's confidences.

"I am very confused and puzzled about it all," she said. "It seems that Dr Thorndyke is trying to get on the track of the man who murdered my father. But whenever I hear any details of his investigations, they always seem to be concerned with somebody else or with something that has no apparent connexion with the crime."

"That is exactly my condition," said I. "He seems to be busily working at problems that are totally irrelevant. As far as I can make out, the murderer has never once come into sight, excepting when he appeared at the studio that terrible night. The people in whom Thorndyke has interested himself are mere outsiders – suspicious characters, no doubt, but not suspected of the murder. This man, Crile, for instance, whose empty coffin was dug up, was certainly a shady character. But he was not the murderer, though he seems to have been associated with the murderer at one time. Then there is that fellow Morris, whose mask was found at the studio. He is another queer customer. But he is certainly not the murderer, though he was also probably an associate. Thorndyke has taken an intense interest in him. But I can't see why. He doesn't seem to me to be in the picture, or at any rate, not in the foreground of it. Of the actual murderer we seem to know nothing at all – at least that is my position."

"Do you think Dr Thorndyke has really got anything to go on?" she asked.

"My dear Marion!" I exclaimed, "I am confident that he has the whole case cut and dried and perfectly clear in his mind. What I was saying referred only to myself. *My* ideas are all in confusion, but *his* are not. He can see quite clearly who is in the picture and in what part of it. The blindness is mine. But let us wait and see what tomorrow brings forth. I have a sort of feeling – in fact he hinted — that this interview is the final move. He may have something to tell you when you arrive."

"I do hope he may," she said earnestly; and with this we dismissed the subject. A few minutes later we parted at the gate of Ivy Cottage and I took my way (by the main thoroughfares) home to my lodgings.

On the following morning I made a point of presenting myself at Thorndyke's chambers well in advance of the appointed time in order that I might have a few words with him before the two ladies arrived. With the same purpose, no doubt, Superintendent Miller took a similar course, the result being that we converged simultaneously on the entry and ascended the stairs together. The "oak" was already open and the inner door was opened by Thorndyke, who smilingly remarked that he seemed thereby to have killed two early birds with one stone.

"So you have, Doctor," assented the superintendent; "two early birds who have come betimes to catch the elusive worm — and I suspect they won't catch him."

"Don't be pessimistic, Miller," said Thorndyke with a quiet chuckle. "He isn't such a slippery worm as that. I suppose you want to know something of the programme?"

"Naturally, I do; and so, I suppose, does Dr Gray."

"Well," said Thorndyke, "I am not going to tell you much."

"I knew it," groaned Miller.

"Because it will be better for everyone to have an open mind —"

"Well," interposed Miller, "mine is open enough. Wide open; and nothing inside."

"And then," pursued Thorndyke, "there is the possibility that we shall not get the result we hope for; and in that case, the less you expect the less you will be disappointed."

"But," persisted Miller, "in general terms, what are we here for? I understand that those two ladies, the witnesses to Bendelow's will, are coming presently. What are they coming for? Do you expect to get any information out of them?"

"I have some hopes," he replied, "of learning something from them. In particular I want to test them in respect of their identification of Bendelow."

"Ha! Then you have got a photograph of him?"

Thorndyke shook his head.

"No," he replied. "I have not been able to get a photograph of him."

"Then you have an exact description of him?"

"No," was the reply. "I have no description of him at all."

The superintendent banged his hat on the table "Then what the deuce have you got, sir?" he demanded distractedly. "You must have something, you know, if you are going to test these witnesses on the question of identification. You haven't got a photograph, you haven't got a description, and you can't have the man himself because he is at present reposing in a little terra-cotta pot in the form of bone-ash. Now, what have you got?"

Thorndyke regarded the exasperated superintendent with an inscrutable smile and then glanced at Polton, who had just stolen into the room and was now listening with an expression of such excessive crinkliness that I wrote him down an accomplice on the spot.

"You had better ask Polton," said Thorndyke. "He is the stage manager on this occasion."

The superintendent turned sharply to confront my fellow-apprentice, whose eyes thereupon disappeared into a labyrinth of crow's feet.

"It's no use asking me, sir," said he. "I'm only an accessory before the fact, so to speak. But you'll know all about it when the ladies arrive – and I rather think I hear 'em coming now."

In corroboration, light footsteps and feminine voices became audible, apparently ascending the stairs. We hastily seated ourselves while Polton took his station by the door and Thorndyke said to me in a low voice:

"Remember, Gray, no comments of any kind. These witnesses must act without any sort of suggestion from anybody."

I gave a quick assent, and at that moment Polton threw open the door with a flourish and announced majestically:

"Miss Dewsnep, Miss Bonnington."

We all rose, and Thorndyke advanced to receive his visitors while Polton placed chairs for them.

"It is exceedingly good of you to take all this trouble to help us," said Thorndyke. "I hope it was not in any way inconvenient for you to come here this morning."

"Oh, not at all," replied Miss Dewsnep; "only we are not quite clear as to what it is that you want us to do."

"We will go into that question presently," said Thorndyke. "Meanwhile, may I introduce to you these two gentlemen, who are interested in our little business: Mr Miller and Dr Gray."

The two ladies bowed, and Miss Dewsnep remarked: "We are already acquainted with Dr Gray. We had the melancholy pleasure of meeting him at Mrs Morris' house on the sad occasion when he came to examine the mortal remains of poor Mr Bendelow, who is now with the angels."

"And no doubt," added Miss Bonnington, "in extremely congenial society."

At this statement of Miss Dewsnep's the superintendent turned and looked at me sharply with an expression of enlightenment; but he made no remark, and the latter lady returned to her original inquiry.

"You were going to tell us what it is that you want us to do."

"Yes," replied Thorndyke. "It is quite a simple matter. We want you to look at the face of a certain person who will be shown to you and to tell us if you recognize and can give a name to that person." '

"Not an insane person, I hope!" exclaimed Miss Dewsnep.

"No," Thorndyke assured her, "not an insane person."

"Nor a criminal person in custody, I trust," added Miss Bonnington.

"Certainly not," replied Thorndyke. "In short, let me assure you that the inspection of this person need not cause you the slightest embarrassment. It will be a perfectly simple affair, as you will see. But perhaps we had better proceed at once. If you two gentlemen will follow Polton, I will conduct the ladies upstairs myself."

On this we rose, and Miller and I followed Polton out on to the landing, where he turned and began to ascend the stairs at a slow and solemn pace, as if he were conducting a funeral. The superintendent walked at my side – and muttered as he went, being evidently in a state of bewilderment fully equal to my own.

"Now, what the blazes," he growled, "can the doctor be up to now. I never saw such a man for springing surprises on one. But who the deuce can he have up there?"

At the top of the second flight we came on to a landing and, proceeding along it, reached a door which Polton unlocked and opened.

"You understand, gentlemen," he said, halting in the doorway, "that no remarks or comments are to be made until the witnesses have gone. Those were my instructions."

With this he entered the room, closely followed by Miller, who, as he crossed the threshold, set at naught Polton's instructions by exclaiming in a startled voice: "Snakes!" I followed quickly, all agog with curiosity; but whatever I had expected to see – if I had expected anything – I was totally unprepared for what I did see.

The room was a smallish room, completely bare and empty of furniture save for four chairs – on two of which Polton firmly seated us; and in the middle of the floor, raised on a pair of trestles, was a coffin covered with a black linen cloth. At this gruesome object Miller and I gazed in speechless astonishment, but, apart from Polton's injunction, there was no opportunity for an exchange of sentiments; for we had hardly taken our seats when we heard the sound of ascending footsteps mingled with Thorndyke's bland and persuasive accents. A few moments later the party reached the door; and as the two ladies came in sight of the coffin, both started back with a cry of alarm.

"Oh, dear!" exclaimed Miss Dewsnep, "it's a dead person! Who is it, sir? Is it anyone we know?"

"That is what we want you to tell us," Thorndyke replied.

"How mysterious!" exclaimed Miss Bonnington, in a hushed voice. How dreadful! Some poor creature who has been found dead, I suppose? I hope it won't be very – er – you know what I mean, sir – when the coffin is opened."

"There will be no need to open the coffin," Thorndyke reassured her. "There is an inspection window in the coffin-lid through which you can see the face. All you have to do is to look through the window and tell us if the face that you see is the face of anyone who is known to you. Are you ready, Polton?"

Polton replied that he was, having taken up his position at the head of the coffin with an air of profound gravity, approaching to gloom. The two ladies shuddered audibly, but their nervousness being now overcome by a devouring curiosity, they advanced, one on either side of the coffin, and taking up a position close to Polton, gazed eagerly at the covered coffin. There was a solemn pause as Polton carefully gathered up the two corners of the linen pall. Then, with a quick movement, he threw it back. The two witnesses simultaneously stooped and peered in at the window. Simultaneously their mouths opened and they sprang back with a shriek.

"Why, it's Mr Bendelow!"

"You are quite sure it is Mr Bendelow?" Thorndyke asked.

"Perfectly," replied Miss Dewsnep. "And yet," she continued with a mystified look, "it can't be; for I saw him pass through the bronze doors into the cremation furnace. I saw him with my own eyes," she added, somewhat unnecessarily. "And what's more, I saw his ashes in the casket."

She gazed with wide-open eyes at Thorndyke and then at her friend, and the two women tip-toed forward and once more stared in at the window with starting eyes and dropped chins.

"It is Mr Bendelow," said Miss Bonnington, in an awe-stricken voice.

"But it can't be," Miss Dewsnep protested in tremulous tones. "You saw him put through those doors yourself, Susan, and you saw his ashes afterwards."

"I can't help that, Sarah," the other lady retorted. "This is Mr Bendelow. You can't deny that it is."

"Our eyes must be deceived," said Miss Dewsnep, the said eyes being still riveted on the face behind the window. "It can't be – and yet it is – but yet it is impossible – "

She paused suddenly and raised a distinctly alarmed face to her friend.

"Susan," she said, in a low, rather shaky voice, "there is something here with which we, as Christian women, are better not concerned. Something against nature. The dead has been recalled from a burning fiery furnace by some means which we may not inquire into. It were better, Susan, that we should now depart from this place."

This was evidently Susan's opinion, too, for she assented with uncommon alacrity and with a distinctly uncomfortable air; and the pair moved with one accord towards the door. But Thorndyke gently detained them.

"Do we understand," he asked, "that, apart from the apparently impossible circumstances, the body in that coffin is, in your opinion, the body of the late Simon Bendelow?"

"You do," Miss Dewsnep replied in a resentfully nervous tone and regarding Thorndyke with very evident alarm. "If it were possible that it could be, I would swear that those unnatural remains were those of my poor friend Mr Bendelow. As it is not possible, it cannot be."

"Thank you," said Thorndyke, with the most extreme suavity of manner. "You have done us a great service by coming here today, and a great service to humanity – how great a service you will learn later. I am afraid it has been a disagreeable experience to both of you, for which I am sincerely sorry; but you must let me assure you that there is nothing unlawful or supernatural in what you have seen. Later, I hope you will be able to realize that. And now

I trust you will allow Mr Polton to accompany you to the dining-room and offer you a little refreshment."

As neither of the ladies raised any objection to this programme, we all took our leave of them and they departed down the stairs, escorted by Polton. When they had gone, Miller stepped across to the coffin and cast a curious glance in at the window.

"So that is Mr Bendelow," said he. "I don't think much of him, and I don't see how he is going to help us. But you have given those two old girls a rare shake-up, and I don't wonder. Of course, this can't be a dead body that you have got in this coffin, but it is a most life-like representation of one, and it took in those poor old Judies properly. What have you got to tell us about this affair, Doctor? I can see that your scheme, whatever it was, has come off. They always do. But what about it? What has this experiment proved?"

"It has turned a mere name into an actual person," was the reply.

"Yes, I know," rejoined Miller. "Very interesting, too. Now we know exactly what he looked like. But what about it? And what is the next move?"

"The next move on my part is to lay a sworn information against him as the murderer of Julius D'Arblay; which I will do now, if you will administer the oath and witness my signature." As he spoke, Thorndyke produced a paper from his pocket and laid it on the coffin.

The superintendent looked at the paper with a surprised grin.

"A little late, isn't it," he said, "to be swearing an information? Of course you can if you like; but when you've done it, what then?"

"Then," replied Thorndyke, "it will be for you to arrest him and bring him to trial."

At this reply the superintendent's eyes opened until his face might have been a symbolic mask of astonishment. Grasping his hair with both hands, he rose slowly from his chair, staring at Thorndyke as if at some alarming apparition.

"You'll be the death of me, Doctor!" he exclaimed. "You really will. I am not fit for these shocks at my time of life. What is it you ask me to do? I am to arrest this man! What man? Here is a wax-work gentleman in a coat – at least, I suppose that is what he is – that might have come straight from Madame Tussaud's. Am I to arrest him? And there is a casket full of ashes somewhere. Am I to arrest those? Or am I off my head or dreaming?"

Thorndyke smiled at him indulgently. "Now, Miller," said he, "don't pretend to be foolish, because you are not. The man whom you are to arrest is a live man, and what is more, he is easily accessible whenever you choose to lay your hands on him."

"Do you know where to find him?"

"Yes," Thorndyke replied. "I, myself, will conduct you to his house, which is in Abbey Road, Hornsey, nearly opposite Miss D'Arblay's studio."

I gave a gasp of amazement on hearing this, which directed the superintendent's attention to me.

"Very well, Doctor," he said, "I will take your information, but you needn't swear to it; just sign your name. I must be off now, but I will look in tonight about nine, if that will do, to get the necessary particulars and settle the arrangements with you. Probably tomorrow afternoon will be a good time to make the arrest. What do you think?"

"I should think it would be an excellent time," Thorndyke replied; "but we can settle definitely tonight."

With this, the superintendent, having taken the signed paper from Thorndyke, shook both our hands and bustled away with the traces of his late surprise still visible on his countenance.

The recognition of the tenant of the coffin as Simon Bendelow had come on me with almost as great a shock as it had on the two witnesses, but for a different reason. My late experiences enabled me to guess at once that the mysterious tenant was a wax-work figure, presumably of Polton's creation. But what I found utterly inexplicable was that such a wax-work should have been produced in the likeness of a man whom neither Polton nor Thorndyke had ever seen. The astonishing conversation between the latter and Miller, had, for the moment, driven this mystery out of my mind; but as soon as the superintendent had gone, I stepped over to the coffin and looked in at the window. And then I was more amazed than ever. For the face that I saw was not the face that I had expected to meet. There, it is true, was the old familiar skull-cap, which Bendelow had worn, pulled down over the temples above the jaw-bandage. But it was the wrong face. (Incidentally I now understood what had become Polton's eyelashes. That conscientious realist had evidently taken no risks.)

"But," I protested, "this is not Bendelow. This is Morris."

Thorndyke nodded. "You have just heard two competent witnesses declare with complete conviction and certainty that this is Simon Bendelow; and, as you yourself pointed out, there can be no doubt as to their knowledge of Bendelow, since they recognized the photograph of him that was shown to them by the American detective."

"That is perfectly true," I admitted. "But it is a most incomprehensible affair. This is not the man who was cremated."

"Evidently not, since he is still alive."

"But these two women saw Bendelow cremated – at least they saw him pass through into the crematorium, which is near enough. And they had seen him in the coffin a few minutes before I saw him in the coffin, and they saw him again a few minutes after Cropper and Morris and I had put him back in the coffin. And the man whom we put into the coffin was certainly not this man."

"Obviously not, since he helped you to put the corpse in."

"And again," I urged, "if the body that we put into the coffin was not the body that was cremated, what has become of it? It wasn't buried, for the other coffin was empty. Those women must have made some mistake."

He shook his head. "The solution of the mystery is staring you in the face," said he. "It is perfectly obvious, and I am not going to give you any further hints now. When we have made the arrest, you shall have a full exposition of the case. But tell me, now; did those two women ever meet Morris?"

I considered for a few moments and then replied: "I have no evidence that they ever met him. They certainly never did in my presence. But even if they had, they would hardly have recognized him as the person they have identified today. He had grown a beard and moustache, you will remember, and his appearance was very much altered from what it was when I first saw him."

Thorndyke nodded. "It would be," he agreed. Then, turning to another subject, he said: "I am afraid it will be necessary for you to be present at the arrest. I would much rather that you were not, for he is a dangerous brute and will probably fight like a wild cat; but you are the only one of us who really knows him by sight in his present state."

"I should like to be in at the death," I said eagerly.

"That is well enough," said he, "so long as it is his death. You must bring your pistol and don't be afraid to use it."

"And how shall I know when I am wanted?" I asked.

"You had better go to the studio tomorrow morning," he replied. "I will send a note by Polton giving you particulars of the time when we shall call for you. And now we may as well help Polton to prepare for our other visitors; and I think, Gray, that we will say as little as possible about this morning's proceedings or those of tomorrow. Explanations will come better after the event."

With this, we went down to the dining-room, where we found Polton sedately laying the table, having just got rid of the two ladies. We made a show of assisting him and I ventured to inquire:

"Who is doing the cooking today, Polton? Or is it to be a cold lunch?"

He looked at me almost reproachfully as he replied:

"It is to be a hot lunch, and I am doing the cooking, of course."

"But," I protested, "you have been up to your eyes in other affairs all the morning."

He regarded me with a patronizing crinkle. "You can do a good deal," said he, "with one or two casseroles, a hay-box and a four-storey cooker on a gas stove. Things don't cook any better for your standing and staring at them."

Events went to prove the soundness of Polton's culinary principles; and the brilliant success of their application in practice gave a direction to the conversation which led it comfortably away from other and less discussable topics.

CHAPTER EIGHTEEN

The Last Act

Shortly before leaving Thorndyke's chambers with Marion and Miss Boler, I managed to secure his permission to confide to them, in general terms, what was to happen on the morrow; and very relieved I was thereat, for I had little doubt that questions would be asked which it would seem ungracious to evade. Events proved that I was not mistaken; indeed, we were hardly clear of the precincts of the Temple when Marion opened the inquisition.

"You said yesterday," she began, "that Dr Thorndyke might have something to tell us today, and I hoped that he might. I even tried to pluck up courage to ask him, but then I was afraid that it might seem intrusive. He isn't the sort of man that you can take liberties with. So I suppose that whatever it was that happened this morning is a dead secret?"

"Not entirely," I replied. "I mustn't go into details at present, but I am allowed to give you the most important item of information. There is going to be an arrest tomorrow."

"Do you mean that Dr Thorndyke has discovered the man?" Marion demanded incredulously.

"He says that he has, and I take it that he knows. What is more, he offered to conduct the police to the house. He has actually given them the address."

"I would give all that I possess," exclaimed Miss Boler, "to be there and see the villain taken."

"Well," I said, "you won't be far away, for the man lives in Abbey Road, nearly opposite the studio."

Marion stopped and looked at me aghast. "What a horrible thing to think of!" she gasped. "Oh, I am glad I didn't know! I could never have gone to the studio if I had. But now we can understand how he managed to find his way to the place that foggy night, and to escape so easily."

"Oh, but it is not that man," I interposed, with a sudden sense of hopeless bewilderment. For I had forgotten this absolute discrepancy when I was talking to Thorndyke about the identification.

"Not that man!" she repeated, gazing at me in wild astonishment. "But that man was my father's murderer. I feel certain of it."

"So do I," was my rather lame rejoinder.

"Besides," she persisted, "if he was not the murderer, who was he, and why should he want to kill me?"

"Exactly," I agreed. "It seems conclusive. But apparently it isn't. At any rate, the man they are going to arrest is the man whose mask Thorndyke found at the studio."

"Then they are going to arrest the wrong man," said she, looking at me with a deeply troubled face. I was uncomfortable, too, for I saw what was in her mind. The memory of the ruffian who had made that murderous attack on her still lingered in her mind as a thing of horror. The thought that he was still at large and might at any moment reappear, made it impossible for her ever to work alone in the studio, or even to walk abroad without protection. She had looked, as I had, to the discovery of the murderer to rid her of this abiding menace. But now it seemed that even after the arrest of the murderer this terrible menace would remain.

"I can't understand it," she said dejectedly. "When you showed me that photograph of the man who tried to kill me, I naturally hoped that Dr Thorndyke had discovered who he was. But now it appears that he is at large and still untraced, yet I am convinced that he is the man who ought to have been followed."

"Never mind, my dear," I said cheerfully. "Let us see the affair out. You don't understand it and neither do I. But Thorndyke does. I have absolute faith in him, and so, I can see, have the police."

She assented without much conviction, and then Miss Boler began to press for further particulars. I mentioned the probable time of the arrest and the part that I was required to play in identifying the accused.

"You don't mean that you are asked to be present when the actual arrest is made, do you?" Marion asked anxiously.

"Yes," I answered. "You see, I am the only person who really knows the man by sight."

"But," she urged, "you are not a policeman. Suppose this man should be violent, like that other man; and he probably will be."

"Oh," I answered airily, "that will be provided for. Besides, I am not asked to arrest him; only to point him out to the police."

"I wish," she said, "you would stay in the studio until they have secured him. Then you could go and identify him. It would be much safer."

"No doubt," I agreed. "But it might lead to their arresting the wrong man and letting the right one slip. No, Marion, we must make sure of him if we can. Surely you are at least as anxious as any of us that he should be caught and made to pay the penalty?"

"Yes," she answered, "if he is really the right man – which I can hardly believe. But still, punishing him will not bring poor Daddy back, whereas if anything were to happen to you, Stephen – Oh! I don't dare to think of it!"

"You needn't think of it, Marion," I rejoined, cheerfully. "I shall be all right. And you wouldn't have your – apprentice hang back when these bobbies are taking the affair as a mere everyday job."

She made no reply beyond another anxious glance; and I was glad enough to let the subject drop, bearing in mind Thorndyke's words with regard to the pistol. As a diversion, I suggested a visit to the National Gallery, which we were now approaching, and the suggestion being adopted, without acclamation, we drifted in and rather listlessly perambulated the galleries, gazing vacantly at the exhibits and exchanging tepid comments. It was a spiritless proceeding, of which I remember very little but some rather severe observations by Miss Boler concerning a certain "hussy" (by one Bronzino) in the great room. But we soon gave up this hollow pretence and went forth to board a yellow bus which was bound for the Archway Tavern; and so home to an early supper.

On the following morning I made my appearance betimes at Ivy Cottage, but it was later than usual when Marion and I started to walk in leisurely fashion to the studio.

"I don't know why we are going at all," said she. "I don't feel like doing any work."

"Let us forget the arrest for the moment," said I. "There is plenty to do. Those arms of Polton's have got to be taken out of the moulds and worked. It will be much better to keep ourselves occupied."

"I suppose it will," she agreed; and then, as we turned a corner and came in sight of the studio, she exclaimed: "Why, what on earth is this? There are some painters at work on the studio! I wonder who sent them. I haven't given any orders. There must be some extraordinary mistake."

There was not, however. As we came up, one of the two linen-coated operators advanced, brush in hand, to meet us and briefly explained that he and his mate had been instructed by Superintendent Miller to wash down the paint-work and keep an eye on the premises opposite. They were, in fact, "plain-clothes" men on special duty.

"We have been here since seven o'clock," our friend informed us, as we made a pretence of examining the window-sashes, "and we took over from a man who had been watching the house all night. My nabs is there all right. He came home early yesterday evening and he hasn't come out since."

"Then you know the man by sight?" Marion asked eagerly.

"Well, miss," was the reply, "we have a description of him, and the man who went into the house seemed to agree with it; and, as far as we know, there isn't any other man living there. But I understand that we are relying on Dr Gray to establish the identity. Could I have a look at the inside woodwork?"

Marion unlocked the door and we entered, followed by the detective, whose interest seemed to be concerned exclusively with the woodwork of windows; and from windows in general finally became concentrated on a small window in the lobby which commanded a view of the houses opposite. Having examined the sashes of this, with his eye cocked on one of the houses aforesaid, he proceeded to operate on it with his brush, which, being wet and dirty and used with a singular lack of care, soon covered the glass so completely with a mass of opaque smears that it was impossible to see through it at all. Then he cautiously raised the sash about an inch, and whipping out a prism binocular from under his apron, stood back a couple of feet and took a leisurely survey through the narrow opening of one of the opposite houses.

"Hallo!" said he. "There is a woman visible at the first-floor window. Just have a look at her, sir. She can't see us through this narrow crack."

He handed me the glass, indicating the house, and I put the instrument to my eyes. It was a powerful glass, and seemed to bring the window and the figure of the woman within a dozen feet of me. But at the moment she had turned her head away, apparently to speak to someone inside the room, and all that I could see was that she seemed to be an elderly woman who wore what looked like an old-fashioned widow's cap. Suddenly she turned and looked out over the half-curtain, giving me a perfectly clear view of her face; and then I felt myself lapsing into the old sense of confusion and bewilderment.

I had, of course, expected to recognize Mrs Morris. But this was evidently not she, although not such a very different-looking woman; an elderly, white-haired widow in a crape cap and spectacles – reading-spectacles they must be, since she was looking over and not through them. She seemed to be a stranger – and yet not quite a stranger; for as I looked at her some chord of memory stirred. But the cup of my confusion was not yet full. As I stared at her, trying vainly to sound a clearer note on that chord of memory, a man slowly emerged from the darkness of the room behind and stood beside her; and him I recognized instantly as the bottle-nosed person whom I had watched from my ambush at the top of Dartmouth Park Hill.

"Well, sir," said the detective, as the man and woman turned away from the window and vanished, "what do you make of 'em? Do you recognize 'em?"

"I recognize the man," I replied, "and I believe I have seen the woman before, but they aren't the people I expected to see."

"Oh, dear!" said he. "That's a bad look-out. Because I don't think there is anybody else there."

"Then," I said, "we have made a false shot; and yet – well, I don't know. I had better think this over and see if I can make anything of it."

I turned into the studio, where I found Marion – who had been listening attentively to this dialogue – in markedly better spirits.

"It seems a regular muddle," she remarked cheerfully. "They have come to arrest the wrong man and now it appears that he isn't there."

"Don't talk to me for a few minutes, Marion, dear," said I. "There is something behind this and I want to think what it can be. I have seen that woman somewhere, I feel certain. Now, where was it?"

I cudgelled my brains for some time without succeeding in recovering the recollections connected with her. I re-visualized the face that I had seen through the glass, with its deep-set, hollow eyes and strong, sharply sloping eyebrows, and tried to connect it with some person whom I had seen, but in vain. And then in a flash it came to me. She was the widow whom I had noticed at the inquest. The identification, indeed, was not very complete, for the veil that she had worn on that occasion had considerably obscured her features. But I had no doubt that I was right, for her present appearance agreed in all that I could see with that of the woman at the inquest.

The next question was, who could she be? Her association with the bottle-nosed man connected her in some way with what Thorndyke would have called "the case"; for that man, whoever he was, had certainly been shadowing me. Then her presence at the inquest had now a sinister suggestiveness. She would seem to have been there to watch developments on behalf of others. Could she be a relative of Mrs Morris? A certain faint resemblance seemed to support this idea. As to the man, I gave him up. Evidently there were several persons concerned in this crime, but I knew too little about the circumstances to be able to make even a profitable guess. Having reached this unsatisfactory conclusion, I turned, a little irritably, to Marion, exclaiming:

"I can make nothing of it. Let us get on with some work to pass the time."

Accordingly we began, in a half-hearted way, upon Polton's two moulds. But the presence of the two detectives was disturbing, especially when, having finished the exterior, they brought their pails and ladders inside and took up their station at the lobby window. We struggled on for a time; but when, about noon, Miss Boler made her appearance with a basket of provisions and a couple of bottles of wine, we abandoned the attempt and occupied ourselves in tidying up and laying a table.

"Don't you think, Marion," I said, as we sat down to lunch (having provided for the needs of the two "painters", who lunched in the lobby), "that it would be best for you and Arabella to go home before any fuss begins?"

"Whatever Miss Marion thinks," Arabella interposed firmly, "*I* am not going home. I came down expressly to see this villain captured, and here I stay until he is safely in custody."

"And I," said Marion, "am going to stay with Arabella. You know why, Stephen. I couldn't bear to go away and leave you here after what you have told me. We shall be quite safe in here."

"Well," I temporised, seeing plainly that they had made up their minds, "you must keep the door bolted until the business is over."

"As to that," said Miss Boler, "we shall be guided by circumstances"; and from this ambiguous position neither she nor Marion would budge.

Shortly after lunch I received a further shock of surprise. In answer to a loud single knock, I hurried out to open the door. A tradesman's van had drawn up at the kerb and two men stood on the threshold, one of them holding a good-sized parcel. I stared at the latter in astonishment, for I recognized him instantly as the second shadower of the Dartmouth Park Hill adventure; but before I could make any comment, both men entered – with the curt explanation "police business" – and the last-comer shut the door, when I heard the van drive off.

"I am Detective-Sergeant Porter," the stranger explained. "You know what I am here for, of course."

"Yes," I replied; and turning to the other man, I said: "I think I have seen you before. Are you a police-officer, too?"

My acquaintance grinned. "Retired Detective Sergeant," he explained, "name of Barber. At present employed by Dr Thorndyke. I think I have seen you before, sir," and he grinned again, somewhat more broadly.

"I should like to know how you were employed when I saw you last," said I. But here Sergeant Porter interposed: "Better leave explanations till later, sir. You've got a back gate, I think."

"Yes," said one of the "painters". "At the bottom of the garden. It opens on an alley that leads into the next road – Chilton Road."

"Can we get into the garden through the studio?" the sergeant asked; and on my answering in the affirmative, he requested permission to inspect the rear premises. I conducted both men to the back door and let them out into the garden, where they passed out at the back gate to reconnoitre the alley. In a minute or two they returned; and they had hardly re-entered the studio when another knock at the door announced more visitors. They turned out to be Thorndyke and Superintendent Miller; of whom the latter inquired of the senior painter:

"Is everything in going order, Jenks?"

"Yes, sir," was the reply. "The man is there all right. Dr Gray saw him; but I should mention, sir, that he doesn't think it's the right man."

"The devil he doesn't!" exclaimed Miller, looking at me uneasily and then glancing at Thorndyke.

"That man isn't Morris," said I. "He is that red-nosed man whom I told you about. You remember."

"I remember," Thorndyke replied calmly. "Well, I suppose we shall have to content ourselves with the red-nosed man;" upon which ex-Sergeant Barber's countenance became wreathed in smiles and the superintendent looked relieved.

"Are all the arrangements complete, Sergeant?" Miller inquired. turning to Sergeant Porter.

"Yes, sir," the latter replied. "Inspector Follett has got some local men, who know the neighbourhood well, posted in the rear watching the back garden, and there are some uniformed men waiting round both the corners to stop him, in case he slips past us. Everything is ready, sir."

"Then," said the superintendent, "we may as well open the ball at once. I hope it will go off quietly. It ought to. We have got enough men on the job."

He nodded to Sergeant Porter, who at once picked up his parcel and went out into the garden, accompanied by Barber. Miller, Thorndyke and I now adjourned to the lobby window, where, with the two painter-detectives, we established a look-out. Presently we saw the sergeant and Barber advancing separately on the opposite side of the road, the latter leading and carrying the parcel. Arrived at the house, he entered the front garden and knocked a loud single knock. Immediately, the mysterious woman appeared at the ground-floor window – it was a bay-window – and took a long, inquisitive look at ex-Sergeant Barber. There ensued a longish pause, during which Sergeant Porter walked slowly past the house. Then the door opened a very short distance – being evidently chained – and the woman appeared in the narrow opening. Barber offered the parcel, which was much too large to go through the opening without unchaining the door, and appeared to be giving explanations. But the woman evidently denied all knowledge of it, and having refused to receive it, tried to shut the door, into the opening of which Barber had inserted his foot; but he withdrew it somewhat hastily as a coal-hammer descended, and before he could recover himself the door shut with a bang and was immediately bolted.

The ball was opened, as Miller had expressed it, and the developments followed with a bewildering rapidity that far outpaced any possible description.

The sergeant returning and joining Barber, the two men were about to force the ground-floor window, when pistol-shots and police whistles from the rear announced a new field of operations. At once Miller opened the studio door and sallied forth, with the two detectives and Thorndyke; and when I had called out to Marion to bolt the door, I followed, shutting it after me. Meanwhile, from the rear of the opposite houses came a confused noise of police-whistles, barking dogs and women's voices, with an occasional report. Following three rapid pistol-shots there came a brief interval; then, suddenly, the door of a house farther down the street burst open and the fugitive rushed out, wild-eyed and terrified, his white face contrasting most singularly with his vividly red nose. Instantly, the two detectives and Miller started in pursuit, followed by the sergeant and Barber; but the man ran like a hare and was speedily drawing ahead when suddenly a party of constables appeared from a side-turning and blocked the road. The fugitive zigzagged and made as if he would try to dodge between them, flinging away his empty pistol and drawing out another. The detectives and Miller were close on him, when in an instant he turned and, with extraordinary agility avoided them. Then, as the two sergeants bore down on him, he fired at them at close range, stopping them both, though neither actually fell. Again he out-ran his pursuers, racing down the road towards us, yelling like a maniac and firing his pistol wildly at Thorndyke and me. And suddenly my left leg doubled up and I fell heavily to the ground nearly opposite the studio door.

The fall confused me for a moment and as I lay, half-dazed, I was horrified to see Marion dart out of the studio. In an instant she was kneeling by my side with her arm around my neck.

"Stephen! Oh, Stephen, darling!" she sobbed and gazed into my face with eyes full of terror and affection, oblivious of everything but my peril. I besought her to go back, and struggled to get out my pistol, for the man, still gaining on his pursuers, was now rapidly approaching. He had flung away his second pistol and had drawn a large knife; and as he bore down on us, mad with rage and terror, he gibbered and grinned like a wild cat.

When he was but a couple of dozen paces away, I saw Thorndyke raise his pistol and take a careful aim. But before he had time to fire, a most singular diversion occurred. From the open door of the studio Miss Boler emerged, swinging a massive stool with amazing ease. The man, whose eyes were fixed on me and Marion, did not observe her until she was within a few paces of him; when, gathering all her strength, she hurled the heavy stool with almost incredible force. It struck him below the knees, knocking his feet from under him, and he fell with a sort of dive or half-somersault, falling with the hand that grasped the knife under him.

He made no attempt to rise, but lay with slightly twitching limbs but otherwise motionless. Miss Boler stalked up to him and stood looking down on him with grim interest until Thorndyke, still holding his pistol, stooped and, grasping one arm, gently turned him over. Then we could see the handle of the knife sticking out from his chest near the right shoulder.

"Ha!" said Thorndyke. "Bad luck to the last. It must have gone through the arch of the aorta. But perhaps it is just as well."

He rose and, stepping across to where I sat, supported by Marion and still nursing my pistol, bent over me with an anxious face.

"What is it, Gray?" he asked. "Not a fracture, I hope?"

"I don't think so," I replied. "Damaged muscle and perhaps nerve. It is all numb at present, but it doesn't seem to be bleeding much. I think I could hobble if you would help me up."

He shook his head and beckoned to a couple of constables, with whose aid he carried me into the studio and deposited me on the sofa. Immediately afterwards the two wounded officers were brought in, and I was relieved to hear that neither of them was dangerously hurt, though the sergeant had a fractured arm and Barber a flesh-wound of the chest and a cracked rib. The ladies having been politely ejected into the garden, Thorndyke examined the various injuries and applied temporary dressings, producing the materials from a very business-like looking bag which he had providently brought with him. While he was thus engaged, three constables entered carrying the corpse, which, with a few words of apology, they deposited on the floor by the side of the sofa.

I looked down on the ill-omened figure with lively curiosity; and especially was I impressed and puzzled by the very singular appearance of the face. Its general colour was of that waxen pallor characteristic of the faces of the dead, particularly of those who have died from haemorrhage. But the nose and the acne patches remained unchanged. Indeed, their colour seemed intensified, for their vivid red "stared" from the surrounding white like the painted patches on a clown's face.

The mystery was solved when, the surgical business being concluded, Barber came and seated himself on the edge of the sofa.

"Masterly make-up, that," said he, nodding at the corpse. "Looks queer enough now; but when he was alive you couldn't spot it, even in daylight."

"Make-up!" I exclaimed. "I didn't know you could make-up off the stage."

"You can't wear a celluloid nose off the stage, or a tie-on beard," he replied. "But when it is done as well as this – a touch or two of nose-paste or toupee-paste, tinted carefully with grease-paint and finished up with powder – it's hard to spot. These experts in make-up are a holy terror to the police."

"Did you know that he was made up?" I asked, looking at Thorndyke.

"I inferred that he was," the latter replied, "and so did Sergeant Barber. But now we had better see what his natural appearance is."

He stooped over the corpse and with a small ivory paper-knife scraped from the end of the nose and the parts adjacent a layer of coloured plastic material about the consistency of modelling-wax. Then with vaseline and cotton-wool he cleaned away the red pigment until the pallid skin showed unsullied.

"Why, it *is* Morris after all!" I exclaimed. "It is perfectly incredible; and you seemed to remove such a very small quantity of paste, too! I wouldn't have believed that it would make such a change."

"Not after that very instructive demonstration that Miss D'Arblay gave us with the clay and the plaster mask?" he asked with a smile.

I smiled sheepishly in return. "I told you I was a fool, sir;" and then, as a new idea burst upon me, I asked: "And that other man – the hook-nosed man?"

"Morris – that is to say, Bendelow," he replied, "with a different, more exaggerated make-up."

I was pondering with profound relief on this answer when one of the painter-detectives entered in search of the superintendent.

"We got into the house from the back, sir," he reported. "The woman is dead. We found her lying on the bed in the first-floor front; and we found a tumbler half-full of water and this by the bedside."

He exhibited a small, wide-mouthed bottle labelled "Potassium Cyanide", which the superintendent took from him.

"I will come and look over the house presently," the latter said. "Don't let anybody in; and let me know when the cabs are here."

"There are two here now, sir," the detective announced, "and they have sent down three wheeled stretchers."

"One cab will carry our two casualties and I expect the Doctor will want the other. The bodies can be put on two of the stretchers, but you had better send the woman here for Dr Gray to see."

The detective saluted and retired, and in a few minutes a stretcher dismounted from its carriage was borne in by two constables and placed on the floor beside Morris' corpse. But even now, prepared as I was, and knowing who the new arrival must be, I looked doubtfully at the pitiful effigy that lay before me so limp and passive, that but an hour since had been a strong, courageous, resourceful woman. Not until the white wig, the cap and the spectacles had been removed, the heavy eyebrows detached with spirit and the dark pigment cleaned away from the eyelids, could I say with certainty that this was the corpse of Mrs Morris.

"Well, Doctor," said the superintendent, when the wounded and the dead had been borne away and we were alone in the studio, "you have done your part to a finish, as usual, but ours is a bit of a failure. I *should* have liked to bring that fellow to trial."

"I sympathize with you, Miller," replied Thorndyke. "The gallows ought to have had him. But yet I am not sure that what has happened is not all for the best. The evidence in both cases – the D'Arblay and the Van Zellen murders – is entirely circumstantial and extremely intricate. That is not good evidence for a jury. A conviction would not have been a certainty either here or in America; and an acquittal would have been a disaster that I don't dare to think of. No, Miller, I think that, on the whole, I am satisfied, and I think that you ought to be, too."

"I suppose I ought," Miller conceded, "but it *would* have been a triumph to put him in the dock, after he had been written off as dead and cremated. However, we must take things as we find them; and now I had better go and look over that house."

With a friendly nod to me, he took himself off, and Thorndyke went off to notify the ladies that the intruders had departed.

As he returned with them I heard Marion cross-examining him with regard to my injuries and listened anxiously for his report.

"So far as I can see, Miss D'Arblay," he answered, "the damage is confined to one or two muscles. If so, there will be no permanent disablement and he should soon be quite well again. But he will want proper surgical treatment without delay. I propose to take him straight to our hospital, if he agrees."

"Miss Boler and I were hoping," said Marion, "that we might have the privilege of nursing him at our house."

"That is very good of you," said Thorndyke, "and perhaps you might look after him during his convalescence. But for the present he needs skilled surgical treatment. If it should not be necessary for him to stay in the hospital after the wound has been attended to, it would be best for him to occupy one of the spare bedrooms at my chambers, where he can be seen daily by the surgeon and I can keep an eye on him. Come," he added coaxingly, "let us make a compromise. You or Miss Boler shall come to the Temple every day for as long as you please and do what nursing is necessary. There is a spare room of which you can take possession; and as to your work here, Polton will give you any help that he can. How will that do?"

Marion accepted the offer gratefully (with my concurrence), but begged to be allowed to accompany me to the hospital.

"That was what I was going to suggest," said Thorndyke. "The cab will hold the four of us, and the sooner we start the better."

Our preparations were very soon made. Then the door was opened, I was assisted out through a lane of hungry-eyed spectators, held at bay by two constables, and deposited in the cab; and when the studio had been locked up, we drove off, leaving the neighbourhood to settle down to its normal condition.

CHAPTER NINETEEN

Thorndyke Disentangles
the Threads

The days of my captivity at Number 5A King's Bench Walk passed with a tranquillity that made me realize the weight of the incubus that had been lifted. Now, in the mornings, when Polton ministered to me – until Arabella arrived and was ungrudgingly installed in office – I could let my untroubled thoughts stray to Marion, working alone in the studio with restored security, free for ever from the hideous menace which hung over her. And later, when she herself, released by her faithful apprentice, came to take her spell of nursing, what a joy it was to see her looking so fresh and rosy, so youthful and buoyant!

Of Thorndyke – the giver of these gifts – I saw little in the first few days, for he had heavy arrears of work to make up. However, he paid me brief visits from time to time, especially in the mornings and at night, when I was alone, and very delightful those visits were. For he had now dropped the investigator and there had come into his manner something new, something fatherly or elder-brotherly; and he managed to convey to me that my presence in his chambers was a source of pleasure to him – a refinement of hospitality that filled up the cup of my gratitude to him.

It was on the fifth day, when I was allowed to sit up in bed – for my injury was no more than a perforating wound of the outer side of the calf, which had missed every important structure – that

I sat watching Marion making somewhat premature preparations for tea, and observed with interest that a third cup had been placed on the tray.

"Yes," Marion replied to my inquiry, "the Doctor is coming to tea with us today. Mr Polton gave me the message when he arrived." She gave a few further touches to the tea-set and continued: "How sweet Dr Thorndyke has been to us, Stephen! He treats me as if I were his daughter, and however busy he is, he always walks with me to the Temple gate and puts me into a cab. I am infinitely grateful to him – almost as grateful as I am to you."

"I don't see what you have got to be grateful to me for," I remarked.

"Don't you?" said she. "Is it nothing to me, do you suppose, that in the moment of my terrible grief and desolation, I found a noble, chivalrous friend whom I trusted instantly, that I have been guarded through all the dangers that threatened me, and that at last I have been rescued from them and set free to go my ways in peace and security? Surely, Stephen, dear, all this is abundant matter for gratitude. And I owe it all to you."

"To me!" I exclaimed in astonishment, recalling secretly what a consummate donkey I had been. "But there, I suppose it is the way of a woman to imagine that her particular gander is a swan."

She smiled a superior smile. "Women," said she, "are very intelligent creatures. They are able to distinguish between swans and ganders, whereas the swans themselves are apt to be muddle-headed and self-depreciatory."

"I agree to the muddle-headed factor," I rejoined, "and I won't be unduly ostentatious as to the ganderism. But to return to Thorndyke, it is extraordinarily good of him to allow himself to be burdened with me."

"With us," she corrected.

"It is the same thing, sweetheart. Do you know if he is going to give us a long visit?"

"I hope so," she replied. "Mr Polton said that he had got through his arrears of work and had this afternoon free."

"Then," said I, "perhaps he will give us the elucidation that he promised me some time ago. I am devoured by curiosity as to how he unravelled the web of mystification that the villain, Bendelow, spun round himself."

"So am I," said she; "and I believe I can hear his footsteps on the stair."

A few moments later Thorndyke entered the room and, having greeted us with quiet geniality, seated himself in the easy-chair by the table and regarded us with a benevolent smile.

"We were just saying, sir," said I, "how very kind it is of you to allow your chambers to be invaded by a stray cripple and his – his belongings."

"I believe you were going to say 'baggage'," Marion murmured.

"Well," said Thorndyke, smiling at the interpolation, "I may tell you both in confidence that you were talking nonsense. It is I who am the beneficiary."

"It is a part of your goodness to say so, sir," I said.

"But," he rejoined, "it is the simple truth. You enable me to combine the undoubted economic advantages of bachelordom with the satisfaction of having a family under my roof; and you even allow me to participate in a way, as a sort of supercargo, in a certain voyage of discovery which is to be undertaken by two young adventurers in the near future – in the very near future, as I hope."

"As I hope, too," said I, glancing at Marion, who had become a little more rosy than usual and who now adroitly diverted the current of the conversation.

"We were also wondering," said she, "if we might hope for some enlightenment on things which have puzzled us so much lately."

"That," he replied, "was in my mind when I arranged to keep this afternoon and evening free. I wanted to give Stephen – who is my professional offspring, so to speak – a full exposition of this very intricate and remarkable case. If you, my dear, will keep my cup charged as occasion arises, I will begin forthwith. I will address myself to Stephen, who has all the facts first-hand; and if, in my exposition, I should seem somewhat callously to ignore the human aspects of this tragic story – aspects which have meant so much in irreparable loss and bereavement to you, poor child – remember that it is an exposition of evidence, and necessarily passionless and impersonal."

"I quite realize that," said Marion, "and you may trust me to understand."

He bowed gravely, and, after a brief pause, began: "I propose to treat the subject historically, so to speak; to take you over the ground that I traversed myself, recounting my observations and inferences in the order in which they occurred. The inquiry falls naturally into certain successive stages, corresponding to the emergence of new facts, of which the first was concerned with the data elicited at the inquest. Let us begin with them.

"First, as to the crime itself. It was a murder of a very distinctive type. There was evidence, not only of premeditation in the bare legal sense, but of careful preparation and planning. It was a considered act and not a crime of impulse or passion. What could be the motive for such a crime? There appeared to be only two alternative possibilities: either it was a crime of revenge or a crime of expediency. The hypothesis of revenge could not be explored, because there were no data excepting the evidence of the victim's daughter, which was to the effect that deceased had no enemies, actual or potential; and this evidence was supported by the very deliberate character of the crime.

"We were therefore thrown back on the hypothesis of expediency, which was, in fact, the more probable one, and which became still more probable as the circumstances were further examined. But having assumed, as a working hypothesis, that this crime had been committed in pursuit of a definite purpose which was not revenge, the next question was, What could that purpose have been? And that question could be answered only by a careful consideration of all that was known of the parties to the crime – the criminal and the victim and their possible relations to one another.

"As to the former, the circumstances indicated that he was a person of some education, that he had an unusual acquaintance with poisons and such social position and personal qualities as would enable him to get possession of them; that he was subtle, ingenious and resourceful, but not far-sighted, since he took risks that could have been avoided. His mentality appeared to be that of the gambler, whose attention tends to be riveted on the winning chances and who makes insufficient provision for possible failure. He staked everything on the chance of the needle-puncture being overlooked and the presence of the poison being undiscovered.

"But the outstanding and most significant quality was his profound criminality. Premeditated murder is the most atrocious of crimes; and murder for expediency is the most atrocious form of murder. This man, then, was of a profoundly criminal type and was, most probably, a practising criminal.

"Turning now to the victim, the evidence showed that he was a man of high moral qualities; honest, industrious, thrifty, kindly and amiable and of good reputation – the exact reverse of the other. Any illicit association between these two men was therefore excluded; and yet there must have been an association of some kind. Of what kind could it have been?

"Now, in the case of this man, as in that of the other, there was one outstanding fact. He was a sculptor. And not only a sculptor but an artist in the highest class of wax-work. And not only this. He was probably the only artist of this kind practising in this country. For wax-work is almost exclusively a French art. So far as I know, all the wax figures and high-class lay figures that are made are produced in France. This man, therefore, appeared to be the unique English practitioner of this very curious art.

"The fact impressed me profoundly. To realize its significance we must realize the unique character of the art. Wax-work is a fine art, but it differs from all other fine arts in that its main purpose is one that is expressly rejected by all those other arts. An ordinary work of sculpture, no matter how realistic, is frankly an object of metal, stone or pottery. Its realism is restricted to truth of form. No deception is aimed at, but, on the contrary, is expressly avoided. But the aim of wax-work is complete deception; and its perfection is measured by the completeness of the deception achieved. How complete that may be can be judged by incidents that have occurred at Madame Tussaud's. When that exhibition was at the old Baker Street Bazaar, the snuff-taker − whose arms, head and eyes were moved by clock-work − used to be seated on an open bench; and it is recorded that, quite frequently, visitors would sit down by him on the bench and try to open conversation with him. So, too, the wax-work policeman near the door was occasionally accosted with questions by arriving visitors.

"Bearing this fact in mind, it is obvious that this art is peculiarly adapted to employment in certain kinds of fraud, such as personation, false alibi and the like; and it is probable that the only reason why it is not so employed is the great difficulty of obtaining first-class wax-works.

"Naturally, then, when I observed this connexion of a criminal with a wax-work artist, I asked myself whether the motive of the murder was not to be sought in that artist's unique powers. Could it be that an attempt had been made to employ the deceased on some work designed for a fraudulent purpose? If such an attempt had been made, whether it had or had not been successful, the deceased would be in possession of knowledge which would be highly dangerous to the criminal; but especially if a work had actually been executed and used as an instrument of fraud.

"But there were other possibilities in the case of a sculptor who was also a medallist. He might have been employed to produce − quite innocently − copies of valuable works which were intended for fraudulent use: and the second stage of the investigation was concerned with these possibilities. That stage was ushered in by Follett's discovery of the guinea; the additional facts that we obtained at the Museum, and later, when we learned that the guinea that had been found was an electrotype copy, and that deceased was an expert electrotyper, all seemed to point to the production of forgeries as the crime in which Julius D'Arblay had been implicated. That was the view to which we seemed to be committed; but it did not seem to me satisfactory, for several reasons. First, the motive was insufficient – there was really nothing to conceal. When the forgeries were offered for sale, it would be obvious that someone had made them and that someone could be traced by the purchaser through the vendor. The killing of the actual maker would give no security to the man who sold the forgeries and who would have to appear in the transaction. And then, although deceased was unique as a wax-worker, he was not as a copyist or electrotyper. For those purposes, much more suitable accomplices might have been found. The execution of copies by deceased appeared to be a fact; but my own feeling was that they had been a mere by-product – that they had been used as a means of introduction to deceased for some other purpose connected with wax-work.

"At the end of this stage we had made some progress. We had identified this unknown man with another unknown man, who was undoubtedly a professional criminal. We had found, in the forged guinea, a possible motive for the murder. But, as I have said, that explanation did not satisfy me, and I still kept a look-out for new evidence connected with the wax-works.

"The next stage opened on that night when you arrived at Cornish's looking like a resuscitated 'found drowned'. Your account of your fall into the canal and the immediately antecedent events made a deep impression on me, though I did not, at the time, connect them with the crime that we were investigating. But the whole affair was so abnormal that it seemed to call for very careful consideration; and the more I considered it, the more abnormal did it appear.

"The theory of an accident could not be entertained, nor could the dropping of that derrick have been a practical joke. Your objection that no one was in sight had no weight, since there was a gate in the wall by which a person could have made his escape. Someone had attempted to murder you, and that attempt had been made immediately after you had signed a cremation certificate.

That was a very impressive fact. As you know, it is my habit to look very narrowly at cremation cases, for the reason that cremation offers great facilities for certain kinds of crime. Poisoners – and particularly arsenic and antimony poisoners – have repeatedly been convicted on evidence furnished by an exhumed body. If such poisoners can get the corpse of the victim cremated, they are virtually safe; for whatever suspicions may thereafter arise, no conviction is possible, since the means of proving the administration have been destroyed.

"Accordingly, I considered very carefully your account of the proceedings, and as I did so, strong suggestions of fraud arose in all directions. There was, for instance, the inspection window in the coffin. What was its object? Inspection windows are usually provided only in cases where the condition of the body is such that it has to be enclosed in a hermetically sealed coffin. But no such condition existed in this case. There was no reason why the friends should not have viewed the body in the usual manner in an open coffin. Again, there was the curious alternation of you and the two witnesses. First they went up and viewed deceased – through the window. Then, after a considerable interval, you and Cropper went up and viewed deceased – through the window. Then you took out the body, examined it and put it back. Again, after a considerable interval, the witnesses went up a second time and viewed the deceased – through the window.

"It was all rather queer and suspicious, especially when considered in conjunction with the attempt on your life. Reflecting on the latter, the question of the gate in the wall by the canal arose in my mind, and I examined the map to see if I could locate it. It was not marked, but the wharf was; and from this and your description it appeared certain that the gate must be in the wall of the garden of Morris' house. Here was another suspicious fact. For Morris – who could have let you out by this side-gate – sent you by a long, roundabout route to the towpath. He knew which way you must be going – westward – and could have slipped out of the gate and waited for you in the hut by the wharf.

It was possible; and there seemed to be no other explanation of what had happened to you. Incidentally, I made another discovery. The map showed that Morris' house had two frontages – one on Field Street and one on Market Street – and that you appeared to have been admitted by the back entrance. Which was another slightly abnormal circumstance.

"I was very much puzzled by the affair. There was a distinct suggestion that some fraud – some deception – had been practised; that what the spinsters saw through the coffin window was not the same thing as that which you saw. And yet, what could the deception have been? There was no question about the body. It was a real body. The disease was undoubtedly genuine and was, at least, the effective cause of death. And the cremation was necessarily genuine; for though you can bury an empty coffin, you can't cremate one. The absence of calcined bone would expose the fraud instantly.

"I considered the possibility of a second body; that of a murdered person, for instance. But that would not do. For if a substitution had been effected, there would still have been a redundant body to dispose of and account for. Nothing would have been gained by the substitution.

"But there was another possibility to which no such objection applied. Assuming a fraud to have been perpetrated, here was a case adapted in the most perfect manner to the use of a wax-work. Of course, a full-length figure would have been impossible because it would have left no calcined bones. But the inspection window would have made it unnecessary. A wax head would have done; or better still, a wax mask, which could have been simply placed over the face of the real corpse. The more I thought about it the more was I impressed by the singular suitability of the arrangements to the use of a wax mask. The inspection window seemed to be designed for the very purpose – to restrict the view to a mere face and to prevent the mask from being touched and the fraud thus discovered – and the alternate inspections by you and the spinsters were quite in keeping with a deception of that kind.

"There was another very queer feature in the case. These people, living at Hoxton, elected to employ a doctor who lived miles away at Bloomsbury. Why did they not call in a neighbouring practitioner? Also, they arranged the days and even the hours at which the visits were to be made. Why? There was an evident suggestion of something that the doctor was not to know – something or somebody that he was not desired to see; that some preparations had to be made for his visits.

"Again, the note was addressed to Dr Stephen Gray, not to Dr Cornish. They knew your name and address, although you had only just come there, and they did not know Dr Cornish, who was an old resident. How was this? The only explanation seemed to be that they had read the report of the inquest, or even been present at it. You there stated publicly that your temporary address was at 61 Mecklenburgh Square; that you were, in fact, a bird of passage; and you gave your full name and your age. Now, if any fraud was being carried out, a bird of passage, who might be difficult to find later, and a young one at that, was just the most suitable kind of doctor.

"To sum up the evidence at this stage: The circumstances, taken as a whole, suggested in the strongest possible manner that there was something fraudulent about this cremation. That fraud must be some kind of substitution or personation with the purpose of obtaining a certificate that some person had been cremated, who in fact had not been cremated. In that case it was nearly certain that the dead man was not Simon Bendelow; for the certificates would be required to agree with the false appearances, not with the true. There was a suggestion – but only a speculative one – that the deception might have been effected by means of a wax mask."

"There were, however, two objections. As to the wax mask, there was the great difficulty of obtaining one. A perfect portrait mask could have been obtained only either from an artist in Paris or from Julius D'Arblay. The objection to the substitution theory was that there was a real body – the body of a real person. If the cremation was in a name which was not the name of that person, then the disappearance of that person would remain unaccounted for.

"So you see that the whole theory of the fraud was purely conjectural. There was not a single particle of direct evidence. You also see that at two points there was a faint hint of a connexion between this case and the murder of Mr D'Arblay. These people seemed to have read of, or attended at, the inquest; and if a wax mask existed, it was quite probably made by him.

"The next stage opens with the discovery of the mask at the studio. But there are certain antecedent matters that must first be glanced at. When the attempt was made to murder Marion, I asked myself four questions: '1. Why did this man want to kill Marion? 2. What did he come to the studio on the preceding night to search for? 3. Did he find it, whatever it was? 4. Why had he delayed so long to make the search?'

"Let us begin with the second question. What had be come to look for? The obvious suggestion was that he had come to get possession of some incriminating object. But what was that object? Could it be the mould of some forged coin or medal? I did not believe that it was. For since the forgery or forgeries were extant, the moulds had no particular significance; and what little significance they had, applied to Mr D'Arblay, who was, technically, the forger. My feeling was that the object was in some way connected with wax-work, and in all probability with a wax portrait mask, as the most likely thing to be used for a fraudulent purpose. And I need hardly say that the cremation case lurked in the back of my mind.

"This view was supported by consideration of the third question. Did he find what he came to seek? If he came for moulds of coins or medals, he must have found them; for none remained. But the fact that he came the next night and attempted to murder Marion – believing her to be alone – suggested that his search had failed. And consideration of the fourth question led – less decisively – to the same conclusion as to the nature of the object sought.

"Why had he waited all this time to make the search? Why had he not entered the studio immediately after the murder, when the place was mostly unoccupied? The most probable explanation appeared to me to be that he had only recently become aware that there was any incriminating object in existence. Proceeding on the hypothesis that he had commissioned Mr D'Arblay to make a wax portrait mask, I further assumed that he knew little of the process, and – perhaps misunderstanding Mr D'Arblay – confused the technique of wax with that of plaster. In making a plaster mask from life – as you probably know by this time – you have to destroy the mould to get the mask out. So when the mask has been delivered to the client, there is nothing left.

"But to make a wax mask, you must first make one of plaster to serve as a matrix from which to make the gelatine mould for the wax. Then, when the wax mask has been delivered to the client, the plaster matrix remains in the possession of the artist.

"The suggestion, then, was that this man had supposed that the mould had been destroyed in making the mask, and that only some time after the murder had he, in some way, discovered his mistake. When he did discover it, he would see what an appalling blunder he had made; for the plaster matrix was the likeness of his own face.

"You see that all this was highly speculative. It was all hypothetical and it might all have been totally fallacious. We still had not a single solid fact; but all the hypothetical matter was consistent, and each inference seemed to support the others."

"And what," I asked, "did you suppose was his motive for trying to make away with Marion?"

"In the first place," he replied, "I inferred that he looked on her as a dangerous person who might have some knowledge of his transactions with her father. This was probably the explanation of his attempt when he cut the brake-wire of her bicycle. But the second, more desperate attack, was made, I assume, when he had realized the existence of the plaster mask, and supposed that she knew of it, too. If he had killed her, he would probably have made another search with the studio fully lighted up.

"To return to our inquiry. You see that I had a mass of hypothesis but not a single real fact. But I still had a firm belief that a wax mask had been made and that – if it had not been destroyed – there must be a plaster mask somewhere in the studio. That was what I came to look for that morning; and as it happens that I am some six inches taller than Bendelow was, I was able to see what had been invisible to him. When I discovered that mask, and when Marion had disclaimed all knowledge of it, my hopes began to rise. But when you identified the face as that of Morris, I felt that our problem was solved. In an instant my card-house of speculative hypothesis was changed into a solid edifice. What had been but bare possibilities had now become so highly probable that they were almost certainties.

"Let us consider what the finding of this mask proved – subject, of course, to verification. It proved that a wax mask of Morris had been made – for here was the matrix, varnished, as you will remember, in readiness for the gelatine mould; and that mask was obviously obtained for the purpose of a fraudulent cremation. And that mask was made by Julius D'Arblay.

"What was the purpose of the fraud? It was perfectly obvious. Morris was clearly the real Simon Bendelow, and the purpose of the fraud was to create undeniable evidence that he was dead. But why did he want to prove that he was dead? Well, we knew that he was the murderer of Van Zellen, for whom the American police were searching, and he might be in more danger than we knew. At any rate, a death-certificate would make him absolutely secure on one condition: that the body was cremated. Mere burial would not be enough; for an exhumation would discover the fraud. But perfect security could be secured only by destruction of all evidence of the fraud. Julius D'Arblay held such evidence. Therefore Julius D'Arblay must be got rid of. Here, then, was an amply sufficient motive for the murder. The only point which remained obscure was the identity of your patient and the means by which his disappearance had been accounted for.

"My hypothesis, then, had been changed into highly probable theory. The next stage was the necessary verification. I began with a rather curious experiment. The man who tried to murder Marion could have been no other than her father's murderer. Then he must have been Morris. But it seemed that he was totally unlike Morris, and the mask evidently suggested to her no resemblance. But yet it was probable that the man was Morris, for the striking features – the hook nose and the heavy brows – would be easily 'made up', especially at night. The question was whether the face was Morris' with these additions. I determined to put that question to the test. And here Polton's new accomplishment came to our aid.

"First, with a pinch of clay, we built up on Morris' mask a nose of the shape described and slightly thickened the brows. Then Polton made a gelatine mould and from this produced a wax mask. He fitted it with glass eyes and attached it to a rough plaster head, with ears which were casts of my own painted. We then fixed on a moustache, beard and wig, and put on a shirt, collar and jacket. It was an extraordinarily crude affair, suggestive of the fifth of November. But it answered the purpose, which was to produce a photograph; for we made the photograph so bad – so confused and ill-focused – that the crudities disappeared, while the essential likeness remained. As you know, that photograph was instantly recognized, without any sort of suggestion. So the first test gave a positive result. Marion's assailant was pretty certainly Morris."

"I should like to have seen Mr Polton's prentice effort," said Marion, who had been listening, enthralled by this description.

"You shall see it now," Thorndyke replied with a smile. "It is in the next room, concealed in a cupboard."

He went out, and presently returned, carrying what looked like an excessively crude hair-dresser's dummy, but a most extraordinarily horrible and repulsive one. As he turned the face towards us, Marion gave a little cry of horror and then tried to laugh – without very striking success.

"It is a dreadful-looking thing!" she exclaimed; "and so hideously like that fiend." She gazed at it with the most extreme repugnance for a while and then said, apologetically: "I hope you won't think me very silly, but – "

"Of course I don't," Thorndyke interrupted. "It is going back to its cupboard at once," and with this he bore it away, returning in a few moments with a smaller object, wrapped in a cloth, which he laid on the table. "Another 'exhibit', as they say in the courts," he explained, "which we shall want presently. Meanwhile we resume the thread of our argument.

"The photograph of this wax-work, then, furnished corroboration of the theory that Morris was the man whom we were seeking. My next move was to inquire at Scotland Yard if there were any fresh developments of the Van Zellen case. The answer was that there were; and Superintendent Miller arranged to come and tell me all about them. You were present at the interview and will remember what passed. His information was highly important, not only by confirming my inference that Bendelow was the murderer, but especially by disposing of the difficulty connected with the disappearance of your patient. For now there came into view a second man – Crile – who had died at Hoxton of an abdominal cancer and had been duly buried; and when you were able to give me this man's address, a glance at the map and at the Post Office Directory showed that the two men had died in the same house. This fact, with the further facts that they had died of virtually the same disease and within a day or two of the same date, left no reasonable doubt that we were really dealing with one man who had died and for whom two death certificates, in different names, and two corresponding burial orders had been obtained. There was only one body, and that was cremated in the name of Bendelow. It followed that the coffin which was buried at Mr Crile's funeral must have been an empty coffin. I was so confident that this must be so that I induced Miller to apply for an exhumation, with the results that you know.

"There now remained only a single point requiring verification: the question as to what face it was that those two ladies saw when they looked into the coffin of Simon Bendelow. Here again Polton's new accomplishments came to our aid. From the plaster mask your apprentice made a most realistic wax mask, which I offer for your critical inspection."

He unfolded the cloth and produced a mask of thin, yellowish wax and of a most cadaverous aspect, which he handed to Marion.

"Yes," she said approvingly, "it is an excellent piece of work; and what beautiful eyelashes. They look exactly like real ones."

"They are real ones," Thorndyke explained with a chuckle.

She looked up at him inquiringly, and then, breaking into a ripple of laughter, exclaimed: "Of course! They are his own! Oh! how like Mr Polton! But he was quite right, you know. He couldn't have got the effect any other way."

"So he declared," said Thorndyke. "Well, we hired a coffin and had an inspection window put in the lid, and we got a black skull-cap. We put a dummy head in the coffin with a wig on it; we laid the mask where the face should have been and we adjusted the jaw-bandage and the skull-cap so as to cover up the edges of the mask, and we got the two ladies here; and showed them the coffin. When they had identified the tenant as Mr Bendelow, the verification was complete, the hypothesis was now converted into ascertained fact, and all that remained to be done was to lay hands on the murderer."

"How did you find out where Morris was living?" I asked.

"Barber did that," he replied. "When I learned that you were being stalked, I employed Barber to shadow you. He, of course, observed Morris on your track and followed him home."

"That was what I supposed," said I; and for a while we were all silent. Presently Marion said: "It is all very involved and confusing. Would you mind telling us exactly what happened?"

"In a direct narrative, you mean?" said he. "Yes; I will try to reconstruct the events in the order of their occurrence. They began with the murder of Van Zellen by Bendelow. There was no evidence against him at the time, but he had to fly from America for other reasons and he left behind him incriminating traces which he knew must presently be discovered and which would fix the murder on him. His friend Crile, who fled with him, developed gastric cancer and only had a month or two to live. Then Bendelow decided that when Crile should die, he would make believe to die at the same time. To this end, he commissioned your father to make a wax mask – a portrait mask of himself with his eyes closed. His wife must then have persuaded the two spinsters to visit him – he, of course, taking to his bed when they called and being represented as a mortally sick man. Then they moved from Hornsey to Hoxton, taking Crile with him. There he engaged two doctors – Usher and Gray, both of whom lived at a distance – to attend Crile and to visit him on alternate days. Crile seems to have been deaf, or at least, hard of hearing, and was kept continuously under the influence of morphia. Usher, who was employed by Mrs Bendelow, whom he knew as Mrs Pepper – came to the front of the house in Field Street to visit Mr Crile, while Stephen, who was employed by the Bendelows, whom he knew by the name of Morris – entered at the rear of the house in Market Street to visit the same man under the name of Bendelow. About the time of the move, Bendelow committed the murder in order to destroy all evidence of the making of the wax mask.

"Eventually Crile died – or was finished off with an extra dose of morphia – on a Thursday. Usher gave the certificate and the funeral took place on the Saturday. But previously – probably on the Friday night – the coffin-lid was unscrewed by Bendelow, the body taken out and replaced by a sack of sawdust with some lead pipe in it.

"On the Monday the body was again produced; this time as that of Simon Bendelow, who was represented as having died on the Sunday afternoon. It was put in a cremation coffin with a celluloid window in the lid. The wax mask was placed over the face; the jaw-bandage and the skullcap adjusted to hide the place where the wax face joined the real face; and the two spinsters were brought up to see Mr Bendelow in his coffin. They looked in through the window and, of course, saw the wax mask of Bendelow. Then they retired. The coffin-lid was taken off, the wax mask removed, the coffin-lid screwed on again, and then the two doctors were brought up. They removed the body from the coffin, examined it and put it back; and Bendelow – or Morris – put on the coffin-lid.

"As soon as the doctors were gone, the coffin-lid was taken off again, the wax mask was put back and adjusted and the coffin-lid replaced and screwed down finally. Then the two ladies were brought up again to take a last look at poor Mr Bendelow; not actually the last look, for, at the funeral, they peeped in at the window and saw the wax face just before the coffin was passed through into the crematorium."

"It was a diabolically clever scheme," said I.

"It was," he agreed. "It was perfectly convincing and consistent. If you and those two ladies had been put in the witness-box, your testimony and theirs would have been in complete agreement. They had seen Simon Bendelow (whom they knew quite well) in his coffin. A few minutes later, you had seen Simon Bendelow in his coffin, had taken the body out, examined it thoroughly and put it back, and had seen the coffin-lid screwed down; and again a few minutes later they had looked in through the coffin-window and had again seen Simon Bendelow. The evidence would appear to be beyond the possibility of a doubt. Simon Bendelow was proved conclusively to be dead and cremated and was doubly certified to have died from natural causes. Nothing could be more complete.

"And yet," he continued, after a pause, "while we are impressed by the astonishing subtlety and ingenuity displayed, we are almost more impressed by the fundamental stupidity exhibited along with it – a stupidity that seems to be characteristic of this type of criminal. For all the security that was gained by one part of the scheme was destroyed by the idiotic efforts to guard against dangers that had no existence. The murder was not only a foul crime; it was a tactical blunder of the most elementary kind. But for that murder, Bendelow would now be alive and in unchallenged security. The cremation scheme was completely successful. It deceived everybody. Even the two detectives, though they felt vague suspicions, saw no loophole. They had to accept the appearances at their face value.

"But it was the old story. The wrong-doer could not keep quiet. He must be forever making himself safer and yet more safe. At each move he laid down fresh tracks. And so, in the end, he delivered himself into our hands."

He paused and for a while seemed to be absorbed in reflection on what he had been telling us. Presently he looked up and, addressing Marion, said in grave, quiet tones:

"We have ended our quest and we have secured retribution. Justice was beyond our reach, for complete justice implies restitution; and to attain that, the dead must have been recalled from the grave. But, at least sometimes, out of evil cometh good. Surely it will seem to you, when, in the happy years which, I trust and confidently believe lie before you, your thoughts turn back to the days of your mourning and grief, that the beloved father, who, when living, made your happiness his chief concern, even in dying bequeathed to you a blessing."

R Austin Freeman

Dr Thorndyke Intervenes

What would you do if you opened a package to find a man's head? What would you do if the headless corpse had been swapped for a case of bullion? What would you do if you knew a brutal murderer was out there, somewhere, and waiting for you? Some people would run. Dr Thorndyke intervenes.

Felo De Se

John Gillam was a gambler. John Gillam faced financial ruin and was the victim of a sinister blackmail attempt. John Gillam is now dead. In this exceptional mystery, Dr Thorndyke is brought in to untangle the secrecy surrounding the death of John Gillam, a man not known for insanity and thoughts of suicide.

R Austin Freeman

Flighty Phyllis

Chronicling the adventures and misadventures of Phyllis Dudley, Richard Austin Freeman brings to life a charming character always getting into scrapes. From impersonating a man to discovering mysterious trap doors, *Flighty Phyllis* is an entertaining glimpse at the times and trials of a wayward woman.

Helen Vardon's Confession

Through the open door of a library, Helen Vardon hears an argument that changes her life forever. Helen's father and a man called Otway argue over missing funds in a trust one night. Otway proposes a marriage between him and Helen in exchange for his co-operation and silence. What transpires is a captivating tale of blackmail, fraud and death. Dr Thorndyke is left to piece together the clues in this enticing mystery.

R Austin Freeman

Mr Pottermack's Oversight

Mr Pottermack is a law-abiding, settled homebody who has nothing to hide until the appearance of the shadowy Lewison, a gambler and blackmailer with an incredible story. It appears that Pottermack is in fact a runaway prisoner, convicted of fraud, and Lewison is about to spill the beans unless he receives a large bribe in return for his silence. But Pottermack protests his innocence, and resolves to shut Lewison up once and for all. Will he do it? And if he does, will he get away with it?

The Mystery of Angelina Frood

A beautiful young woman is in shock. She calls John Strangeways, a medical lawyer who must piece together the strange disparate facts of her case and in turn, becomes fearful for his life. Only Dr Thorndyke, a master of detection, may be able to solve the baffling mystery of Angelina Frood.

'Bright, ingenious and amusing' – *The Times Literary Supplement*.

OTHER TITLES BY R AUSTIN FREEMAN AVAILABLE DIRECT FROM HOUSE OF STRATUS

Quantity		£	$(US)	$(CAN)	€
☐	A CERTAIN DR THORNDYKE	6.99	11.50	16.95	11.50
☐	DR THORNDYKE INTERVENES	6.99	11.50	16.95	11.50
☐	DR THORNDYKE'S CASEBOOK	6.99	11.50	16.95	11.50
☐	THE EYE OF OSIRIS	6.99	11.50	16.95	11.50
☐	FELO DE SE	6.99	11.50	16.95	11.50
☐	FLIGHTY PHYLLIS	6.99	11.50	16.95	11.50
☐	THE GOLDEN POOL: THE STORY OF A FORGOTTEN MINE	6.99	11.50	16.95	11.50
☐	THE GREAT PORTRAIT MYSTERY	6.99	11.50	16.95	11.50
☐	HELEN VARDON'S CONFESSION	6.99	11.50	16.95	11.50

ALL HOUSE OF STRATUS BOOKS ARE AVAILABLE FROM GOOD BOOKSHOPS OR DIRECT FROM THE PUBLISHER:

Internet: www.houseofstratus.com including author interviews, reviews, features.

Email: sales@houseofstratus.com please quote author, title and credit card details.

OTHER TITLES BY R AUSTIN FREEMAN AVAILABLE DIRECT
FROM HOUSE OF STRATUS

Quantity		£	$(US)	$(CAN)	€
	Mr Polton Explains	6.99	11.50	16.95	11.50
	Mr Pottermack's Oversight	6.99	11.50	16.95	11.50
	The Mystery of 31 New Inn	6.99	11.50	16.95	11.50
	The Mystery of Angelina Frood	6.99	11.50	16.95	11.50
	The Penrose Mystery	6.99	11.50	16.95	11.50
	The Puzzle Lock	6.99	11.50	16.95	11.50
	The Red Thumb Mark	6.99	11.50	16.95	11.50
	The Shadow of the Wolf	6.99	11.50	16.95	11.50
	A Silent Witness	6.99	11.50	16.95	11.50
	The Singing Bone	6.99	11.50	16.95	11.50

ALL HOUSE OF STRATUS BOOKS ARE AVAILABLE FROM GOOD BOOKSHOPS
OR DIRECT FROM THE PUBLISHER:

Hotline: UK ONLY: 0800 169 1780, please quote author, title and credit card details.
INTERNATIONAL: +44 (0) 20 7494 6400, please quote author, title, and credit card details.

Send to: **House of Stratus Sales Department**
24c Old Burlington Street
London
W1X 1RL
UK

Please allow for postage costs charged per order plus an amount per book as set out in the tables below:

	£(Sterling)	$(US)	$(CAN)	€(Euros)
Cost per order				
UK	2.00	3.00	4.50	3.30
Europe	3.00	4.50	6.75	5.00
North America	3.00	4.50	6.75	5.00
Rest of World	3.00	4.50	6.75	5.00
Additional cost per book				
UK	0.50	0.75	1.15	0.85
Europe	1.00	1.50	2.30	1.70
North America	2.00	3.00	4.60	3.40
Rest of World	2.50	3.75	5.75	4.25

PLEASE SEND CHEQUE, POSTAL ORDER (STERLING ONLY), EUROCHEQUE, OR INTERNATIONAL MONEY ORDER (PLEASE CIRCLE METHOD OF PAYMENT YOU WISH TO USE)
MAKE PAYABLE TO: STRATUS HOLDINGS plc

Cost of book(s): —————————— Example: 3 x books at £6.99 each: £20.97

Cost of order: —————————— Example: £2.00 (Delivery to UK address)

Additional cost per book: —————————— Example: 3 x £0.50: £1.50

Order total including postage: —————————— Example: £24.47

Please tick currency you wish to use and add total amount of order:

☐ £ (Sterling)   ☐ $ (US)   ☐ $ (CAN)   ☐ € (EUROS)

VISA, MASTERCARD, SWITCH, AMEX, SOLO, JCB:

☐☐☐☐☐☐☐☐☐☐☐☐☐☐☐☐☐☐

Issue number (Switch only):

☐☐☐

Start Date: Expiry Date:

☐☐ / ☐☐   ☐☐ / ☐☐

Signature: _____

NAME: _____

ADDRESS: _____

_____

POSTCODE: _____

Please allow 28 days for delivery.

Prices subject to change without notice.
Please tick box if you do not wish to receive any additional information. ☐

House of Stratus publishes many other titles in this genre; please check our website (**www.houseofstratus.com**) for more details.